Claimed for Their Pleasure

A fantasy barbarian romance

Coveted Prey
Book 6

L.V. Lane

Created with Vellum

Contents

Prologue	1
Chapter 1	9
Chapter 2	21
Chapter 3	33
Chapter 4	47
Chapter 5	57
Chapter 6	65
Chapter 7	77
Chapter 8	83
Chapter 9	93
Chapter 10	99
Chapter 11	109
Chapter 12	119
Chapter 13	127
Chapter 14	133
Chapter 15	143
Chapter 16	153
Chapter 17	159
Chapter 18	167
Chapter 19	175
Chapter 20	183
Chapter 21	189
Chapter 22	203
Chapter 23	209
Chapter 24	221
Chapter 25	231
Chapter 26	239
Chapter 27	245
Chapter 28	253
Chapter 29	263
Chapter 30	271

Chapter 31   279
Chapter 32   289
Chapter 33   303
Chapter 34   317
Chapter 35   323
Chapter 36   333
Chapter 37   345
Epilogue   351

About the Author   363
Also by L.V. Lane   365

Prologue

Jessa

A faint rustling rouses me from a deep sleep.

As I open my eyes, I see a brown rabbit watching me with interest. A slim clover leaf disappears between its teeth before it leans down and snatches up another clump.

Sitting no more than a handspan from my face, it shows not a bit of fear.

"Uhhh!" As I heave myself to a sitting position, the bunny bounds off, its white tail flashing.

I am outside, curled up against the roots of a great oak tree. The forest around me is cast into shades of grey. A few birds have begun to chatter, signifying dawn's approach.

I am stiff and cold. Not for the first time, I have sleep-walked, and I do not recognize where I am.

My lips tremble as the fear crashes in. Stupid tears spring and spill over my cheeks.

I quickly brush the tears away. I'm fifteen, too old for self-pity.

Papa will be rousing by now. As a carpenter, he always has plenty of work to do in the workshop adjoining our home. My mother will be up and about, too, making biscuits to go with the porridge. My younger siblings might still be napping or awake and making their noisy demands.

Only they will be doing none of their usual things, for by now they will have realized I have gone.

My nightgown is covered in dirty smudges, leaves, and bits of twig. Heaving myself to my feet, I brush it off, although it is assuredly beyond saving. No matter how well they lock and bolt doors, nothing defeats my sleep-driven ingenuity when it comes to escaping our home.

Molly, the omega from the Baxter clan, says I have a wanderer's soul and am searching for something. The women-folk of the clan often go to her for advice, for she is both old and wise.

Well, I wish I could find the blasted thing so that I might not wander anymore.

Turning full circle, I try to orientate myself. Sickness settles in my tummy. I need to try and find my way home.

Thirsty and shivering, I make my way down a slope.

Is that water?

I think it is.

Following the sound of water, I emerge onto a rocky gorge, from which water cascades into a river far below. A thick tree has fallen over the rocks but is weather-worn and long since stripped of branches.

I do not know this place.

The river appears to curve, although it is hard to see far in the dawn light made darker by thick cloud cover.

Everything about this feels wrong, and panic brings a tightness to my chest. I am thirsty and tired, and my feet have blistered such that every step is like a knife. The rocks are steep and treacherous here, and I cannot even reach the water to drink. Since I woke, I have covered a fair distance, and I am no longer sure I can find my way back.

A deep growl sets the hairs rising on the back of my neck. No, not a single deep growl; there are several.

Turning slowly, I face this new trouble.

"Goddess!" I whisper as three wolves emerge between the trees. Beautiful and deadly; they are wary, watching me through their cold eyes. I am small for my age. Happen they like their chances of taking me for a meal.

The coarse ground around me offers a few smaller rocks that might make a weapon. Trembling, I slowly bend and pick up one, comforted by its weight in my hand.

Should I throw it now? Should I wait and see if they leave? Should I shout and wave my arms?

Wolves never come near the village. They do not like the scent of the shifters living within our community. When I was little, I remember fearing for my papa when he would go into the forest with the men of the village to cut trees. A small child at the time, he had sat me on his lap and explained that wolves rarely attacked humans who are far too big to be seen as prey. Further, he explained that wolves are nocturnal and mostly hunt at night.

We are not yet into spring, the nights are long, and as our hunters attest, game is scarce.

The central wolf lifts his head and howls. The other two take up the cry.

The sound chills me more deeply than the icy rocks under my feet. I grip my weapon-rock so fiercely that my fingers begin to ache.

I will not become their next meal.

With a roar, I toss the rock with all my might. It skitters across the stones harmlessly. The nearest wolf nimbly dodges it before returning his attention to me. The rightmost wolf howls again.

The cry is returned by another wolf in the distance.

They are calling their pack!

I'm about to throw another rock when a great snarling beast leaps from the trees for the leading wolf. They clash together in a twisting ball of fur and teeth. The two smaller wolves dance back, snarling, circling, and nipping at the newcomer.

The newcomer is far too large to be a natural wolf.

Shifter.

My heart pounds furiously as they engage in a deadly dance, growling and snapping their teeth.

A smaller wolf dives for the shifter. But he is taken savagely by the throat, shaken, and tossed aside.

Yipping with pain, the downed wolf struggles to its feet.

As the shifter moves to stand between the wolves and me, he throws his head back and howls. A chilling sound that sends a great shudder through my body.

The wolves turn and flee, darting back into the forest.

The shifter wolf throws a look over his shoulder at me. There is blood covering his snout and beautiful tawny coat.

The rock drops from my fingers. I recognize his coat, although I have never seen it bloody.

I swallow past the lump in my throat. *Brandon.* Oh, why does it have to be Brandon, the handsome lad from our village that can tie my tongue in knots simply by glancing my way!

He shifts.

Naked and covered in blood, his face remains stern with censure as he stalks toward me.

"It is not my fault!" I say before he can utter a word. Brow furrowed and jaw tight, he stalks closer.

My eyes lower. I don't mean for them to lower, but they have a mind of their own. It is not polite to look at a naked shifter who has not had a chance to dress. Children are naturally curious. I admit I peeked on occasions when I was younger. As I matured, I understood the rudeness of it and have not looked in many years.

Goddess save me. I do not think I have seen Brandon's cock before. It hangs fat and long between his legs, swinging with every step in the most arresting way.

"Eyes up!" Brandon snaps as he closes in on me.

I back up a step. My eyes lift to meet his narrowed ones briefly before they dart back down. How does it fit...

I yelp as he fists my arm.

"You are a fucking test," he growls before tossing me over the nearby fallen tree and landing a firm spank to my bottom.

"It is not polite to look at an undressed shifter who is not your mate!"

Spank!

"I have scouted all over the territory looking for you!"

Spank!

"Your parents are beside themselves!"

Spank!

"You assuredly did not get all the way over here during your sleepwalk."

Spank!

"Had you stayed put, I would have found you long ago."

Spank! Spank! Spank!

"I am sorry!" I wail. My nightgown barely shields me from his palm. Papa has never disciplined me, for I am never naughty. I am shocked by how greatly this stings.

"I am still fucking furious!" he growls. "Gods, I cannot get the fear out of my mind from when I saw they had cornered you!"

The dam breaks inside me, and I fall to sobbing. I feel both his anger and fear as if it were my own. A small, deeply tucked place inside my chest blooms to awareness. My bottom throbs, but so does my head and my heart.

He stops. Heaving me from the tree, he takes a seat and puts me on his lap. "There, lass," he says, pressing my cheek into his chest and making the sweet rumbly sound all shifters can make. "You are too old for this nonsense."

"I thought I recognized where I was," I mumble into his chest, shaking violently as the magnitude of what just happened comes crashing in.

"Aye," Brandon says. "You know what thought did. He followed a muck cart and thought it was a wedding."

I chuckle.

Brandon chuckles, too, a pleasant rumble under my ear.

"That is a terrible saying," I say. The warmth from his big body is seeping into me, making me wish I could burrow under his skin.

"Aye, that it is," Brandon says. "But things are going to change. From now on, I will be watching your house of a night. And rest assured, I will put you straight back inside should you try wandering in your sleep again."

"Thank you," I say. The little place tucked inside my chest blossoms further. I take comfort that he will watch over me. There is a rightness about it.

His arms make a gentle cage around me, inside which I am safe. I become aware that I am sitting on his lap and that he is still naked. Many lasses in the village swoon over Brandon, for he is very handsome. Further, he is best friends with our clan king's brother and has a high status.

I can admit that I have noticed him. Papa says I am too young to be thinking about boys. Although, my mother always winks behind his back whenever he voices this determination.

When I peep at Brandon through my lashes, I notice he's watching me. His eyes are a bright clear blue. Wolf eyes, they call them, for all shifters have them.

"Half the village is out looking for you," he says gruffly. "We need to get back."

Only he doesn't move, and I don't either. My gaze lowers to his lips.

"Don't fucking look at me like that, lass," he says.

I swallow. This close, his sharp white fangs are visible when he speaks.

Then I glance up and find he is staring at my mouth. My lips part on a gasp. Is he going to kiss me?

"Oh!" I am unceremoniously dumped onto the ground as he stands. Not yet having a chance to right myself, he shifts to a wolf and closes his teeth over my nightgown. "Goddess!"

He tugs, pulling me over again with a warning growl.

I try to bat him away, but he is far too big and far too strong. Pushing me onto my stomach, he closes his teeth over the back of my nightgown and lifts me clear from the ground. He is so huge that I dangle thus.

"Brandon!" I wail. "What are you doing?" Oh, he can't mean to carry me all the way home like this, can he? At his low growl, I still, arms and legs hanging. This is assuredly not a comfortable way to travel.

Just as I am about to demand he put me down, he bounds off into the forest.

Chapter One

Three years later...

Jessa

Ever since he rescued me, I can't stop thinking about Brandon. Now every time I see him in the village, the memories of that day come crashing back.

The confusing mixture of emotions as his big hand spanked my bottom.

The sweet, safe comfort as I nestled upon his lap.

Both memories bring a little flutter, although it manifests in different ways.

It has been three years since he imprinted upon me and my obsession became fully-fledged...three long years.

At first, I thought he ignored me because he was older and I was only a girl. But I am eighteen now, and soon I will be expected to choose a husband.

To make matters worse, Brandon lives with his parents, whose cottage is on the opposite side of the lane.

As I exit my home, sibling brats clinging to my hide skirt, I see Brandon outside his home. Sturdy ax in his hands, he is busy splitting wood. It is a warm summer day, and he has stripped his leather jerkin and tossed it over the nearby post.

A gaggle of lasses are leaning over the fence of the sheep paddock, pretending to be doing things. They are not doing anything other than staring at Brandon's rippling muscles.

Goddess help me, now I am also staring at his rippling muscles.

"Jessa! Take this over to Doreen," my mother says, bustling out of our cottage. There is a giant pie in her hands that she baked earlier this morning.

Doreen is Brandon's mother. Ordinarily, I would not mind popping over to take a pie, for I know Doreen has not been so well. But it means walking past Brandon.

"I am busy, Mother," I say, mind scrambling for a reason why I might be too busy to carry a pie a small distance and coming up short. I am a dutiful child who is always willing and helpful.

My mother looks past me to where Brandon works up a sweat.

"My," she says. "What a strapping lad!" Then she winks and hands over the cherry pie. "At least you have a good excuse, unlike the shameless hussies gawking."

I think my mama knows I like Brandon. I think my papa does too, but they handle my obsession in very different ways.

"Everyone else inside," my mother says. "You too, Greta. Go and wash your hands afore lunch."

Greta has a soft spot for Brandon, and Mama corrals my youngest sibling back inside when she tries to dart off.

With no choice now, I make my way across the lane, face heating the closer I draw.

Brandon stops his wood splitting, eyes tracking my progress in a way that reminds me that he is not only a man, but a wolf and a predator at heart.

He wipes the sweat from his brow with the back of his forearm, letting the ax blade rest against the cutting block. Goddess, he is sinful in his beauty with his dark hair reaching his shoulders and bright blue eyes. His hair has a tendency toward messy curls that his mother is always threatening to cut. He keeps his beard short, but if he has been away scouting with Fen, it looks a cute kind of furry when he returns.

I get a little squirmy as I approach. I can smell his clean musky sweat, and it makes me tingly inside my belly. Lower, I feel the dampness that has been happening more often of late and has become a source of acute embarrassment.

"Something smells good," Brandon says as I draw level.

Realizing that he is looking at me and not the pie, my cheeks go up in flames. I trip on an invisible obstacle. "Uff!"

I fear the cherry pie my mother baked especially for his, will go flying. But within the space of a heartbeat, Brandon stows the ax, closes the distance on me, and snatches the flying pie from my hands.

My momentum is such that I'm flattened against his sweat-dampened chest.

Behind, I hear the tinkling laughter of the girls who were ogling Brandon. I will never live this down!

Brandon smirks. "That was close," he says, voice a husky drawl that sets the fluttering off again.

I always thought sweat was a disgusting thing, but Brandon smells divine. Staring into his pretty eyes, I get a little lost. He stares back before his focus lowers to my lips. Does he want to kiss me? I'm hoping that he'll kiss me. My life would be complete if Brandon would kiss me even once.

Also, it will show the shameless hussies who are always batting their lashes at him.

His gaze suddenly shifts to something over my shoulder, and I'm set aside so swiftly I nearly topple over again.

When I glance back, I see Papa standing in the open doorway of his workshop, hands on hips, glaring at Brandon.

Brandon's lips twitch. "Your papa looks fit to cave my head in with my own ax. Best you run back home, lass, afore we get blood over this delicious pie." Smirking, he about faces before stomping toward his cottage.

"Ma! Betty sent you a pie," he calls as he takes the steps two at a time.

"Jessa!" My father's gruff call startles me from my perusing of Brandon's ass. "Help your mother with the brats!"

My father, still scowling, returns to his workshop. The noisy sounds of hammering ensue. Feeling disgruntled on a thousand different levels, I slink back home.

"She can't get a lad without throwing herself at one," Nola says loudly enough to ensure that I hear.

I do not like Nola. Given she is full of airs and graces, few lasses of the clan do. Except for her posse, who hang on her every word and laugh now at my expense.

Nola thinks she is better than everyone else because her father died defending the clan.

Her father was much respected, and Nola has presumed that respect to be her due. When the clan king's wife died last fall, Nola all but announced herself as the future mate.

I cannot see that happening. Jack cared deeply for his late mate, who was a kind-hearted beta and loved by all.

Jack is a good king, and I pray he does not mate the witchy

Nola. She is nasty enough now and sure to be a thousand times worse should she claim the lofty title of mate to the king.

Their laughter follows me as I stomp up the steps into my home. My siblings are all seated at the table, eating bread and jam, and supping on milk.

"What was that about?" my mother asks, nudging her head toward the door.

"I tripped," I say, face flushing. "I nearly dropped the pie! They were making fun of me."

My mother shakes her head, wiping Greta's fingers, which are covered in jam.

"The lass is a test," my mother agrees.

"Who is a test?" Greta demands.

"Never you mind," my mother says, lips tugging up as she sees what William is doing. William is a year older than Greta, and he is licking all the jam from the bread, which has set Greta to doing the same. "Doesn't matter what I feed them. They make a mess with it."

"I don't understand why everyone tiptoes around her," I say. My voice lowers to a whisper. "You don't think Jack will mate her, do you?"

My mother places an arm around my shoulder and hugs me. "No, lass, I don't. A fool could see Jack is in no state to think about mating again. I think he is hoping that Nola will step up as a leader within the clan. Her father was well-loved and held a high status afore he died a hero."

"I don't think she will ever step up," I say sadly.

"Me neither," my mother agrees.

A sudden wailing brings a halt to the conversation. William has tipped his milk, and it has spilled all over Greta.

The children keep me busy for the next while. Then I spend the afternoon with some of the clanswomen in the herb

13

cottage, as it is called, where we keep all the healing roots and herbs.

I return home at dinner time and help my mother with my siblings. There are six of us in total. Greta and William are the youngest and stay with my mother and me most of the time. While the older three boys, Amos, Karl, and Doug, help my father in the workshop. Doug is only eight, but loves to watch my father and brothers when there are no lighter duties for him to do. When my father goes out logging, only Amos, as the oldest, is allowed to go with him. The other two mope around when they must stay behind, although it won't be long before Karl can join him.

Ordinarily, I love the banter between my siblings, but I'm feeling out of sorts. Once dinner is over, and we have cleared up, I go to my bedding nook with a lamp, pull my curtain across, and read my treasured book. It's a story of a princess who mates with a shifter lord. Together, they have wondrous adventures. I never get bored despite reading it so many times that the pages are worn. The wolf lord has been betrayed and captured by the Orcs. His daring mate must lead the rescue. It is a fanciful tale, and I enjoy it very much. I imagine I am the princess, disguising myself as a boy as I infiltrate the Orc citadel where my mate is held.

They have chained the shifter lord, for everyone knows a bound shifter cannot shift. All our heroine needs to do is free his bound wrists, and he will be able to take them both to safety.

I know what will happen. I have read the book many times, but I still get a wriggly sort of tense when the Orc guards pass the alcove where the princess is hiding.

"Lamp out, Jessa," my mother calls.

Engrossed in my story, I didn't realize that it had gone quiet on the other side of the curtain. Turning out my lamp, I return it to the hook before placing my book on the small alcove where I keep my personal treasures.

I wriggle deeper into my bed.

Usually, I fall straight asleep, diving into a dream world I conjure for myself. But tonight, the dreams won't settle as my mind keeps looping over the day's events.

I can hear Nola's laughter as she spitefully made fun of my stumble. But I don't linger on that.

I have dreamed of Brandon for so long. He has starred as the hero in every story I have ever played inside my head. I want him so badly, but he barely notices me. And when he does notice, it is only so that he might tease me.

Restless, I toss and turn, but sleep still evades me.

I find another story weaving in and out of my mind. One with a great alpha and a beta shifter who fight to claim a lass. The two men hate each other, for their clans are at war. I push and pull at this story of my making, but I can't find a pattern that will give it the happy ending it deserves.

The gentle murmur of my parent's conversation rouses me when I hear my name. I do not listen in on them often, but I am curious and carefully clamber around in the bed so that my ear is against the wall nearest to them.

"She is growing up, Ed," my mother says softly. "She's not our baby anymore."

I hear my father's huff. "She has shown no signs yet then?" he asks.

My interest piques at this question. Is Papa talking about my moon blood? I am eighteen, most lasses have bled by now, but I have shown no signs. I try not to worry about it. My mother told me I am small and that some lasses naturally start later.

"We both know what she is," my mother says. "Molly told us as much, years ago. She has a sense of such things."

I frown.

Molly is the mate of the Baxter clan king. She is a kindly, older omega who visits from time to time to speak to our clanswomen. I remember seeing her talking to Mama when I was younger. I feel a little sick and betrayed that they have been discussing me thus.

I wonder what it is they think I am?

"She has been wrong before," my father says gruffly. "Has Jessa shown any inclination toward nesting?"

My frown deepens, and a cold prickling sensation skitters down my spine.

"No, none," says my mother. "But Molly said not all of them nest until they go through the change."

My mind blanks out. I feel sick. Change? What is this change? I do not want to change. I do not want to build a stupid nest like an animal might.

"She is still sweet on Brandon," my father says. "But she will need an alpha if she does change. I'm yet to be convinced she will reveal thus. Either way, Brandon is not a suitable match. The lad is always up to mischief with Fen. The king's brother is half wild and a poor influence, in my opinion. Neither lad is inclined toward settling down, and Jessa will only be hurt."

"Ah, Ed," my mother says. "I don't think Brandon is so bad."

I cover my mouth to stifle my cry. It is like a knife twisting in my chest, sharp and vicious. I assuredly do not want to be forced to pick an alpha from the clan. They are all huge and frightening. But my father has already determined that Brandon is not for me.

Worse, I know he is right in all he says about Brandon. I have seen the beta shifter sneaking off with the older lasses to the barns. He could have his pick of many. Why would he ever pick me?

I do not want to hear more of the conversation. I am heart-sore that I have heard this much.

Sliding back into my cold bed, I pull the covers over my head. I turn, wriggling around until I am nestled at the bottom in a ball where the blankets are tucked tight.

Here, I sob silently, broken-hearted for the broken dream where Brandon claims me, and we wed.

It was a stupid dream, for he has never done anything to suggest he might return my feelings. I am eighteen, and I have not even kissed a boy!

My hurt gives way to anger. How dare my parents keep this from me. How dare they plot about me behind my back. I will assuredly run away before I am handed over to some alpha like a prize.

Alphas. My mind immediately latches onto an image of the great, stern alpha from the Lyon clan. His name is Gage, and he is the younger son of the Lyon clan king. He comes here on occasion to speak with our king. The Lyon clan are not well-liked. They are aggressive and easily twice our number since they claimed the Born clan territory a year back. Their leader is a warmonger, or so I have heard other clansfolk say.

Yet, something about Gage has drawn my interest since he started visiting a few years ago.

My tears have dried up, but inside, my chest feels raw.

I am not alone in noticing Gage, just as I am not alone in noticing Brandon.

An idea unfurls... What if I could have both? What if I did change, and they both claimed me?

My belly tightens, and dampness gathers between my legs. Fingers shaking, I lift my nightgown, finding my feminine place is slick. I move very slowly, circling the little bud that feels so good. I don't even need to touch it. Touching close is enough to make the sensations awake.

It is a dream, and in my dream, I can have anyone I want.

And I want them both, Brandon and Gage. It doesn't matter that they hate one another, or that our clans are near at war. I imagine them crowding in on either side of me, kissing me, fingers where mine are now, stroking me softly...encouraging me to come.

I come, biting my lower lip to stifle the sounds as my pussy gushes a flood of stickiness.

Chest heaving, I still. This is the second time that has happened, and I have drenched my nightgown. Heat fills my cheeks. This is assuredly not normal. Maybe something is wrong with me?

I shuffle around, pushing my head out of the covers. I'm tired but also sad, for neither Brandon nor Gage will be mine. How can they be?

Amid these troubling thoughts, I drift into sleep.

Chapter Two

Five years earlier...

Brandon

"I think we should take his pants," Fen says.

"What? Are you crazy? Why would we take his pants?" I ask, scowling at the lad who has been my best friend my whole life.

Fen is an alpha, and the younger brother of our clan king.

It is natural for a beta shifter to find an alpha to latch. I bonded with Fen when he was but a lad, and I, a pup. I would follow Fen to the ends of the world if he asked me to.

Most often, I follow him into trouble that does not start out with that intent.

I suspect today might be one such day.

We lay in the cover of the thick ferns carpeting the forest floor, scoping out our quarry.

"He stole our fucking buck," Fen says. "I say we steal his pants...and the buck."

"How the fuck will we take the buck?" I ask. "It is big and we will not carry it far. Even supposing Gage was not twenty paces away from it."

Gage.

We have gotten up to mischief with the alpha from the Lyon clan for as long back as I can remember. Fen is convinced Gage has been poaching deer from our lands. Maybe he has. Maybe he hasn't. Fen has never let the truth of a matter interrupt his plans for mischief.

Gage is in the stream washing off. His clothing rests on a nearby rock. A short distance away, his horse crops the lush grass. On the forest floor beside the horse is a plump buck and the rest of Gage's things.

"I'll bring the horses," Fen says. "Your wolf can snatch his pants off that rock. He will chase after you. While he chases you, I will take the buck."

"That is a reasonable plan," I say. "But if Gage gets a hold of you, he will put a beating on you. After, Jack will beat you again when we get home for causing trouble with their clan."

"He stole our fucking buck," Fen repeats.

"Fine," I say. "I will go and steal his pants. But don't blame me if this does not go to plan."

It does not go to plan. Mischief with Fen rarely does.

I shift, I snatch Gage's pants. The huge alpha roars and shakes his fist at me, but he does not give chase.

Fen aborts. I run on for a mile or so before catching up with him and the horses.

Dropping Gage's pants to the floor, I shift.

"That did not go so well," Fen says.

Shaking my head at him, I grin.

22

"Do you think he recognized your wolf?" Fen asks as I shuck into my pants.

I pause. "I doubt it. What makes you say that?"

"Nothing," Fen says too casually for my liking. "Pity about the buck."

We ride home, and I forget all about Gage and his buck.

∮

"Gage is here," Fen hisses.

My head snaps around. I am in the Ralston clan hall where a sweet lass is asking me to take her to the barn.

The lass scurries off.

"He was looking pissed when he was talking to Glen," Fen says.

Glen is second in command to our king, Jack.

Both Jack and Glen have berated the pair of us more times than I can count for our mischief.

"Fuck!" I say. "Do you think Gage will tell Glen that I stole his pants?"

"No," Fen says. "More likely, he will just thump you."

My eyes widen as this comment sinks in.

"Mutt!"

I turn, realizing this was a bad idea the moment Gage's fist connects.

Pain explodes. It feels like my eyeball has exploded in the socket. I stagger a step back before landing on my ass.

"Fuck!" Fen's voice is ripe with stress.

I squint and blink as an enraged Gage descends upon me. Dragging me from the floor, he punches me again. I only stagger this time before locking my knees.

"Dumb fucking whelp," Gage growls. "Did it not cross your mind that I might have more than one pair of pants? Did you not think that I might recognize your mangy pelt? Take what is mine again, and I will skin you and use your pelt to wipe my fucking boots!"

"You stole our buck!" I say, although I'm now suspecting that Fen made this up.

"I did not steal your buck!" Gage says. Through my left eye, I see his nostrils flare like he is thinking of punching me again.

Huffing out a breath, he about faces and storms from the hall.

I growl, ready to spring my wolf and go at him.

"Don't," Fen puts a hand on my shoulder. "You stand no chance as a man, and I don't much like your chances as a wolf, either."

"Thanks," I say dryly.

Fen winces. "Maybe shift to heal your eye, though. It doesn't look so good."

Before I can shift, Glen enters the hall.

"What was that about?" Glen asks, gesturing toward my eye. "What did you do to piss off Gage?"

"Brandon stole his pants while he was in the river," Fen says.

Great! Now I am blamed! It was not even my idea.

"What are you, a five-year-old whelp?" Glen says, frowning and shaking his head.

"It was Fen's idea!" I say.

"Well, don't listen to aught he tells you," Glen says. "The average goat has more brains than Fen and twice the common sense."

Fen growls. I huff out a laugh despite the pain radiating from my busted eye.

"Don't piss Gage off," Glen continues. "He is a big bastard, and likely I couldn't stop him if he decided to strangle your whelp ass."

Glen about faces but stops at the open hall doors. Looking over his shoulder, he waves his hand in my general direction. "And for fuck's sake, shift afore you lose an eye."

§

Present day...

Gage

The great hall is awash with merriment as I push my way inside. A drunk alpha waves a full tankard in my face. I shove the asshole aside, sending him tumbling to the floor.

His beer sloshes all over him, and he tries to rise with a roar.

Planting my boot against his throat, I pin him to the ground.

His glazed eyes finally see *me*, and he raises both hands.

Lifting my boot, I shove my way toward the blazing fire. My father, the clan king, is seated on his throne. Pale chest lost under the swirling tattoos that evidence his battle kills. There is more grey than red in his hair and beard now, but he still has the body of a warrior in his prime. My brother, Danon, sits to his right, slumped in the chair where a mate should sit.

Our late mother would turn in her grave to see what has become of our clan.

"Come and sup with us!" My father cries, making himself heard over the din.

I have been negotiating with the Baxter clan today, and I come home to this madness. "Is it true?" I demand. The air is ripe with weed and beer. I have no problem with either in the right circumstance.

"Aye," my father says, nodding. "Snatched her right off

Halket lands. Old Karry is weak. Letting his lasses wander unattended. They deserve to be snatched."

My nostrils flare. I had hoped it was a tall tale greeting me, but now I see it is the truth.

"Take her back," I say. "Take her back, or there will be a war."

"Let them come," Danon sneers. Two years older than me, he has been the favored son his whole life in ways that go beyond being firstborn. He chuckles as he raises his beer to his lips, draining it before calling a serving lass for more.

My brother is the image of my father with red hair and temper to match, while I'm the image of my late grandfather on my mother's side. With dark hair and eyes, I'm the tallest man in our clan. I have a temper too, but I rarely let it out.

Things and people tend to get fucked up when I let my darkness loose.

Swiping a hand down my face, I plant my ass on a stool beside them. Snatching up the beer intended for my brother, I drink deeply, ignoring his protests. Before us, the great oak table is crowded with raucous warriors deep into their beer. Around the periphery, more men stand or sit in clusters. Servers bustle in and out, dodging roving hands... Not always successfully.

I cannot lay all blame with Danon for his ways. He has spent his life bending to the will of my father and his fists. There was a time when I thought Danon was a weak alpha. But I understand his journey through life was not the same as mine. The firstborn is favored, which might be a blessing or a curse.

In Danon's case, it is assuredly a curse.

My father pats my shoulder. I resist the urge to shrug him off.

An illness swept through our clan a decade ago, killing more women than men. Now we find ourselves with too many warriors and not enough lasses to slake our lust. It is little wonder we are warring so much of late.

"It is done now," my father says. "The lass is mated. She will say it was her choice."

"Was it?" I ask.

My father grins and shrugs. He doesn't care whether she was willing or not. "We need womenfolk. We need mates for our warriors. We are a strong clan, and a strong clan takes what other clans are too weak to protect."

I don't argue with him. I have argued with him before, and it rarely ends well. We each have our opinion on this matter. My father sees me as weak because I'm unwilling to take what I want. I see myself as strong because I can resist taking what is not mine.

I sup my beer, then I drain it, and call a serving lass for more.

In the dark, depraved corners of my mind, I recognize that I am not so different from my father and brother in many ways. I am frightened by how much I want the sweet little beta from the Ralston clan. An alpha is ever a determined beast when he sets his sights upon prey.

How often have I heard that saying?

It is an excuse for weak alphas to embrace their basal side, forget social constructs, and succumb to their animal instincts.

I could become a beast too easily over Jessa, although we have yet to be formally introduced. Assuredly, I do not allow my eyes to linger on the lass whenever I notice her peeping at me from the crowd. I only know her name because I heard Brandon, the bastard I have clashed with more times than I can count, calling her away.

It doesn't matter that the tiny slip of a girl is not yet quite of age. Well, she might be by now. I wouldn't know either way given no one from her clan would venture to discuss her with me. Soon, she will be expected to take a mate or husband, depending on whether he is an alpha or a beta.

The rage inside me builds as I wonder if it will be Brandon who gets to claim the lass neither of us is worthy of. I have pictured caving the shifter's head between my bare hands too many times to be objective anymore.

The cocky bastard would be only too happy to close his wolf jaws around my throat. It is a mutual hatred that burns based on many years of mischief and altercation. He is in thick with the brother of the Ralston king. The pair of them take nothing seriously and seem hellbent upon pissing every clan off. It is only their king's steadying influence that has stopped them from finding themselves at war.

Still, things are changing for them. Their king's mate died last fall, and he has not been himself since.

I call the serving lass for another drink, and when she brings it over, I snatch up the lass as well.

She giggles prettily as she tumbles onto my lap, her small hands stroking my cock through my hide pants as I sup on my beer.

"You look tense," she says. Mara is enthusiastic for rutting... which is a blessing given how many lusty men we have within the clan.

As I sup my beer, I give her a side-eye.

Smirking, she dips her hand inside my pants and liberates my cock.

"Oh!" she says. Taking me in both hands, she pumps slowly up and down. "That looks painful. Let me help you with that."

Wasting no time, the lass sinks to her knees and takes me deep into her throat.

I lean back, stroking a hand through her hair as I take another sup of beer. The lass has skills in cock sucking, so I'm not about to complain. I am not alone in enjoying the unmated lasses of the clan. The room sinks into debauchery, as it is often wont to do when weed and beer are in ready supply. There are too many men and not enough mates. Men without bonds or hope of bonds fall prey to drunken revelry and infighting.

Mara does a twirling thing with her tongue, and I feel my balls tighten.

"I am going to come," I say. The greedy lass sucks harder.

Closing my eyes, I give in to the bliss as I come down her throat. For that single moment, I am no longer burdened with the fall of our once-great clan nor my father's warmongering ways.

Then it is over, and a growl rouses me from that brief peace.

Mara squeals happily as Danon scoops her up. Tossing the lass over his shoulder, he stalks for his room.

I sigh as I shove my cock back into my pants before taking another sup of beer.

"You should take her before it's too late," my father says.

I growl.

He grins. Little fazes my father, certainly not my disrespect.

The bastard knows I am keen on the little Ralston beta. A foolish slip on my part one night while drunk when I spilled my feelings to Danon, who, in turn, told our father.

"She is too young," I say.

"If you wait, then she will be given over to an alpha in their clan, and you will need to fight for her. Not that there's anything wrong with challenging for what you want. I killed your mother's betrothed, and she was ever grateful for it."

I could point out that my mother's betrothed was a worse bastard than my father by all accounts. She was an omega born to beta parents and revealed her dynamic late. Her road to claiming was not an easy one. I am not my father, and I will not claim a lass unless she agrees. Jack Ralston is unlikely to hand Jessa over to any male she does not accept willingly, for it is not the way of their clan.

I don't offer my opinion.

Tonight, I am tired of it all.

I have spent the day negotiating only to have all the good work undone by a selfish warrior claiming a Halket lass as his mate. It is but the beginning, I realize. Now that one has stolen a lass and gotten away with it, more will follow his lead. Soon, we will be at war, for although old Karry, the Halket king, is every bit as weak as my father suggests, his son is not. The young warriors of the Halket clan will demand recompense.

We have lost the way of the Goddess.

We have fallen far from honorable men, and the sliding is not yet done.

The Blighten often raid the clans to replenish their slave ranks. When it last happened, I was but a boy. Barely did we get through the last raid when illness came. It was our women-folk who paid the price. We should be working together with the other clans to protect everyone from our common enemy. Then we would not need to snatch a lass, for they would come to us willingly.

A fight breaks out on the far side of the room. Cackling, my father raises his drink, cheering them on.

I watch the men beat on one another with jaundiced eyes.

One way or another, this is coming to a head.

Chapter Three

Gage

When I pass through the great hall the following day, I find my father asleep, slumped and snoring on his throne. Danon is nowhere to be seen, but a beta whelp clearing the mess from the revelry informs me he has gone hunting.

It is typical of Danon to slink off when there are matters to be dealt with.

I go alone to speak to the alpha who took the Halket lass. Part of me wants no involvement in this foolishness, but another part of me knows I need to face this. I ask him outright if he took the lass against her will.

He denies it. So, I speak to the lass in question.

I'm not sure what I expect to get from this. She seems shy and sweet and does not appear fearful of the alpha. Then he slips his arm around her waist, and she blushes a pretty shade of pink. I don't claim to have exhaustive knowledge of lasses or how they behave under duress. But there is nothing to indicate that she is seeking to pull away, and further, she peeks at her new mate under her lashes.

"You know that this might lead to war," I say.

It is only now that the lass' lips tremble as she meets my gaze. "My parents would not let me leave," she says. "For they do not like the Lyon clan. I did not mean for it to come to this. Please, do not send me back."

I sigh, now wishing that she did not want to be here, for this is sure to end poorly for all involved. Sending her back with an apology would be bad enough. Keeping her here will be worse.

My father would not care if she was snatched, but I assuredly do. I also fear that it will encourage others to do the same, only next time, the lass might not be willing.

Against this backdrop, I leave, intending to visit the Ralston clan so I can subtly scope for any backlash about the stolen lass. Then I will head for the Halket clan and do my best to temper this mess.

Jessa

We are almost out of blackroot, and I decide to go and do a little foraging on the northern side of the village. Basket over my arm, I make my way along the lane that leads out of the village. There is an old abandoned storage barn here, and as I near, I hear noises coming from inside.

I know lads and lasses sneak in here for rutting.

Usually, I hasten straight past as quickly as I can. But something draws me today.

I shouldn't look. I can sense that this is a mistake. Yet a rebelliousness is building inside me as I rail against the directions my life continues to take me. I worry that I will be wedded to an alpha from another clan I do not know, or worse, one from this clan that I do not want. There are a few lads who have come of age, and I assuredly want none of them.

Ever since the pie incident with Brandon and that overheard conversation between my parents, there is also a budding curiosity for all things carnal.

At night, I pull the curtain across my bedding nook and wait for everyone to go to sleep. Then I touch myself, exploring the sensations, glorying in the strange awakening and awareness unfurling within me.

Sometimes, I imagine Brandon, the handsome wolf shifter who has been my obsession for so long. Before, he might take on a heroic role in an adventure. Lately, I imagine him spanking me...or kissing me...or that it is his hand where mine is.

Sometimes I also imagine it is Gage, the great bear of an alpha who visits our clan from time to time.

And sometimes, I feel this restless urgency building within me, and it does not matter how I touch or pet myself, I cannot come... On those occasions, I think of them both.

Thankfully, I have been washing my own clothes for a few years, and my mother does not notice that I need to clean certain things more than I ought to.

Placing the basket on the ground, I check that I am alone before sneaking closer to the ruined barn door.

I blink a few times as they come into view. *Brandon.* I would recognize his dark, too-long, tousled hair anywhere. My heart thuds wildly within the cage of my ribs, and my breath catches in my lungs.

They are laying over some old, dry hay that has been strewn out on the floor. He is on one side, braced over the lass, kissing her deeply. Their mouths open around each other's, tongues tangling before the kiss deepens again. His hand is under her skirt, moving in a slow rhythm. Her hips lift to meet every stroke, and she moans into his mouth.

I should back away. I have already seen too much. But her pleasure is fascinating and shocking to my innocent mind.

I have thought about rutting.

I have touched myself often of late, deep in the night. It felt nice, but it did not look like this breath-stealing, body-writhing pleasure Brandon is bestowing on this young lass.

He changes the movement, doing something I can't quite see. Her legs part further, and her groans turn wild.

She is going to come.

She is going to come, and it will be a thousand times better than anything I have experienced by my own hand.

Stepping away, I gather my basket and run for the woods.

I do not want to see the lass getting pleasured. I wish I had not seen as much as I have. Why did I look at them? Why did I do such a foolish thing?

I stop only when my chest burns for breath and my legs are cramping with the strain.

Dropping the basket, I brace my hands to my knees and suck air into my starved lungs.

I hate the lass. I hate her more than I have hated anyone in my life. I am a good girl. Everyone is always telling me as much, but I do not feel good today.

Today, I want to scratch her eyes out. I want to rake Brandon with my nails for giving another lass pleasure that should be mine.

Tears spill down my cheeks. I am heart sore and sick of spilling tears.

Sitting on the forest floor, I give myself a talking to. If I want Brandon, I will need to make him notice me. I will need to be bold like the other lasses are when they want to catch a lad's eye.

Only, I don't think I am very bold. And I'm not sure I have the nerve to pursue a lad like Brandon when I am all but choked by a fear that he will laugh.

Being laughed at does not hurt a person, only their pride. I am not prideful, and reason that it cannot hurt me so much to try.

And I want to try. I might regret it for my whole life if I do not.

Standing, I dust off my skirt and gather my basket once again. How I will gain Brandon's attention is yet to be determined. But I shall.

Resolute, I begin searching for the yellow leaves that signify blackroot. Soon, I am singing to myself as I plot how I might make Brandon mine.

Gage

My life is shitty enough without stumbling upon an Orc after riding for half a day. It is not unusual to cross paths with the odd straggler, given our lands are closest to the mountains. Still, I am currently close to the Ralston lands, and I have never seen one this far south unless in a raiding party.

It is the wrong time of year for raiding parties. He is on the smaller side for an Orc but a big bastard nevertheless, and he appears to be alone.

Black eyes narrowing and nostrils flared, the Orc hefts his club. They can run fast when they have a mind to. He will be faster than my horse in this scrubby, rock-strewn part of the forest. Retreat is not an option.

Squeezing my horse's flanks, I draw my sword and charge.

My sword catches his shoulder, and blood sprays. But he takes the hit willingly as his club sweeps me from the saddle.

"Uff!" I land on my back, winded. My horse rears and dances out of the way. I do not have time to worry about that because a monstrous club is swinging toward my head.

I roll to my left, my sword in a fierce grip. He smashes his club for me again, and I roll back the other way before jumping to my feet.

I don't stay upright for long before his club sweeps out my feet.

"Fucking Blighten scum!" I growl. Bringing my blade up, I stab blindly. It is a poor strike, but it finds flesh and more blood sprays.

Staggering to my feet, I face the Orc. He is limping, bloody wounds at his shoulder and thigh. I am bruised and battered where the club knocked me from the horse and tossed me to the floor.

Roaring, he charges. We trade blows that force me backward. The bastard is head and shoulders above me and easily twice my weight.

His attack lacks finesse, and this may be my only hope. Meeting each mighty blow saps my energy. I feint left, then step right to slash his side. Issuing a savage roar, he smashes me with his club. The blow connects with my shoulder and back, heavy enough to drive air from my lungs. I roll with it, ready when he comes in for the kill.

Sword gripped in both hands, I ram it upward into his gut.

He grunts. Blood gushes and innards spill out in loopy coils. The stink is enough to make me want to hurl. His damn club is still swinging, clipping the side of my head.

I see stars.

Fingers cramped with the strain of holding the slick hilt, I twist the blade embedded in his gut. The hilt turns slippery under my fingers. My head is ringing, and my rib and shoulder ache like a bastard! If I do not end the Orc now, I'm going to blackout, and we will both fucking die.

His club swings again, but he has lost strength. Face comical in confusion, he collapses to the forest floor.

I collapse too, but it's a partially controlled collapse because I am still mostly conscious.

"Fuck!" I grunt. Sprawled out on my back, I breathe. That is the limit of my capability.

I hope the Blighten bastard didn't bring a friend because I will be well and truly fucked.

A shadow passes over me. My horse's head comes into view as he puffs air into my face. Grabbing hold of the reins, I motion him to back up and use his strength to heave up.

I assess myself and my location. I am nearer to the Ralston community than I am to my home. Either option will be a struggle in my current condition. So much for me mending the alliance between us. They will not be impressed if I arrive like this.

But I do not have a choice.

I make my way south slowly, ribs aching like a bastard with every step of the horse. I cough up some blood. That is a bad sign.

As I ride, I worry about the Orc and that there might be more. He looked young, and the young ones often venture to make a name for themselves. It is seen as a rite of passage taking back a human skull.

Needing to replenish my water, I stop by the stream. Letting my horse take a drink, I plant my ass on the ground.

Which is when I hear the singing...sweet, high, feminine. The sound of the Goddess herself or one of her sacred angels. Perhaps I am in worse shape than I thought, and she has come for me?

"Oh!" Emerging through the trees, the lass-angel stops with a gasp.

Dark hair and forest green eyes, she is a little slip of nothing.

Jessa. What the fuck is a child doing out alone in the forest?

Rushing to me, she throws herself to her knees, discarding her herb and root-laden basket on the forest ground.

"Oh! What has happened to you!"

"An Orc, lass," I say.

Her eyes widen, and she glances over my shoulder like she is expecting an imminent attack.

"I killed it," I add.

"Goddess!" Her pretty eyes grow round. "On your own?"

"Aye," I say, frowning. "What the fuck are you doing out alone?"

She stands, planting her tiny fists to her hips. "I am of age. What I do is none of your business," she says, lifting her pert nose in the air.

What the fuck?

She bends over, presenting me with a nice view of her ass in her tight hide dress as she rummages in the basket. Her dress falls to her knees when standing but rides high on her thigh while bent. What is wrong with her? I'm an alpha from another clan, and she is all but presenting me with her too-fucking-young charms.

She has just said she is of age, the devil on my shoulder reminds me.

I drag my gaze away, eventually.

She hastens to the stream. Here, she mashes a root on some rocks before mixing it with a little water and some crushed herbs in a giant leaf.

She returns to me.

"Careful, lass," I say, trying not to breathe in her sweet scent when she gets too close. "You will get blood on you."

"Stop fussing," she says, voice taking on an air of authority.

I blink a few times, wondering if the Orc blow has addled my mind or this young beta lass really has just scolded me.

Her face softens, and her lips tremble as she takes in the damage on my chest. "This will hurt some," she says, her small hand petting my undamaged shoulder gently like she is calming a wild beast.

A pained wheeze escapes me as she places the leaf over the bruising on my chest. Her other hand remains on my shoulder, rubbing soothing circles that I admit take my mind off the pain.

I am disarmed by this small, sweet lass who I am yet to determine is an angel. I am gentled by her in ways I did not think myself capable of. A lifetime of rage seeps from me with nothing more than a touch.

Lashes lowering to make a pretty fan against her cheeks, she mumbles what sounds like a prayer. I want to scoff, for I believe the Goddess has neither time nor inclination to listen to prayer on my behalf. But the lass' face is solemn, and I don't wish to disrespect her tender care.

The mashed root begins to tingle and cool my skin. The pain, much to my surprise, eases, and she moves it onto the next place.

I endure this healing attention with a sense of wonder. I am sitting on the forest floor while she stands, yet she is barely taller than me. Gods save my mind from wandering to weak thoughts, for she is a sweet young lass, and I am a mountain of dark violence before her.

More mashed root is applied to the next area of bruising. And each time she pets the nearest undamaged part of me with her soft, warm, tiny hand.

"There, that is better," she announces with a nod before her eyes settle on my temple. "Is it very sore?"

Leaning over me, she inspects the scratch on my temple like my life might be under threat. Her small tits are in my face, and I'm trying not to look.

I look.

I like big tits, something to fill my big hands. She barely has more than a gentle swell, yet they hang down, perfect, round, and tipped by stiff nipples that tent her hide top.

My mouth fucking waters.

"No, lass," I say, voice gruff. "I am fine thanks to your skilled ministrations." The cut to my forehead feels small and troubles me much less than her soft fingers against the skin of my forehead as she brushes my hair aside.

Her natural scent fills my lungs. I am an alpha who recognizes the faint hint of her lust.

"Okay," she says, leaning even closer.

The fuck! Did she just kiss me?

I have her by the waist to thrust her away quicker than a flash, surging to my feet. Now that I'm standing, I realize how tiny she is. Her scent is stuck in my nose, and I cannot breathe it out. "What the fuck are you doing?" I demand.

"Kissing it better," she says, face turning red as she wrings her small hands.

"Well, don't fucking kiss a man better!" My hands are still on her waist...her tiny little waist. They go all the way around. I thrust her further away, chest heaving with the strain. "Do you do that often?" I demand. I am ready to end whoever the fuck she has put her lips upon.

"Only Brandon," she says.

My nostrils flare. Fucking Brandon! I would love to snap that weak beta's neck for having her kiss. Not that he is a weak beta, the bastard is a strapping man, but he is not an alpha, so weak compared to me. He does not have my strength, nor my scent, nor my knot.

I envy the lack of knot given he could fill this cute little beta lass up in ways I could not without a great deal of training.

Fuck! I will not think about that while her scent is in my lungs and her small trembling body within reaching distance.

"I am sorry," she says. "It seemed natural that I should kiss you." Her hands clamp tightly together, and her lips tremble like she might burst into tears. "I can see it was not appropriate for me to kiss a man from another clan, even an injured one. It was very forward of me. I don't know why I did it."

Now I have fucking upset the angel who was being kind to me. By rights, she should have run screaming at the sight of a bloody male from another clan.

"Hush, lass," I say. I do not know what foolishness is going through my mind, but her tears are near enough to unman me, and I gather her into my arms. "Thank you for your care."

Instinctively, I purr, although I have long understood that betas find such a sound annoying. It makes my chest swell with joy when she softens against me.

"I was on my way to your clan when the Orc attacked me. It is not safe for you out here," I say. "Allow me to escort you home."

"Okay," she says.

Reluctantly, I let her leave my arms.

She scrubs her damp cheeks.

"Oh!" Her gasp accompanies me lifting her into the saddle. I should be in terrible pain, but there is only the slightest twinge to my ribs.

I glance down, frowning as I notice the bruising has faded and nearly gone. The hairs on the back of my neck rise to attention. I do not worship the Goddess as often as I should. But I am humbled as I realize her presence has indeed been here today. When I meet the young lass' eyes, I find she looks as shocked as I am.

"What is your name, lass?" I ask. I know her name, but it would reveal more than appropriate interest, should I admit as much.

"Jessa," she says softly. She won't look at me anymore.

Taking her chin gently, I turn her to face me, waiting patiently until her pretty green eyes meet mine.

"Thank you, Jessa," I say. "I am Gage of the Lyon clan. Has this happened before?"

"No," she says, earnest eyes holding mine. "What does it mean?"

"It means you are Goddess blessed," I say gruffly, aware of how soft her skin is under my rough fingers. "It will be our secret, Jessa."

"Okay," she agrees.

I pass her basket to her, which she takes with a nod and mumbled thanks. I should lead the fucking horse, but I mount behind her instead. And even knowing it will cause trouble if I arrive at Ralston with one of their lasses before me on the horse, I continue anyway.

Chapter Four

Brandon

"You mean for us to leave now?" I ask. It is late afternoon and an unusual time of day to begin a trek. "I have not eaten yet."

I'm a shifter and eat large amounts compared to everyday folks. I guess I can grab a snack while we are out...

Grinning, Fen tosses me an apple from the bowl on the oak table.

I catch it instinctively...and put it right back. "What the fuck is wrong with you?" I say. "Shifters don't eat fruit."

He laughs, the bastard. But it is a good-humored laugh.

Fen's brother, Jack, is our clan king, and their home is the grandest within the community. The great hall where we stand talking has been turned into a workspace as a couple of men are busy making repairs to the hearth while Jack is away.

Jack is away...which means his second, Glen, has been left in charge of the clan.

It also means we have a chance to do some deep scouting without drawing attention.

I notice one of Jessa's friends disappearing into the 'herb cottage' through the hall's open double doors.

"I don't want to leave until Jessa returns," I say, frowning. I do not often challenge a decision made by Fen, but I make an exception for Jessa. I overheard the women mentioning that she had gone to collect medicinal plants after noticing the stocks were low. She has matured since I found her surrounded by hungry wolves. But she still has no sense of danger. While she knows better than to venture too far, she also gets distracted. Likely, the lass is currently singing her heart out and not paying a bit of attention to where the fuck she is.

It is not my place to tell her where she can and cannot go, but I get ants under my skin whenever they let her go anywhere alone. My palm also itches. I wholeheartedly believe the lass could do with some loving discipline to aid her in developing a sense of caution.

"She is sweet on you," Fen says with a smirk as we walk down the steps of his home.

"Who?" I ask, scowling, although I already know he is talking about Jessa.

"Jessa," he says. Grinning, he bumps his shoulder to mine. "She is of age."

"Do not fucking go there," I say. "Her father does not like me well. She slipped while bringing a cherry pie over for Ma yesterday, and the bastard looked fit to bust my balls. I can picture my wolf hide pinned over his mantle like a fucking war prize after he has finished with me."

Fen chuckles. He does not take much seriously except for making mischief and rutting, which he takes very seriously indeed.

"You do like her, though?" he asks.

"What's not to like about Jessa?" I counter. Her father will never let me near the lass. For all Jessa's mother and mine are friends, I was not wholly joking when I said he would sooner skin me than let me claim his daughter. It is a sore point all around.

I hear Fen chuckling. I refuse to make eye contact with the bastard.

"Everyone likes Jessa," he says. "She is sweet, pretty, and always smiling. She is of age. With all her sibling brats, her pa is sure to marry her off soon."

He is baiting me, I reason, but I still growl and turn to him with murder in my eyes. We may be best friends, but he knows baiting me about Jessa is off-limits.

A call on the other side of the village square rouses our attention before we come to blows. Our heads swing in the direction of the forest as a great horse bearing a warrior comes into view.

"What the fuck?" I growl. My inner wolf battles to spring from my flesh.

Not only a horse and a warrior, but Jessa smeared in blood.

Jessa

One look at Brandon's face, and I know this is going to be a disaster.

Brandon, who I watched earlier this morning pleasuring a lass in ways that made me green with rage.

Brandon, who I have often wished was pleasuring me in such a way.

Then there is Gage, whose body cages mine and who does not even realize he has become a similar star in my lustful dreams. I can still remember the flash of anger on his face when told him I had kissed Brandon, even though I haven't. Why did I do that?

Oh, this is such a mess!

Gage's growl reverberates through me where we are pressed together. His arms are around my waist so that he can hold the reins, but now they tighten.

Fen tries to cut Brandon off, but he barely notices the larger alpha as he storms down the steps of the king's home and hall.

"Get down from the fucking horse, Jessa!"

Gage's hands tighten further, and his growl rattles with menace. Violence coils in his body. The same in Brandon as his wolf threatens to burst. If he shifts... No, he cannot shift. It will start a clan war, and we are barely civil as it is.

"Let me go," I say to Gage.

"I am not letting you down. The mutt is un-fucking-stable."

"Let me down!" My voice carries authority. I sense this moment is important in ways more than stopping a fight. "He won't hurt me."

Brandon is nearly upon us when Gage slips from the saddle, hauls me down, and shoves me behind him. His great horse dances beside us.

"No!" Slipping under Gage's arm, I plant myself between them. One hand against the warm, firm flesh of Gage's stomach behind me. The other landing in the center of Brandon's chest as he barrels forward.

They both still instantly, although they continue growling at one another over my head. Goddess, it sets my body tingling in ways naught to do with fear of being between these two dominant males. Brandon is head and shoulders over me, and Gage is head and shoulders over Brandon. I feel tiny and yet powerful between these two towering walls of muscle. My belly turns over, and my pussy clenches so sharply, I have to bite back my whimper.

Brandon's nostrils flare, and he flicks a glance at me before returning his glare to Gage. "Jessa, move aside."

"No!" I repeat. "Not until you stop acting like a pair of whelps!"

Heat fills my cheeks that I dare to call a grown man a whelp. I am a polite, dutiful lass. I have no idea where this rogue madness comes from.

I hear a chuckle, low and masculine. Fen is standing a few paces away. "The lass has the measure of you both by the looks of it," he says, and still smirking, folds his arms like he is getting ready for a show.

"Stand down the pair of you!" The newcomer is Jack's second, Glen. The alpha does not look amused by the nonsense happening in our village square. A frown crosses his face. "What has happened to you? Did you get into a fight with a bear?"

"Orc," Gage says gruffly. "I killed it."

I hear collective gasps from the nosy villagers watching. Fen straightens, and the smile is wiped from his face.

Gage is no longer growling, and neither is Brandon. The tension leaves the two men I touch in slow, hard-won increments.

"I was at the ford and closer to your village than mine," Gage continues. "I found Jessa and thought it best to bring her home."

Brandon growls at the mention of me being found away from home.

Gage takes a step back. I miss the connection. No sooner do my hands drop to my sides then Brandon snatches me up.

"Oh!"

Brandon tosses me over his shoulder. Behind, I can hear Gage's low warning growl.

I bounce about over Brandon's shoulder as he stalks from the village square. Pushing my hair aside, I strain to look back.

I can *sense* Gage's fury. Both Fen and Glen shift to cut him off. Goddess, Gage is so powerful, I think if he set his mind to it, they could not stop him.

"Oh! Put me down!"

I get a spank to my bottom for my wriggling. I get another when I curse.

"Quieten down, lass," Brandon says, voice a barely tempered growl. "Or you will be getting a lot more than my palm against your bottom."

"Goddess!" I mutter, feeling that unmistakable wetness pooling between my legs. Does he mean to spank me again?

He makes a sharp cut to the left into a nearby hay barn, mostly empty at this time of year with a few bales scattered about the ground. Sitting on one, he tosses me over his lap.

Spank! Spank! Spank!

"What the fuck were you doing so far away from the village?"

"Oh! I was looking for blackroot!"

Spank! Spank! Spank!

"That is not a good enough reason for putting yourself in danger!"

Spank! Spank! Spank!

"It did not escape my notice that you scented of arousal when you were between us!"

"Goddess," I mutter weakly, having no idea how to respond to that.

"Do you like that, Jessa? Like driving males to growl and fight over you?"

Spank! Spank! Spank!

"No!" This conversation has taken a very alarming turn, and it was assuredly not nice to start with.

"Don't fucking lie to me," Brandon growls between spanks. My hide skirt offers little protection from his firm chastisement, and my poor bottom is on fire. "His scent is all fucking over you. I thought you were a good girl Jessa. Good girls do not drive men to lose their fucking minds!"

"I am a good girl!" I would say anything to stop the punishment. It stings far worse than my memories.

"You are not a fucking good girl," he says between yet more spanks. "You are very fucking naughty!"

"Enough!"

At my father's gruff voice, Brandon surges to his feet, sending me tumbling to the floor. He towers over me, chest heaving with the strain as I scramble to my feet.

My father's eyes seem to bulge in his face. I have only seen him this livid once, and that was when William pushed Greta off the jetty into the loch, and she nearly drowned. "Home, Jessa. Now!"

I do not want to leave them alone, but one look at my father's face, and I flee.

As I round the corner and my home comes into view, I see my mother waiting on the steps. I throw myself into her arms.

"There, lass," she says, holding me as I try to get the words out between stuttered sobs. "I have heard all about it! Goddess knows folks love to gossip. Come inside, and let's shut the door."

"Brandon spanked me!" I wail. "And now Papa is going to kill him!"

My mother's chuckle disarms me. She draws me into our home, enclosing us inside where it is unnaturally quiet. I am guessing she asked a clanswoman to look after the brats after learning of the trouble.

Pulling out a seat for me at the oak table, she pours me a glass of milk.

My tears have turned to hiccups, and I try to sip a little.

"Your father will not kill him. There, and you know as much. Your papa is a sensible man who suffers occasional bouts of protective rage on behalf of his first, and much loved, daughter." With gentle fingers, she brushes the tears from my cheeks. "Happen he might thump the lad a few times. But I dare say Brandon will cope."

"I am so confused," I say.

"I know, love. It will work out, I promise you."

"How? How can it possibly work out? Papa hates Brandon. Now he will never let us wed!" I want to cut off my tongue for spilling this out. But my mother only smiles kindly.

"Is that what you want?" She asks. "To wed Brandon?"

I nod, feeling foolish. I have long been certain that Brandon shares no similar affection toward me. The events of this morning are still fresh in my mind. But everything has gotten muddled up. My thoughts spin over all he said as he spanked me in the barn. Maybe he is only furious because it was an alpha from another clan? Maybe this is merely hopefulness on my part that he spanked me and said all those things because he cares?

I wanted so badly for Brandon to notice me. Now I fear he might have noticed me in ways more than I can handle.

"Leave it to me," my mother says. When I glance up, she winks.

I hiccup loudly. My mother chuckles.

I can't make head or tails of what has just happened, but for the first time in forever, I feel the tiniest bit of hope.

Chapter Five

Brandon

I do not have a fucking hope with Jessa.

Her father did not like me well before the spanking incident. Now he fucking hates me.

"What is going on with you, Jessa, and Gage?" Fen asks as we make our way through the forest toward the Halket clan. Leaving our horses tied off, we continue on foot.

I don't know what Fen has planned. I spent yesterday eve brooding and most of this morning too.

"I thought you were going to challenge Gage then and there," Fen continues. The lad has a hard time with personal boundaries when it comes to discussions and is a worse gossip than any lass. "I'll be honest, I wouldn't like your chances in wolf form, and you have less than none as a human."

"Thanks," I say dryly. "I needed further insult to add to the bounty I have acquired over the past day."

He chuckles.

"How come you didn't shift to heal it?"

Fen rarely lets a matter drop until he has gotten all the details. He is talking about my black eye, which aches like a bastard.

Better I get this over with.

"Her pa told me a man should never discipline a lass while angry," I say.

Fen whistles. "He has a point," he agrees.

"He also said a man should never discipline a lass because he is jealous of another man."

Fen grimaces.

Yeah, that one stung as well. "Then he said if I put my hands on Jessa again, he would nail me to the barn wall by my balls and leave me there until I learned a lick of sense."

Fen chuckles.

"Then he thumped me. The bastard has been a carpenter his whole life and has big fucking hands."

Fen's chuckle turns into a deep guffaw. "How the fuck does that work?" he asks.

"How does what work?" I say, scowling. I want to forget the whole fucking thing. I do not want to talk about it.

"Nailing a man to a wall by his balls?" Fen elaborates. "Surely you would just drop off the wall?"

I cut him a scowl. Every time I think about that threat, I swear my cock shrivels, and my balls try to crawl up my ass. "I don't fucking know," I say. "I believe it was said to inspire fear rather than something he would actually do. It is working. I will not touch the lass."

"But you do want to?" Fen presses because he is too dense to know when to let a matter go.

I *do* want to. But I also understand when want is without hope. Her pa will not let me near the lass. She is of age now, although her father has yet to announce it officially. If I am honest with myself, I do not feel worthy after spanking her as I did. I resolve to put Jessa out of my mind. Better for all involved if I do for nothing could ever come of it. She deserves a better man who does not succumb to jealousy because another man's scent is all over her.

I swallow, thinking about her arousal as she stood between the two of us.

Some lasses need more than one mate, just as some men need more than one lass. It is the way of the clans that we do not judge. I think Jessa, for all she is still innocent, will need more than one mate. I have caught the occasional hints of arousal on her, more often of late. But nothing like the heady saturation that every shifter and alpha in the fucking square must have scented when Jessa was between Gage and me.

He sensed it. And *he* wants her too.

My wolf is not inclined toward sharing, and definitely not with the son of the Lyon clan king.

Better for everyone that I back the fuck away.

"No," I say. "I do not want her."

"Good," Fen says decisively and in a way that piques my concerns. "That will make my plans easier."

"What plans?" I ask.

The bastard only grins.

I am a beta wolf, so it is in my nature to latch with an alpha and follow. Yet, I still do not have a fucking clue how I end up rutting a lass in the forest a short distance from the huts and cottages of her home.

This is all because Fen is hellbent on causing mischief with their king's son, Eric.

Eric is besotted with Gwen. I heard that he gifted her

flowers the other day. What a fool! Gwen is as tall as most beta men and has better combat skills than half of Eric's clan. The idiot should have claimed her long ago. He doesn't even have an enraged father getting in his way.

Fen has determined that Eric needs a little push. Also, Fen is Eric's rival as far back as time and cannot help but bait him about the lass.

He cannot help baiting everyone, truth be told.

The lass' name is Gwen, and she is a warrior maiden from the Halket clan.

The only thing I get out of this mischief is a clear determination that I don't want any lass but Jessa. The fire flashing in her pretty eyes as she boldly stood between Gage and me, and called us a pair of whelps. The feel of her small, soft hand as she pressed it against my chest. And her aroused scent as she found herself between two warring males... Finally, Jessa over my lap, her plump ass jiggling under her hide dress as I spanked her.

Gods, her fucking scent was like wildfire through my veins.

I am roused from my daydreams and thrust back into reality. A few paces away, Gwen curses her outrage at Fen who has managed to get cum in the poor lass's hair.

"We were rutting," Fen points out. "What did you expect to happen?"

At a sudden roar, we all look left.

Eric.

He has not come alone.

I snatch Gwen out of the way just in time as Eric slams Fen into a tree.

"Fuck!" Fen growls as they wrestle.

I wince as Eric gets a few good blows in. He is a crazy bastard at the best of times and fully enraged presently.

"Separate them! For fuck's sake," I yell. I grab hold of

Gwen, who looks like she wants to beat on Fen as well. "Before he kills Fen!"

Eric's crew try and wade in, but it is near impossible with the wild, swinging fists.

"Oh! Look at my hair!" Gwen wails as she aims a kick at Fen's shin.

Everyone is fucking shouting. Gods, this is a calamity of the highest order!

"Do not blame Brandon!" Fen shouts before Eric lands a brain-rattling fist to his chin. "Do not blame Gwen either!" Fen adds. "The lass is lusty and cannot help herself—uff!"

I wince as a purple-faced Eric slugs Fen in the gut.

I don't see what the fuck happens next. It is like one giant melee. Gwen is still bewailing the state of her hair. The blow I'm sure she intended for Fen lands on Eric, and both men end up on the floor grappling like a pair of drunk bears.

"Oh! Stop them!" Gwen yells.

"I am fucking trying!" one of Eric's crew yells back.

More wild wrestling ensues. Legs thrash, and fists fly as though in slow motion. They are both grunting and wheezing for breath. I think they might be tiring out. Thank fuck because it is exhausting to watch.

Then Fen grunts in a pained wheeze, and Eric shoves him off.

Everyone stills as they both lie there panting. Fen is holding his nuts, and Eric is holding his bloody nose. Finally, Eric's crew wade in and drag Eric up. As Fen staggers to his feet, I plant a hand on his chest and search for signs of reason in his flushed face.

Heaving deep breaths, he waves me off him.

"Best get yourself a second when you mate the lass," Fen says. "One cock is definitely not going to be enough."

The crowd surges to try and cut the two men off. But alas, Eric is powerfully enraged, and the blow sends Fen sprawling.

"This was not a fair fight," Fen says, scowling. "It is well known that only a coward challenges a man who has just rutted a wench."

This time, Eric's crew cut off his charge. There is yet more roaring and cursed threats from Eric as Fen staggers to his feet.

I shake my head at him, although I cannot help my small grin. Life is never dull with Fen.

Eric stabs a finger in our direction and barks, "Fuck off my lands."

Pivoting, he snatches up the bedraggled Gwen, who has washed most of the seed off courtesy of an offered waterskin. She squeals as he tosses her over his shoulder before stalking off toward their home.

Given she is a hefty lass, and much of her weight is muscle, I admit to being impressed.

As they disappear through the trees, I finally let my laughter out. "I have never seen Eric that purple of face. I think you hit a sore spot telling him she would need a second mate."

Fen chuckles. "Eric has a powerful right hook. I should not bait him with the lass."

"I don't think you will have the chance to bait him again," I say, grinning. It is good to think about other people's problems instead of worrying about mine. "Something tells me Eric's father's plans to bond him to a foreign lass are about to come undone."

But as Fen gathers his discarded things, I know my own troubles are far from over.

I thought this might purge me of thoughts pertaining to Jessa. But all it has done is stir them up.

I don't want another lass, I realize. I want Jessa. She might have responded to Gage, but she responded to me first. I know a lot about pleasuring a lass. By the time I have wooed and plea-sured her, she won't even remember Gage's name.

As we return to the horses, I begin to plan.

Chapter Six

Jessa

After the spanking incident, Brandon left with Fen, and I have not seen him since. I tell myself it is for the best, given nothing can come of it, but it hurts all the same.

Worse, Papa is in a bad mood and works until late in his workshop every evening. The brats all have a nose for trouble and are acting up.

My mother says to trust her and that it will work out. I cannot see how.

Then, yesterday, Jack returned, and everyone is talking about how Fen and Brandon are still gone.

I am hanging out the washing when Suka saunters past. She is part of Nola's posse, and I do not like her well. Still, she is hard to avoid, given she lives two cottages away.

"Did you hear that Jack brought a slave with him?" she says, leaning against the sheep paddock fence.

I pause my washing hanging. "No," I say. "I did not hear

that. What does he want a slave for?" We have few slaves in the village. The only folks who become slaves are those who have committed particularly heinous crimes. Usually, the king will gift the criminal to another clan, and they will live as a slave there. "Where is she from?"

"From the western lands," Suka says. "I heard she is from Oxenford."

I frown. This does not make any sense. Why would Jack bring a slave back from Oxenford? That is not even where his sister lives.

"Why would he do such a thing? Slaves come from other clans, not from the western lands."

Suka smirks. "A pleasure slave. The king has broken his year-long abstinence from rutting. Nola says he will soon cast the slave aside, likely hand her over to the unmated men or gift her to another clan. It will not be long before he claims Nola as his mate."

"Maybe he just wants to rut the pleasure slave?" I say a little spitefully. I feel sick to my core thinking that Nola might become Jack's mate.

Suka chuckles. "For certain, he wants to rut her. But it is only temporary. Why else would he have given Nola responsibility for the slave?"

"Goddess," I mutter. I do not know this slave, nor what crime she committed to become one. But I instantly feel sorry for her being given over to Nola. She must have committed a truly heinous act to be treated thus. "Did Jack's spirits seem lifted?"

I go back to hanging washing. Jack has been melancholic since his mate died last year. Some said he would never take another mate.

"Aye, until he learned about Fen and Brandon getting into a fight with Eric of the Halket clan over a lass."

My head snaps up.

Suka smirks again. "They were both rutting her when Eric found them. Jack is furious and has ridden over to Halket to try and smooth things over."

"It cannot be both of them," I say as my world seems to tilt. I was so sure that Brandon might have feelings for me after he spanked me. All the words Brandon said that day have plagued my mind. I know Papa is in a bad mood because my mother seeks to soften him toward Brandon. Now, Brandon is off rutting other lasses, and I feel such a fool.

Suka gives me a smug look. "You can't be *that* innocent, Jessa. Fen and Brandon have shared lasses on plenty of occasions." She makes like she is fanning herself. "They have shared me a time or two. But I dare say a sweet lass like yourself will be married off and never have such fun. Jessa, the good girl, always doing what her mama and papa say. Jessa, who will be wedded to a respectable farmer who knows more about crops than pleasuring a lass."

"Jessa!" My mother's call startles me.

"Run along, good girl," Suka says, and turning, she saunters off.

My heart is racing, and my lips are trembling.

"Jessa!"

Dropping the washing in the basket, I turn and head for home. I have not even kissed a boy, and I am of age to be married.

I don't want to be a good girl anymore. I want my share of the fun.

My mother is frowning when I near the door. "What's wrong, love?" Her eyes pass over my head to where Suka is.

"Did you hear about Fen and Brandon?" I blurt out before I can think better of it.

"Aye, I did hear about some mischief between them and a

Halket lass," she says, her face softening. "But that is all it is as yet, a bit of gossip that folks are wont to exaggerate."

I want to cling to the innocent version of me that believes in love ever after, but I can feel it slipping away.

Suka was telling the truth. About all of it.

I have no interest in Fen, never have had, but I am jealous she has gotten to be with Brandon. Maybe she was the lass he was pleasuring in the barn?

"Your father has not yet spoken to Brandon. No formal agreement has been made, and the lad is free to get up to mischief."

"I know that," I say. But in my heart, I thought that Brandon's words and the firm discipline meant that he cared about me. How can he care about me and be with another lass?

A flush heats my cheeks. Am I not also thinking of another man and alpha even as I berate Brandon for being with someone else? Maybe Brandon is the kind of man who needs two lasses? I try to imagine how it might be to share him with another lass, and it makes me feel sick.

"I need to go," I say.

"Where?" my mother asks, worry lining her face.

"A walk. I won't go any farther than the old lane," I promise. "I just need time to think."

"Okay, Jessa," she says. "It has taken me a week to talk your father around to the idea of Brandon. But I will tell him to do naught yet."

"Thank you," I say, and leaning up on my toes, I press a kiss to my mother's cheek.

❧

As I pass the infamous barn, my resentment grows. How dare Brandon spank me and then go to another lass!

My temper further charges with every step that I take. My route leads out of the village before curving north. I don't realize where I am going until I arrive.

Before me is the sacred pool, surrounded by smooth, mossy rocks. A waterfall, weak at this time of year, sends a fine mist into the air as it crashes into the water. On the right of the waterfall is a great shimmering oval that spins and warbles, sparkling blue and golden light.

The portal. A place where the Goddess can hear our prayers. I come once a month with an offering, but people often visit whenever they need Her guidance.

There are other portals within the lands of the world, not here in the eastern clans, but far away in the western kingdoms of Hydornia. Those portals lead to other worlds and to other portals within this world.

I have seen the portal often, living as we are so close to this wondrous site. I've also heard tales about it from elders who visit our village from time to time. They talk of the travelers who pass through portals and what they find on the other side.

Many leave for adventure.

Sometimes, they return.

More often, they are never seen again.

On the other side, you might find desolation, utopia, and everything in between.

Monsters more fearsome than Orcs.

Wise and ancient Fae.

You never really know, for it does not lead to the same location twice.

Not this portal, for this one is lost. It is said that if you try and step through, you come back out here again. I know children have games doing it, although it is forbidden.

I sigh.

Maybe I do need some of Her guidance today.

A faint splash draws my attention. Goddess! Is there someone in the pool?

When I was a young lass of Greta's age, I threw a rock into the pool. I got a stern talking to and went to bed without supper that night.

Confusion incapacitates me, and rather than approaching, I move off the path and a little way into the trees. I have never seen anyone in the sacred pool and have no idea what to do.

The pool is forbidden.

It must be a child. I wonder if I can coax them from their mischief before they get into trouble.

"Oh," I murmur, seeing the back of a blonde head just visible around a rock. With long hair the color of sunshine and a petite frame, the lass is sitting on the mossy bank splashing her feet in the pool!

"Mnnnnn!"

An arm snakes around my waist, and a huge hand smothers my scream. Lifted, I am carried a short distance away from the pool. Panic rushes and then collapses as I recognize the scent.

How do I recognize the scent? How is such a thing even possible?

Yet, I know even before he speaks that the man holding me is Gage.

"Do not scream, lass," Gage says gruffly. "Or I will end up getting skewered."

I struggle a little, elated to discover there is no give. I revel in the feeling of his strong arm around my waist and his warm hand over my mouth. The ease with which he restrains me should instill fear, yet his great strength over me is a source of heady arousal.

"Stop wriggling, lass. Your aroused scent is enough of a test without you stirring my need to subdue."

I still, although it is not fear that drives my compliance.

Strangely, I like this feeling of submission to the will of this stern alpha. Like it is the natural order of things. This time, I only suffer a token amount of shame that he can tell I'm aroused.

"I'm going to take my hand away. Do not fucking scream."

I consider screaming. A good girl would scream. But as his fingers slowly peel away from my mouth, I don't make a peep. I like this very much, being a bad girl with an alpha from another clan. The heat from his body behind me sets off a pleasant buzz low in my belly. His big hand lowers to rest at the base of my throat.

A sudden thought strikes me.

"Were you watching the lass at the pool?" I demand, trying to peer back.

"What lass?" His fingers tighten on my waist, pinning me to him more securely. "The only lass I have been watching is you. I was trying to gain your attention as you hung out the washing, but you were singing your heart out and oblivious to the world. I did not know a laundry basket could contain so many items!"

I don't remember singing, but I often sing while doing chores. It helps to pass the time.

"Then that other lass came over, and you went back inside. I was returning to my horse to quit my foolishness when you stomped off muttering and waving your arms like you were fit to strangle someone."

I giggle. I don't remember waving my arms about, but I might have done. I was cross because I was thinking about Brandon rutting a lass.

"I was cross," I say. My gaze lowers to where his hand holds me securely to him. A big, broad hand that spans my tummy. His other hand rests against my throat. He has no reason to hold me now, but I like that he does.

71

I wonder how Gage would look while rutting a lass. He is so big and powerful. I imagine the lass would be like a little doll compared to his great bulk. I think he would be rough with her, would hold her down and force her to take his cock and knot.

"Goddess," I whisper as the fluttery sensation kicks off between my legs. I do not even need to check to know that the strange slick is gathering there.

He makes a low rumbling noise deep in his chest, half growl, half purr. His fingers, spread wide over my tummy, clench a little like he cannot help himself. I want him to pleasure me the way I saw Brandon pleasuring that lass. To lay me upon the floor, to kiss me deeply, to tangle his tongue with mine and swallow my moans of pleasure as he slides his hand under the hem of my hide skirt.

I am set aside so swiftly, I stumble a few steps.

When I turn, I find a wild version of Gage I barely recognize with chest heaving, nostrils flared, and dark eyes, hungry.

"You are a fucking test," he growls. "Don't look at me like that unless you want to find yourself on the forest floor with your skirt lifted and my face buried between."

Goddess! I don't even know why a man would want to put his face between a lass' legs, but I very much want to find out.

He heaves a great breath in and swipes a hand down his face. "I just wanted to see you," he says. "To make sure you were okay after the mutt carried you off."

My lips tug up in a smile. "Brandon is not a mutt." A warm determination settles inside me that Gage, despite his despicable clan, is a noble alpha.

"He *is* a fucking mutt who is off rutting some Halket lass and all but starting a war."

My smile fades.

"Fuck," he mutters, eyes widening as I march over and poke him in the chest.

It is closer to his stomach, but it is as far as I can easily reach. "At least he is not invading territory and claiming it as his own."

"That is the least of our transgressions, lass," he says, voice softening like he is sad.

I do not want to fight with Gage any more than I want to fight with Brandon. But Gage knows secrets about me, and I worry about what would happen should he tell.

"It is our secret," he says like he can read my mind. "I have no desire to quarrel with you, Jessa. I should not have spoken of Brandon so. We have clashed in the past, Brandon and me. Does he have a claim to you?"

He grimaces when he says *clashed*. I know Brandon gets up to mischief with Fen and so this does not surprise me. I wish Brandon had a claim on me. I wish for many things that are unlikely to come to pass.

His fingers under my chin, gently tipping it so I meet his eyes, sets off a little spark under my skin.

"Does he have a claim on you, Jessa?"

"No," I say. "Not yet."

A weight settles in my stomach as I watch the shutter come down over Gage's face. His hand drops away, and I miss his touch.

"I will still fucking end him if he does not treat you well, and even if it starts a war."

I think he is going to kiss me then. I sway a little like I am being drawn toward him by an invisible force.

But he turns and disappears into the forest, leaving me alone and twice as confused.

He came all the way over here. I do not think he had a reason today. Given the tensions between all the clans at present, I think he could be in great danger should he have been found.

I think he could have been in worse danger should they have discovered he came to see me.

He came to see *me*.

I'm glad he came to see me, although it stung that he rubbed salt in the wound of Brandon and the Halket lass. But it only stung a little the second time, and as my mother said, there was no agreement made. Likely Brandon has put me out of his mind for good after Papa had *words* with him.

Only I think if a man cares for a woman, he should fight for that. Maybe he doesn't want me enough?

I get the impression that Gage would fight for me, even if it brought our clans to war.

"I thought you were a good girl, Jessa," Brandon said as he spanked my bottom. *"Good girls do not drive men to lose their fucking minds!"*

My lips tug up. I think that Brandon would fight for me, too.

Chapter Seven

Jessa

Needing to clear my mind, I end up walking to the river. When I return home, the sun is beginning to set, and a great commotion is coming from the direction of the village square.

My father is stowing his woodcutting gear having been out all day in the forest with the men. My mother is at the workshop door wringing her hands, seeming torn between ushering the brats inside and talking to my father.

"I need to put a stop to this madness," my father says. "I do not care if the lass is a slave or not. She belongs to Jack, and he will be the one to see to her discipline, not Nola."

"What has happened?" My younger siblings are crying, the older ones ashen-faced. Amos, the oldest of my brothers, has been with my father all day. He is as tall as Ma, and even he looks shaken.

"A lot of nonsense that will not end well for Nola," my

father says gruffly. "Take the children inside and keep the doors locked, Betty."

"Please, be careful, Ed," my mother says. "Nola has infected a few of the younger warriors and village folk with her madness. With Glen accompanying Jack, there was no one to reason with them."

My father presses a kiss to my mother's forehead. "I have to try," he says. "Come with me, Amos."

They leave.

"Inside, everyone," I say, gathering William and Greta by the hand. They are the most likely to be naughty. Sickness settles in my stomach. No sooner do I get the brats indoors than I hear the thunder of approaching horses.

"Thank the Goddess!" my mother says as we watch Jack, Glen, and the other warriors of the clan thunder past.

Not long after, my father and Amos return.

"She was no slave," my father says. "The lass being punished by Nola was Jack's new mate."

The following day, Jack sends for me.

I admit to being terrified after all the troubles surrounding last night. The lass I spotted by the pool yesterday was Jack's new mate. Had I only gone to her and warned her that the site was sacred, she would not have been hurt.

"It will be fine," my mother says. "You did no wrong. Likely Jack is seeking a companion for his new mate."

I find Jack in his great hall talking to Glen, his second in command. They are both huge alphas, and I contemplate slinking off.

Spotting me, Jack curls his fingers to beckon me in.

"No need to be fearful, lass," he says, frowning as he notices me quaking.

"How is your new mate?" I blurt out before considering how it might be a delicate subject likely to lead to his rage.

"She is not well," he says sadly. "But she will recover with a little time."

"I saw her," I say before I can stop myself. "I was going to pray, and I saw a lass near the sacred pool."

Goddess, why am I telling him this? Now I have backed myself into a corner!

"Then I bumped into...a friend." My cheeks grow so hot, I am sure they will catch fire. "And I forgot about the lass...your mate. Had I warned her, she would not have been hurt."

Hot, shameful tears begin to pool behind my eyes.

"Steady, lass," Jack says, placing his big hand upon my shoulder. "This mischief is not your fault. Nola was seeking an excuse to have Hazel punished. Happen she would have done something else, maybe more spiteful, had you thwarted her plans. And anyway, how were you to know what would happen? No, lass, I am her mate and made a poor choice in a companion."

He squeezes my shoulder gently before letting his hand drop.

"I was hoping you might be able to accompany Hazel while I must deal with clan business. She is not from the clans and does not know our ways. I made a poor choice last time, thinking a certain lass was due respect because her father once held some. I must live with that mistake. But this time, I would like a gentler companion. I've only ever heard good things said about you, Jessa. I've had a chat with your parents to see if they can manage with a little less of your time. And it would make me very happy if you could show Hazel a better side of clan life."

"Oh!" I say, feeling a smile split my face. "I would be delighted to! When will I meet her?"

"She is resting now, lass," he says. "But after she has eaten some breakfast, perhaps you could return." He looks a little shifty-eyed before he adds. "She likes soft things for her bedding. See what pelts we have in the stores as might be suitable."

"I will, sire," I gladly agree.

❦

Arms laden with the softest pelts within the village, I return to find Jack and his mate are in the bedding chamber.

I wait a while, making sure they are not *busy*. When I hear talking, I venture to knock on the entrance.

"I have the pelts, sire," I say, glancing at the lass on the bed before lowering my lashes.

"Come in, lass," Jack calls. "This is my mate, Hazel. Hazel, meet Jessa."

I bob another bow, feeling nervous.

As Jack takes his leave, Hazel smiles at me. She has long blonde hair and the prettiest hazel eyes.

She is naked, and I immediately see the welts upon her skin.

I wonder if I were to kiss her like I did Gage, whether it would heal her, too?

"Did Nola do that?" I ask. My lips tremble with shame to be part of a clan that would do such a terrible thing to a lass.

"Yes," she says. "But she has been well punished. A gifted slave to the Halket clan, at Jack's determination."

"Good," I say. "She was a witchy lass and not well liked. That she would do such a thing horrifies me."

"I do not wish anyone the life of a slave," Hazel says. Then her lips twitch in a small smile. "But she *was* a witchy lass."

Soon, we are firm friends, and I wonder at how her arrival has brightened everyone within the clan, especially her new mate.

But then Fen and Brandon return.

My heart races when I learn this. It has only been a few weeks, but it feels like the world has turned on its head since I last saw Brandon.

But they bring with them troubling news.

And those wild dreams and forbidden thoughts that still fill my mind at night are now unceremoniously quashed.

Warriors from the Lyon clan—Gage's clan—have been caught trying to snatch a Halket lass.

The tentative alliance is over. Gage and his clan are no longer welcome here.

Chapter Eight

Brandon

Tempers have been flared ever since our return. The Halket clan do not like us well after our mischief with Gwen and Eric. Now we may also be on the verge of war with the Lyon clan after we caught and stopped four of their warriors from snatching a Halket lass.

Before Fen and I left, there were rumors that the Lyon clan had taken a Halket lass. Supposedly, it was her choice. Now with this second attempt, everything is in doubt. They hold no respect for other clans nor the women they try to take by force.

Jack hates the Lyon clan. Their leader, Rend is a blood-thirsty heathen who rules his people with fear.

As if this were not enough to contend with, Jack has gotten himself a mate.

A mate he is now sharing with Fen.

I am in a state of wonder at Fen's sudden dive into mated life. But I have my own problems to deal with. I did a lot of thinking while we were scouting, and I'm determined to woo

Jessa at any cost. A task made worse since news of what happened with Gwen has spread throughout the clan.

Groveling is going to be required.

But before such plans can be put in place, I see Jessa returning from the forest, a basket in her arms.

She has been out in the forest again.

❦

Jessa

I have had a pleasant morning with Hazel, and I am returning home with a basket full of berries when an arm shoots out to block my path.

"Where have you been, Jessa?"

As I look up into Brandon's handsome face, my tummy ties in knots even as my eyes narrow. A tic thumps in his jaw. He is a little furry, as he often is when he has been traveling.

I want to pet the scruff on his jaw.

I also want to slap his face.

"None of your business, Brandon," I say, looking away like I am bored.

"Jessa."

There is a warning in his voice, and it brings a sense of thrill.

"Brandon," I say, sending a fake smile his way.

"What has gotten into you lately?" he says, frowning. "You are not a reckless lass."

"Maybe it is time I started being more reckless. Why do you care anyway? Don't you have a Halket lass to rut?" I can't believe I just said that, but I won't take it back.

Brandon's cheeks take on a ruddy glow. "I'm sorry," he says.

That just makes me madder, and my temper spills out.

"You spanked me, Brandon," I hiss. "You said all those things to me like you cared. Only you didn't care."

"I did. I do! Fuck! Your pa threatened to thump me if I so much as looked at you again."

"Well, I suppose that is that then. You always do what my pa says."

"Jessa!"

He sounds exasperated now, but I don't care about that either. I thought I had reconciled myself to what happened, but seeing him has brought forth all the hurt.

"Don't tell me where to walk, Brandon," I say, poking him in the chest. "I'm of age now. You are not the only lad who has ever caught my eye. And to think, my papa was going to talk to yours."

He growls, a low, rumbly sound that is part fury and part hurt. "I was stupid. I didn't think I had a chance with you."

My finger still touches his chest. It shakes. Vision blurred with tears, I don't notice his hand has moved until I feel it enclose mine. By then, I am lost in the tentative connection that makes my fool heart sing.

"Jessa, I'd like to court you," he says.

I huff out a breath.

"Please, if I came, would you walk with me this evening?"

I don't pull my hand away.

Brandon's head lowers as he stares at my hand clasped within his larger ones.

There is intimacy in the gentle touch. I want him. But I am also a little wounded inside.

"If I came?" he persists.

"I don't know," I say. As my mother said, there was no agreement made between us. Yet, it still hurts more than I expected.

"That is not a no," he says.

When I glance up, I find him watching me with a tentative smile.

"I don't know," I repeat, withdrawing my hand from his.

With gentle fingers, he tucks my hair behind my ear. "Then I will come, and I will keep coming until you do."

§♠

Brandon

I knew groveling was going to be required, but I still feel like the worst kind of sap as I dress in my best leather pants and jerkin, brush the dust from my boots, and gather the flowers I picked.

My mother is in the rocker by the fire, knitting, a smile on her lips. My father, who sits at the table smoking his pipe, doesn't offer an opinion or smile. Given he sups beer with Jessa's father on occasion, I've no doubt they have been discussing me and my ways.

"I'm going out for a bit," I say. Why the fuck do I feel the need to announce this? I've been of age for several years and long since stopped announcing my activity to my parents. Half the time, I don't even come home.

"Good luck, son," my father says between puffs on his pipe. "You're going to need it."

Then the bastard smiles.

"Gods," I mutter under my breath, stomping over to the door with my father's low chuckle following me.

It's not a great distance. Jessa's family lives directly opposite us. I have seen Jessa most days of my life. Yet it is the strangest experience to cross the small lane as I do today, flowers in hand and belly full of nerves.

Their door is shut. I can't decide if that is better or worse. It is early evening, so I dare say they are relaxing after dinner. Not so long ago, I'd have knocked and continued straight in. Now, I stand like a fool before knocking and holding my breath.

I hear a chair scrape back on the other side and footsteps approaching, *heavy* footsteps. It was too much to hope that Betty might come to the fucking door.

It opens, and a stony-faced Ed stands on the other side.

"I was hoping to see Jessa," I wheeze past my tight, dry throat.

Ed's narrowed eyes lower to the flowers in my hand before rising and pinning me to the spot. "Not a fucking chance," he growls.

"Ed!" a stern, but feminine, voice calls. Thank the Goddess Betty is on my side.

A tic thumps in Ed's jaw. He glares at me like he is imagining nailing my balls to the barn wall.

My butt cheeks clench and my balls try to crawl up into the non-existent crack of my ass.

"Jessa, there's a young *whelp* to see you. Say the word, and I'll toss him off the porch."

I hear another chair scrape and the patter of lighter feet before Jessa appears at her father's side.

She looks from me to the flowers, much like her father did, only it is done slowly. I see the emotions on her pretty face, for she has ever been an open book. I see hurt, and I hate myself for causing it, but there is also a little hope.

"Are they for me?" she says, indicating the flowers.

I follow her line of sight, belatedly remembering that there are flowers in my fucking hand that I am supposed to give to her. "Aye."

As I hand them over, her father rolls his eyes and stomps back into the cottage.

"Would you like to walk with me?"

"Walk?" She smiles as she lifts the flowers to her nose to sniff. It is a sly smile like she is weighing up my fate.

Gods, how have I not noticed how pretty she is until now?

"Aye, a walk, and that is all. I like my balls attached, and your father has made enough threats toward them already."

She laughs, and it transforms her face from pretty to stunning.

I'm convinced she is about to slam the door in my face when she hops down from the step.

"Okay," she says before calling to her parents that she is going for a walk.

I hear muttered threats from her father and well wishes from her mother before Jessa shuts the door with another sweet giggle.

She peeps at me through her lashes. On any other lass, I would think she was being coy. Maybe she is? I feel like I don't know the lass who has lived across the lane from me her whole life. She is so tiny, the top of her head barely reaching my shoulders. As I take her small hand in mine, I feel my chest swell.

"You seem to be in a better disposition?" I venture to ask.

She nods. "A little."

We walk in silence all the way down the lane until we come out where the river meets the loch. It is quiet here, although it is not unusual for lads and lasses to get up to mischief a little further along.

Stopping, we sit down on the grassy outcropping that gives views across the loch. Fishing boats are tied off at the jetty at this time of day. They bob gently as a light breeze stirs the water.

"I am sorry," I say, staring out at the water glistening in the early evening sun.

"About the Halket lass?" she asks.

"A lot of things," I say. "About spanking you when I was angry, for one."

"You should not spank a lass when angry," she agrees. Then her face turns a pretty shade of pink. "Although, I do not mind spanking so much, even so."

"You don't?" the words come out unnaturally high in pitch.

She shrugs, grinning impishly as she turns to face the loch. "We will need to try it again to be sure."

Fuck!

"I want to kiss you, Jessa," I say. "I want to kiss you more than I want my next breath."

"Okay," she says.

Fuck! I have never been this nervous about a kiss in my life. Leaning in, I cup her cheeks and press my lips to hers.

"That was not a proper kiss," she says as I lift my head.

"What do you know about proper kissing?" I say, frowning.

"What do *you* know about proper kissing?" she counters.

Chuckling, I lean up. "Little brat," I mutter without heat. "You know I want to toss you over my lap and spank your bottom when I think of you kissing another man. Best you tell me who it is so I can thump them instead."

"I have never kissed a lad before," she says, surprising me.

I have no rights to Jessa, nor to be jealous of her kissing another man. That she has agreed to walk with me this evening and allowed me to kiss her is all the claim I have. Yet I am staggered that such a pretty lass has never kissed before.

"But I saw you once in the old barn with a lass," she continues. "And it was a different sort of kissing."

The fuck?

Her face flushes again.

My face heats, too, and my throat becomes unnaturally tight. "I was only kissing her?"

When she doesn't answer, blood begins thumping in my

temple. She doesn't sound angry about whatever the fuck I was doing, only curious. Turning, I catch hold of her chin. "Jessa, do you want me to kiss you like that?"

She nods. "And the other stuff."

"Fuck!" I groan, feeling a little sick but also hard at the thoughts of her seeing me with another lass. Mostly sick. "Other stuff?"

"I don't know exactly what it was for I could not see," she says, her eyes never leaving mine. "But you were touching her under her skirt, and she liked it."

I swallow.

"She liked it very much, and I was so jealous that it wasn't me."

Gods, I hate myself all over again for making her feel jealous. I want to give her everything, all the pleasure, all the kisses, both the sweet ones and the hot, dirty ones.

This time when my lips meet hers, she emits a small groan. She parts beneath me, and her tongue lifts to touch mine. I'm lost. She is like feasting on moon-berries, and I feel fucking drunk on her bold response. Her small hand tangles in my hair, and she grips like she doesn't want me to leave. Our mouths move over each other with an instinctive rhythm that lacks the awkwardness of a lass new to kissing. My heart thuds wildly and my dick is so hard that I swear I could use it as a hammer.

She groans, and her fingers tighten. I need to stop before I rut the lass on the shore of the loch where anyone might pass. The thought of her father nailing my balls to the barn wall helps me to get the urge under control.

Dragging my mouth from hers, I suck in a gusty breath.

"Brandon," she mumbles, pressing kisses to my throat that stoke the flames higher. "The other stuff. You owe me the other stuff."

Capturing a handful of her hair, I gently tug, bringing her franticness to a stop.

"Not today, Jessa," I say, pressing my forehead to hers. "Your father is barely comfortable with me talking to you, let alone kissing...and the other stuff."

"But I want it," she says softly, weakening my resolve.

"Aye, I want it too. I want to make you feel good. But we need to take this slow if we want this to last the rest of our lives."

She bursts into tears.

"What the fuck?" I say, near mindless in seeing her distress. "What did I say wrong?"

"I am happy!" she sobs.

"Could have fooled me," I say as I drag her onto my lap and hold her tightly. Pressing her cheek to my chest, I offer her my purr. "There now, stop the tears, or your father will not let me see you again, and you won't get the kisses, never mind the other stuff you want."

She hiccups, and it sounds adorable.

"I like this," I say. "Not the tears, but holding you is nice."

Her tears soon dry up, and she sneaks a little kiss against the open collar of my jerkin. I try not to think about how soft she feels against me. It takes every bit of self-restraint I have not to let my hands wander.

"Did you mean it when you said the rest of our lives?" she whispers.

"I did mean forever, Jessa. But you are barely of age...and I need to do a bit of groveling to prove myself worthy before I ask you for a commitment."

"Okay," she says. "I would be happy for that."

Chapter Nine

Gage

I have spent too much fucking time brooding over Jessa, the lass I cannot have. She is sweet. I am a rough man who has lived a life full of violence. I would need to temper my natural ways to be with her.

I could do it for her if she accepted me.

But our clans are barely civil, and it will never come to be.

Needing time to clear my head, I leave to hunt. We are a large clan with many mouths to feed, so although we farm and keep sheep, we supplement it with game where we can. I return home having spent a few days alone, resolved, but still miserable. With a nice plump buck and a brace of rabbits over my horse, I ride into the stables.

Dismounting, I call a stable lad over to see to my horse. I toss the buck to a nearby servant, who staggers off under the weight.

Pete, my second, and one of the few alphas in the clan I trust to have my back, joins me as I exit and gives me the news.

"An envoy came from the Halket clan about the lass that was taken," he says. "Your father, in his wisdom, had the man executed and sent his body back tied to his horse."

A tic thumps in my jaw.

War. It is coming, and there is no avoiding that. But I find it is not the other clans I wish to war with. No, my rage is all directed at the monsters within my home.

"There is worse," he says. "Four warriors took it upon themselves to try and snatch another lass. There is no word from the Halket clan yet, but given we sent their envoy back dead, I am not surprised."

"Tried?" I ask. "They were not successful?"

"They had a run-in with Fen and Brandon."

My eyes widen.

"They fought. One of our warriors was injured. He will recover."

"Fuck!" Now we are at war with the Halket clan, and likely Ralston too, given they came to the lass' aid.

I should not need to spell out to grown men that taking a woman against her will is not the way of the Goddess. Even if I had, it would have been a wasted breath. My father encouraged it, and he is still the fucking king.

But everything pales beside the dead envoy. I cannot reconcile that my father's lust for blood drives him to take this road. "Had he allowed the envoy to speak to the lass taken, he would have left satisfied, as I was, that there was no ill-intent. Some recompense would have been needed. But a couple of mules laden with supplies would have seen the matter dropped. By killing the envoy, he is declaring war."

"We need mates," Pete says, meeting my steady gaze. "The taking of lasses from other clans has been a threat hanging over us long since. We took over the Bron lands, but they were a small clan and were few in number."

I know he speaks the truth, but there are ways to find our clan mates and wives that do not involve a fucking war. The tic in my jaw pulses harder. Confronting my father now will lead to an unrecoverable rift. Yet, I am sick to my gut with news of these events.

A dead space opens inside my chest. I am broken and cannot be remade. My father is not a man who inspires love, but there was a time when he had my respect. As I think back over my life since my mother passed, I find it hard to pinpoint where this all began to unravel. Certainly, the illness a decade ago played a part, but he was warmongering even then. As a lad, the events were viewed differently. Disjointed scenes playback, all of them awash with brutality.

"Where is my father now?" Blood pounds through my veins. I need to cool off before speaking to him, but I find myself welcoming whatever will come.

"Your father has left," Pete says, eyes wary like he senses my intentions. "He is planning something, maybe something as bold as the takeover of the Halket clan. He has sent Danon off to make mischief, I have no doubt. They did not leave together."

My rage rises further, like ants under my skin. It needs an outlet.

"Who tried to take the lass?" I demand.

"Four warriors," he says, listing their names.

Two are alphas, and two are betas. All four of them should know better.

"Are the idiots still here?" I ask.

"Two of them," Pete says, his lips forming a wry smile. "Your father was concerned about retaliation, so there are still enough warriors to defend the clan. Want me to round them up?"

I nod.

My father has left, so too, Danon, which means the warriors responsible for starting a clan war will get the full brunt of my fury. Those that are here, anyway.

Pete brings the two warriors to the great hall. It is quiet, for there is no merriment to be had with the threats in the air. The few servants attending duties in the room soon scurry off. We have been teetering on the edge of anarchy for a long while, and the lesser betas have a sense for trouble and make themselves scarce.

I think about asking the two men questions, but I happen they know why they have been called. I have the ringleader by the throat while his whelp companion cowers out the reach of my fist. I put a good beating on him, enjoying every blow. It is not only about this man nor his reckless deed. It is about the lost hope of clan peace that stands between a certain tiny beta and me. My chances were slight before this happened, now they are none.

I don't stop until his face looks like raw meat, and he has pissed himself with fear.

Then I repeat my punishment for his companion. This man is injured, but I don't let his weakened state stop me.

As I lose myself in the savagery, I imagine Brandon telling Jessa about the low, despicable nature of the Lyon clan. If not now, then soon, the Ralston clan will learn of the dead envoy.

I had little hope to start with, but now the crushing of my desire is absolute.

Fists and booted feet are used to remind the warriors of their place. I don't care that my father has led them astray. I'm sickened to be part of any plan to rape and claim a lass. I'm sickened that we would kill an envoy sent in good faith to ensure his clanswoman was not taken by force.

It feels good to let the dark side of me out. Rarely do I

unleash it on the people of my clan. But of late, they do not feel like my people, not all of them, anyway.

Chest heaving, I finally stop realizing that neither man moves.

Dead.

I have killed them, and I do not even fucking care. Maybe my father will be displeased. I no longer care about that either.

When I look toward Pete, I see understanding in his face. Maybe my temper will have cooled some before my father returns, or maybe it won't. Maybe my father will laugh when he learns what I did to the warriors who tried to take the lass.

Or maybe his fury will rise to meet and clash with mine.

"I will spread the word," Pete says. "To those loyal to you."

He accepts what is done and what is yet to unfold without question. Conflict comes for us from all directions. Our people and clan are rotten, and the sickness needs to be purged.

I nod.

He leaves, and as I look from the broken bodies to my raw knuckles, I feel the pieces fall into place.

Events are escalating, shifting, fluid, and where they will finally land is anyone's guess.

Chapter Ten

Jessa

When Brandon comes to collect me the following evening, I am waiting to answer the door.

My father mutters about unworthy whelps.

My mother wishes me a good time.

Bounding down the steps, I throw my arms around his neck, and on my tiptoes, plant a kiss upon his lips. I badly want to pet his short beard that tickles my face.

A broad smile lights his face. As his hands settle on my waist, my tummy flutters with anticipation. "That was quite a welcome," he says, eyes lowering to my lips. "But I think I can do better."

There is a wicked glint in his eyes as his lips lower to mine.

My heart rate quickens as we kiss. His familiar scent invades my nose as I sink into him and the kiss. A rushing heat sweeps through me as his tongue tangles with mine. Deep inside, I feel the sweet tickling sensation as my body prepares for what it wants and needs.

As his head lifts, my lashes flutter open.

"I'm not sure that was better," I say, peeping at him through the slits of my eyes. "You might want to try it again."

He chuckles. Taking my hand in his, he begins to walk, giving a little tug when I remain rooted to the spot.

"Where are we going?" I ask as we make our way down the lane. "To the rutting barn?"

His head whips around to face me. "The what? What the fuck, Jessa."

I chuckle. "What do you call it then?"

This is fun, both the kissing and shocking of Brandon. Happen he will be more shocked soon when he finds out what I have done.

If he finds out what I have done.

I'm certainly hoping things will progress enough so that he will. I could barely sleep last night thinking about kissing and all things rutting. I made myself come twice, and I still wanted more. But I wanted more with Brandon and not by myself.

"It is just the old barn, and we are not going there," he says, giving me a stern glare that only makes me grin. "But we will find a quieter spot by the river where we can talk."

"Brandon," I say, waiting until he glances my way. "I don't want to talk."

"Aye, I'm getting the idea that you are an insatiable lass."

"I really am," I agree. Brandon is only holding my hand and already my body thrums. Maybe tonight I will not need to make myself come.

"And bolder than I was expecting," he continues with a smirk.

"My mother told me long ago that it is natural for a lass to have such thoughts, and that I was not to be ashamed. She also said that if I did not, that was all right too."

"Well, your mother talks sense," he agrees.

As we near the small path to the wood, we take the left-hand track. Part of me feels I should be aggrieved that Brandon knows these quiet places because he went there with other lasses. But I don't. I am glad he knows where to go and how to kiss. And I'm sure he knows about the other stuff that I have yet to experience.

"She also said it was natural for a lass to kiss a lad and...and other things if she wished to and if it felt natural and right to her. As long as she wasn't doing it because she felt pressured to please the boy."

"Jessa," he says softly, like it is a warning...like he might be in pain.

He comes to a stop by a giant oak tree with a view of the riverbank. It is peaceful, and the evening air, warm. He sits, tugging me down beside him.

"Brandon?" He looks a little flushed and stares at the river like he is terrified to look at me.

He glances across and groans a little when he notices my smirk. "You are going to fucking test me this evening. I can see the mischief in your eyes."

"I do not want to sit beside you." Rising to my knees, I nimbly slip over his lap so that I am straddling his muscular thighs, and our faces are inches apart. "I would rather sit here."

His hands settle on my waist. Mine settle on his shoulders. Eyes lowering, he gently squeezes as if testing how it feels. "I'd rather you sit here, too."

"I have never wanted to kiss or touch anyone," I say. "I thought perhaps I never would. But things have changed of late, and I do want to." My voice lowers to a whisper. "Sometimes, when I lie in bed, and everyone else is asleep, I touch myself and imagine it is you."

He groans again, and I wonder if he is getting hard? I can still remember how his cock looked as he strode toward me the day wolves trapped me in the forest.

Leaning forward, I brush my lips over his rough beard on his left cheek, skimming them back and forth and delighting in the tingly feeling. "I want the kisses and the other stuff," I whisper close to his ear before pressing a gentle kiss to his cheek.

As I lean up, our eyes meet and hold.

He nods.

His hands glide down my thighs, his eyes lowering to watch them pass over the stretched material of my hide skirt until they meet my skin.

I watch, too, mesmerized by his broad, tanned hands against my paler skin. They feel warm and a little roughened. My cheeks heat. I begin to worry that I have been too bold. But then his hands slip under the hem of my skirt and skim upward. I am so thrilled to have his hands on me that I scarcely can breathe.

"Is this the other stuff that you want, Jessa?" he asks. His voice low and growly, and it makes the wetness gather between my thighs.

"Yes," I say, tearing my gaze away to find he is once more watching me...watching my reaction. "Goddess, yes, this is exactly what I want."

Then his big broad hands are cupping my ass.

He stills.

I bite my bottom lip. *Oops!*

"Jessa, where the fuck are your panties?" His hands move again, gliding all over my ass in a most arresting way as he verifies what he suspects—that I am not wearing any panties.

"They are always getting wet," I say, breathless now.

"Fuck!" he mutters gruffly. His fingers squeeze the flesh of my ass. "That was very naughty, Jessa. Happen this might be one of those punishment times we spoke of."

"What punishment?" I ask. It comes out a little whiny as I think about how it felt when he put me over his lap and spanked me. It stung a great deal, but it also felt a squirmy kind of good. I very much did not like the stinging pain, but I *did* like being mastered, being put over his lap, and held helpless for whatever he might decide to do.

"I do not mind the spanking so much, is what you said, Jessa," he reminds me before stealing a swift kiss. "We will need to try it again to be sure, you added."

Tugging up the back of my skirt, his big hand lands against my ass cheek with a crack.

"Goddess!" I gasp. It stings only a little. It was more of a shock. Between my thighs, I can feel my slickness. Perhaps taking my panties off was a bad idea? I now fear I may embarrass myself.

His hand lifts and falls again with another sharp crack.

I groan. Oh, I like this very much. Not painful, more a light sting that warms my bottom and makes my pussy clench.

"I can smell your arousal," he growls before sneaking another kiss.

Spank.

"Tell me you like it, Jessa, or tell me to stop."

"Goddess! I like it."

Spank.

"You've been a very naughty girl, Jessa," he continues. His palm lands against the other cheek, and I gasp at the new stimulation. "Leaving your home without your panties on." He begins to spank a little firmer, alternating between each side, and the heat begins to grow. "Good girls wear panties.

Bad girls get their naughty bottom spanked until they repent."

"Oh! I am very much not sorry!"

I swear here and now that I shall never wear my panties again if he puts his hands upon me like this. Only I'm growing restless, and I want and need more.

Then I feel it, a gush as the wetness trickles down my inner thigh. I clamp my hand there lest it spill out.

He stops. He is breathing heavily. We are both breathing heavily.

"Jessa, take your hand away this instant, or I will spank your bottom in the sharp way you do not like."

I shake my head, cheeks as hot and flushed as my bottom. "I can't," I whisper. "It is going to make a mess."

"Let it make a mess. I don't give a fuck. Now, move your hand away."

I have only heard his stern voice a few times. My pussy clenches, and more wetness escapes. Slowly, I pull my fingers away.

He catches my wrist, and I watch with numb compliance as he lifts my hand to inspect the glistening stickiness coating my fingers. Eyes locked with mine, he brings my fingers to his lips... and licks them clean.

My chest saws unsteadily, and my pussy gushes like it wants to give him more. Eyes closed, he purr-growls with pleasure as he laps up all the mess.

When he opens them again, I can barely see through the haze of lust.

"Do you want me to make you feel good?"

"Yes," I say. "Please, yes. Make me feel good. Please, touch me there, like you did with that lass. Please, kiss me. Please, do all of the things."

He growls. Tipping me onto my back, he braces over me.

"Do not mention that lass again. I do not care about that lass. I only want to think about you—about pleasuring you."

I nod.

"I'm going to make you feel so good," he says, lips lowering to my throat where he presses kisses and sucks gently upon the flesh. "But first, I'm going to need to clean up all the mess you have made. I'm going to need to lick up all the slick that is weeping from your pussy. Every little bit of it. And you are going to lay there like a good girl while I do it."

I groan, my fingers clasping his silken hair.

"You will be good and still, and you will not come until I'm ready. If you come, I will need to punish you again."

I am near insensible. I think I might come without Brandon touching me at all. His lips trail lower, over my collarbone, exploring the limits of my clothing before rising once more. Palming my cheek within one strong hand, he kisses me. A deep, lusty kiss with tongues and teeth nipping against my lips. I sink into it, elated by the awakening sensations that are a thousand times more glorious than anything I imagined.

Our breath mingles. I want to meld with him, to tumble into this kiss and into him, to press against him until our flesh becomes one.

His lips tear from mine. He moves lower, kissing my throat, sucking the flesh into his mouth as his hand slides under the waist of my hide top. Big, warm hand skimming over flesh until he cups my right breast.

"Goddess, please," I whimper, pushing my breasts into his hand. Then his thumb brushes across the stiff peak of my nipple, and I groan.

His lips return to capture mine in a drugging kiss as he brushes his thumb back and forth, lifting the urgency within me, making me restless and impatient.

An unearthly wildness invades me. I want everything, and I want it now.

His mouth wrenches from mine. Fingers shaking with impatience, he tugs my top up and encloses my nipple and a good portion of my breast in the hot wetness of his mouth.

"Goddess!" The air leaves my lungs. I feel a thread of hot need pulse between my nipple and my clit. Hot waves of pleasure pulse and pulse. The urgency builds. I think I might come...

His head lifts abruptly, and he stares at me, chest heaving, eyes near black in an echo of the lust I feel coursing through me. "Lay very still for me," he says. "And do not fucking come."

My skirt is already rucked up, but he pushes it higher, exposing me to his lustful gaze. His lips twist in a wicked smirk as he stares at what he has exposed. "What a naughty, wet little pussy."

His smile drops as his eyes rise to meet mine. "You are so fucking beautiful, Jessa," he says. "Here, like this, in your sweet awakening. You are the most beautiful thing in the world."

My breath catches in my lungs. The place deep inside that belongs to Brandon blossoms to life, growing into a great warm sphere that encompasses us both.

He shifts, moving back, sinking lower, lips pressing to my inner knee. He works upward, gentle kisses that take him closer and closer to the place where I ache.

My fingers sink into the springy forest floor as he begins to lap. Groaning and growling, he does exactly as he promised. Carefully, he cleans all the sticky mess, one searing lick at a time, moving ever closer to my drenched pussy.

"Lay very still," he warns when I grow even more restless. Then he licks the length of my pussy slit.

"Goddess!" It sets a thousand nerves rushing to life. Sweet, wondrous sensations consume me as he laps gently over the swollen folds of my pussy. His fingers enclose my thighs, holding me open, spreading me wider so he might have full access. My hips want to lift. I want more of what he is doing. I want faster and deeper.

I want to come.

I want to come more than I want to breathe.

"Don't come," he growls against my pussy.

I sob. I beg.

He changes, no longer licking and lapping. No, now he is kissing me there. Lips, tongue, and the gentle nip of his teeth. Growling, he feasts upon me.

My breathing turns to gasped pants. The coil is tightening, pulling me in closer and closer. I try to wriggle away. "Goddess, I'm going to come. I can't stop it."

"Come for me," he growls. A hand slides under my top to grasp my nipple. He tugs and twists it hard just as his lips enclose my engorged clit, and he sucks.

I come. Groaning, my head tips back as the sweet rhythmic pleasure crashes through me.

He laps gently at my clit until it is too sensitive, and I push him away.

Lifting his head, he smirks at me. "You have made another mess, Jessa. Looks like I'm going to have to start all over again."

And Goddess help me, he does.

Chapter Eleven

Brandon

"I need you to step up to your place, Fen," Jack says. "And you, Brandon."

Fen and I have been summoned to the great hall to discuss tomorrow's plans.

"I will do what needs to be done," Fen says, scowling at his brother. "Even if it kills me."

He does not like being reminded of his abstinence from clan business, although the facts are hard to dispute. Neither of us has taken responsibility for negotiating or meeting with other clans. Other than the odd bit of mischief, which does little for our standing.

The actions of the Lyon clan cannot go ignored. So, although Fen and Jack are newly mated, we must face into this challenge.

"It will not kill you unless you fuck up," Jack says. "Do not fuck up."

Jack is the older of the two brothers by many years. A big

brawny alpha, he is measured in his handling of matters unless you incur his wrath, as the bitch Nola will attest. After her mischief with their mate, Nola was gifted as a slave to the Halket clan. Angering Jack is in no one's best interest.

Jack's stern gaze shifts to me, and his eyes narrow. "I heard Jessa's father has given his permission for you to wed. I hope you will likewise remember you have a lass as well as family counting on you not to fail."

I look toward Fen, who shrugs with a smirk. I consider pointing out that I follow Fen's lead and so have diminished responsibility in this. Still, I don't believe Jack would appreciate any humor or backtalk at this point.

"We will do what we need to do," Fen says. "They need allies as much as us. Old Karry has long been seen as a gentle king. Some consider it his weakness. But Eric is not cut from the same cloth. I do not think Karry's peaceful ways will serve him well. We all fear that the Lyons are building up to an attack. Their actions suggest as much. We need to support each other, and I will tell him as much. Only do not tell me to apologize to Eric. The bastard has already put a good beating on me. I will not grovel as well."

Jack's lips twitch. "Goddess forbid you should lower yourself so," he says. "Just negotiate with a civil tongue and don't get into a fight with Eric is all I'm asking."

Melancholy since the death of his late mate, Jack has begun to find humor and joy again since the arrival of their sweet little beta mate. Fen spent many years angry after his parents died. I know much of his rebelliousness was because he thought the Goddess had abandoned him. Their beta mate, Hazel, has been good for them both. It's unusual for two alphas to mate with a single beta. More often, they would take two as mates. But if the frequent sounds of pleasure and rutting emanating from their home are anything to go by, she is not suffering from their attention.

"We can do that," Fen agrees.

"We will," I add.

Any further conversation is interrupted by the arrival of Jessa and Hazel. The two lasses have been together much of late and have become firm friends. As I study them side by side, I realize how tiny Jessa is.

"If we have finished talking..." Fen trails off as he scoops Hazel up into his arms. She squeals and giggles as he makes a beeline for the bedding chamber.

Jack rolls his eyes, although he is looking longingly after the pair of them.

"If I'm excused, sire, I'll walk Jessa home."

"Aye," Jack says, only half-listening as he follows Fen and his mate. More sounds of giggling emanate from the bedding chamber.

Jessa peeps at me under her lashes, and we both burst out laughing.

"It's a good job the lass is lusty," I say. Taking Jessa's hand, we take the wooden steps before heading out into the village square.

"You're not really taking me home, are you?" Jessa asks.

Glancing over, I see mischief shining in her face. I raise a brow. "Why, what else did you have in mind?" I subtly swap her hand and slide the other over her ass...just to check. "Have you got any panties on today?"

"I have," she says. "But I can soon change that."

My dick is already rising to hopeful attention even though it has yet to get a look in. I am determined to go slowly with her, to show her as much pleasure as I can before claiming pleasure for myself. Guilt still consumes me that I spanked her in a jealous rage. Afterward, I convinced myself that I wasn't worthy, and further, had no chance of claiming Jessa as mine. Foolishly, I went and rutted another lass.

A shifter is a complex beast. We are half animal, and at times, those instincts rule our thoughts and actions.

I will pay my dues with a cock that aches to the point of pain every time I escort Jessa back to her home well sated from my attention.

We walk hand in hand all the way to our favorite place underneath the giant oak tree. It is a warm afternoon, and the air is full of sweet scents from the flowering creepers.

"I want to try something different today," she says with an impish smile.

I raise my brows, instantly suspicious. I have done everything a man can do to a lass except for rutting and touching her little puckered back hole. I have thought about both. I have thought about a thousand fucking things with my cock in my own hand as I jack off after leaving her on the steps of her home.

It doesn't satisfy me, but I will be patient with the lass if it kills me.

Likely, it *will* kill me. Before, I was worried about Ed nailing my balls to the barn wall. Now it is death by blue balls that I fear.

So, I greet her enthusiastic determination that she wants to try something new with a measure of dread and curiosity. The lass has taken well to the 'other things', as she calls them, but I sense her impatience. I don't even know why I'm hesitating. Her father has given his blessing. We have pledged commitment to one another. The wedding is a formality now. No one would care if we were to take the next step...except maybe her pa, who suffers begrudging tolerance toward me. Happen he could tip back into rage should I fuck up.

"What sort of thing?" I ask, bracing myself for this future torment.

Her answer is a giggle that does nothing to ease my concerns.

On reaching the tree, I sit, tugging her down beside me, and fighting my natural urge to thrust her little hide skirt up and bury my face in between.

We should talk, maybe...

Fuck it!

She squeals and laughs as I tip her onto her back. Caging her tiny, lush body beneath mine, I kiss her until we are both breathless. My hand slips under her hide skirt. I groan on discovering that she is not wearing any fucking panties. The lass is a shameless hussy of the highest order. My blue balls thank the Goddess for sending this treasure to me.

I tell myself I can go slowly, but her pussy is addictive and tastes fucking delicious. Thrusting her skirt up, I get ready to feast.

"Brandon, stop."

Her gasped command brings me to a halt. My mouth hovers inches over her wet folds, and my nose is full of her scent. I want badly to pin her to the forest floor and lick all the juices up.

When I glance up, I find her eyes so dark with lust, they appear almost black.

She wriggles, sitting up, pushing me backward, and crawling over me.

"I want to try something different," she says, her breath a gusty pant. "Please."

I am sprawled out on my back, at her mercy, although I am twice her size. "No rutting," I say seriously.

Her lips tug up. "No rutting," she agrees.

I nod.

Her small hands are on my belt buckle before I realize her intent. I try to peel her off, but she is fucking fast and nimble when she has a mind to be.

"Goddess!" she says.

I groan and lose all will to fight as she grasps my dick within her tiny hands. I am so fucking primed. If I so much as breathe heavily, she is going to find herself smothered in my cum.

"Gods!" I say, flinging an arm across my eyes. I cannot fucking look.

It's no use, I can still see her kneeling between my splayed legs with my ruddy dick clasped within her tiny hands, her cheeks pink, and lips parted in shock.

"It looks painful," she says, giving a tentative pump.

"Aye," I say, voice a roughened grunt. I am so close to spilling my load like a green whelp. I try thinking about the rotting sheep carcass I found in the ditch last week, but it only helps so much.

"It is so soft," she says, hands moving up and down a little bolder. She is talking to herself, her future husband all but forgotten.

Goddess help me find the will to endure this tentative exploration!

I lift my arm and take a swift glance.

Bad idea, but I have seen now, and I cannot force my eyes to avert. My cock is leaking like a tap all over her tiny, pumping hands. Her focus is absolute on what she is doing. She does not look afraid. She looks fucking hungry.

"Does that help?" she asks.

"Some," I say. It is a torturous kind of helping truth be told. "You need to stop now, Jessa."

"What? Why?" Eyes flashing to meet mine, she grasps me tighter like I might take her prize away.

"I'm going to fucking come," I say.

"Good," she says decisively. "That is what I want."

Turning back to the prize in her hands, she lowers her head and licks the crown.

I feel like the top of my head has just exploded off. My lower spine tingles, and my balls tighten. I fight the urge to come in a way that is nothing short of heroic.

Then she sucks half the length into the hot cavern of her mouth.

I can't hold it. I don't have a fucking chance, and what feels like a gallon of cum shoots down her throat.

I groan-growl, mind empty to everything but the heady sensation of cum ejecting from the tip of my dick. Blindly, I grasp a handful of her hair and try to pull her off before she chokes herself. My cock won't stop spewing. I see stars, and my capacity for clear thinking is lost.

"Spit it out," I say, poking a finger in her mouth to try and scoop the worst of it out.

The little brat bites me. Finger throbbing, I blink a few times trying to assimilate the vision before me. My chest saws. My dick jerks with renewed interest at the arresting sight of Jessa high on my cum. Eyes hooded in bliss, she is stuffing her sticky fingers into her mouth and sucking it all down. My rough hold of her hair barely registers as she licks her fingers clean.

"Gods, you are a lusty lass," I say. "How the fuck did I get so lucky?"

She gives me an impish grin before her eyes lower. "Oh," she says, closing her small hand around my length. "Can we do that again?"

"Not a chance," I say. "It is my turn."

Using her hair as I leash, I haul her onto her back. The little minx groans as she tugs up her hide skirt. "Goddess, yes! Please, yes, Brandon."

"That was very naughty, Jessa," I say as I thrust two thick fingers into her sopping cunt.

Her hips lift as she tries to get more.

I pump slowly. Too slowly to get her off. "I told you to stop, and you ignored me. Happen you have earned yourself another spanking."

"Yes, please, yes! Spank me. I am such a bad girl."

As I brace over her on my hands and knees, she waits, cheeks a pretty shade of pink and eyes closed in anticipation of what I will do.

I want to laugh at her wild enthusiasm. I want to offer prayers to the Goddess that this wonder will soon join with me for life. I want to discover all the things that please her. I want to rut her. I want to watch her belly grow fat with child. I want a whole fucking brood of brats running around. I want all the pleasure as I sow each one in her perfect pussy. I want to grow old with her and watch our children grow.

Not so long ago, I desired none of these things. Now they are all that matter.

My eyes lower to where her legs are spread wide, and I see how slick and needy she is.

I still want all the things, but they are for tomorrow and the next day.

Here, in this moment, I just want to eat her out until we are both too exhausted to worry about tomorrow and the danger that it brings.

Chapter Twelve

Jessa

As we quit the old oak tree, I am happy, chest full of love, and body buzzing after all the pleasure Brandon has made me feel. It is not yet dark when we return home, hand in hand. But with every step, a weight seems to settle upon Brandon's shoulders.

As we arrive at the steps of my cottage, I ask him what is wrong.

"Fen and I will be leaving tomorrow," he says. "We need to talk to the Halket clan."

Confused, I study him. Standing as I am, facing him on the first step, our eyes are nearly level. It is not unusual for him to travel with Fen. I will miss him while he is away, but this is a normal part of clan life.

"Jack is also leaving to speak with the Baxters. We will need alliances now."

I shake my head, a sickness settling in my tummy.

He puts his hands upon my shoulders, letting them run all

the way down until they capture my hands. His sad eyes track the movement.

"A warrior from the Lyon clan snatched a Halket lass a while ago. They claimed it was her choice. While Fen and I were out scouting, we happened upon four Lyon warriors trying to snatch another within sight of the Halket village. Had we not been there, the lass would have been raped and taken as a prize."

Cold sweeps the length of my spine. I had not heard this. I'd learned about Brandon because Suka came over and shared the gossip with spiteful intent.

"There must be a mistake." Behind my eyes, hot tears are forming.

"I was there, Jessa. We stopped it. The lass was screaming, mouth bloody from where they had slapped her to quieten her. I don't like to talk to you about such things. I don't want to scare you. But you need to stay close to the village tomorrow, and for the next few days while we are away. This cannot go unaddressed. The Lyon clan are heathens with no respect for the Goddess' ways," he says, bitterness entering his voice. "It has been a few years since they took the Bron clan, but Jack believes they have set their sights on larger prey. Maybe Halket since their king is seen as weak. But maybe also our clan if we do not send a clear message now."

My lips tremble. *War.*

War is bad enough, but this war is with the Lyon clan—Gage's clan.

Today was the best of days.

Tomorrow, not so much.

I have tried to push thoughts of Gage from my mind, not always with the greatest success. I can't deny that I am drawn to the alpha from the Lyon clan. He was kind to me, *gentle,* in handling my shock when I healed him in the forest that day.

Why would the Goddess gift me the ability to heal him if he were bad?

My distress rises. Brandon smooths his hands up and down my arms, but it does not take the chill away.

Gage accused Brandon of starting a war that day after his mischief with the Halket clan. But now Brandon is telling me that Gage has done far worse.

Not Gage, someone from his clan.

I wonder if my attraction toward him has addled my mind such that I cannot see the truth.

In my heart, he is a proud and noble alpha. He came all the way to our clan at great risk to check that I was well. That is not the action of a monster. He had his hands upon me twice. He could have snatched me either time had he been of mind. These are not the actions of a man who watches while his clansmen rape a lass.

Conflict consumes me. I want to argue with Brandon, but I know mentioning Gage's name will do nothing to prevent the war. More likely, it will only anger Brandon.

He doesn't know Gage like I do, although I admit, I do not know Gage well either.

I only know that Gage had the opportunity to harm me. He did not harm me, and further, was fiercely protective, thrusting me behind his back when Brandon stormed toward us. The two men do not like each other well. They hate each other, truth be told. That fool fantasy where they both loved me seems twice as foolish on reflection.

"Gage is not a bad man," I say quietly.

Brandon's jaw tightens. "Do not mention his fucking name."

"He is not a monster, and I won't let you say that he is." I feel my temper rising, clashing with the sorrow, and mashing it all up into a great eruption of distress. "If these men from his clan hurt a lass, then they did it without his permission."

"It doesn't matter," Brandon says. "He is not the king of his clan. He is not even the firstborn son. He is nothing, and less than nothing if he stands by and watches while his clansmen commit such acts."

He heaves a great breath and lets it out on a sigh. "I do not want to quarrel with you, Jessa, not tonight and not now. It is not my decision that we war. I am but a beta and do not even sit at Jack's table. I am bound to Fen, have been since I was but a pup. For all that, I would argue with them if I thought their actions were wrong. The Lyon clan has lost its way. I will not sit by idle. Not after what I witnessed."

His sadness and conviction bring a tightness to my chest. No matter what I think of Gage, men of his clan hurt a lass. I am sorry that Brandon had to witness such a thing, but heartened that he was there to stop it. I step closer to him, and placing my arms around his neck, press my nose into the crook of his shoulder. His scent, rich and spicy, soothes me. "I am sorry," I say. "Sorry that it has come to this. You are right. They have lost their way."

I feel the tension leave his body. He purrs.

But it only soothes me a little bit, for tomorrow will bring war.

When I slip back into the cottage, I find my parents talking quietly at the table. My sibling brats are in bed, except for my younger brother Amos, who will likely still be out with his friends.

They don't ask what is wrong with me as I get ready for

bed. Perhaps they similarly know about the men leaving tomorrow. I expect that they must do.

I wash up, change into my nightgown, and head for my bedding nook. Slipping inside the cool sheets, I pull the curtain closed. I lay awake for a long time, listening to the rumble of my parent's conversation. The lights go out, quietness descends, and still, I cannot sleep.

Tossing and turning, my mind wallows in turmoil. My thoughts are like pebbles upon the loch shore, sifting and clashing and shifting again.

It is still dark behind my bedding nook curtain when I rise from my bed. Brandon said he was leaving early, but I might still catch him before he goes.

As I carefully draw my curtain back, I find my father is up, supping a brew as he throws the shutters open to let the weak morning light in.

He does a double-take as he sees me. I must look terrible, face ravaged by tears and worry, and hair a knotty mess. His face softens. Without a word, he puts his cup of brew on the counter and gathers me into his arms. "There, lass," he says. "They will be back afore you know it."

It has been a few years since I was cuddled by my papa, and it feels so nice.

"I'm so worried," I say. "I feel sick with it. And Brandon won't rut me until after because he is worried he's going to die!" He didn't actually say this, but I'm convinced it's the reason.

My father chuckles softly. Drawing me away so he can see my face, he brushes the fresh tears away with the pad of his thumbs. "Ah, lass. Not sure your pa is the best person for this discussion. I was fit to nail the whelp to the barn door by his balls when I caught him spanking you. But he has stepped up in committing to you, and I am heartened by the way he is with you."

"He makes me happy," I say, feeling the tears threaten to spill again. I don't remember being as happy as I have been these last few weeks. First, Hazel arrived, and in the same breath, Nola was banished from the clan.

There was a brief, painful dip in my joy when Brandon and Fen returned and I learned he had rutted another lass. Suka, the former member of Nola's posse, had been eager to spill the gossip.

But that very same day, I met Gage in the woods. And then the next day, Brandon arrived at my door with flowers in his hands.

My heart hurts.

For both the men I have come to care for. One, I have loved all my life—have obsessed over. The other, I have watched from afar for many years only to have him crash into my world after he was attacked by an Orc.

I healed him.

Why would the Goddess work through me to heal a man who was not good?

"*It means you are Goddess blessed,*" Gage had said gruffly. "*It will be our secret, Jessa.*"

I should not be thinking of another man when Brandon will be leaving, possibly heading into danger. Yet my heart does not care for reason.

My heart still wants them both.

I suffer so much guilt.

"I was going to see him now," I say. "Do you think they will have left yet?"

He glances out the window before winking at me. "If you are quick, you might catch him afore he leaves."

"Shoes!" he calls when I race for the door still in my nightgown.

Huffing, I shove my feet into my boots, fling the door open, and clatter down the steps.

I come to an abrupt stop when I find Brandon outside staring at my home.

He blinks slowly like he is as shocked to find me there as I similarly am.

A broad smile splits his face as he takes a few steps to me and gathers me into his arms. "I was going to knock on the door but was worried your father would kick my ass for waking everyone up."

"I have not slept a wink," I say. "I'm glad you are here, and I can see you before you go."

"Me too," he says, lips against my hair and deep rumbly purr coming from his chest.

Chapter Thirteen

Jessa

I go through the motion of helping my mother with my sibling brats. I am busy tidying their bedding but have half an eye on the table. Greta is full of mischief this morning. But I am tired and not in the mood. She is using her biscuit like a spoon to scoop the porridge, and it is going everywhere. William thinks this is funny. Greta pokes her tongue out at him. He retaliates by scooping a spoonful of porridge and flicking it over Greta.

A great dollop lands on her forehead...and slowly trickles down.

My mother gasps. There is a delay before Greta opens her mouth and emits an ear-splitting wail.

William grins and goes back to eating his porridge.

"William, clear the table," my mother says as she takes a cloth to wipe a wailing Greta up.

"I've not finished yet!" William announces.

"You should have considered that afore you threw it over

your sister," my mother says, lips thinned. "A hungry lad does not toss his food about like an animal. Happen you will be ready to eat like a good boy at lunchtime. Or if there is any more of this nonsense, you will be going hungry until supper, and I'll be telling your father why."

I bite back a laugh as William jumps down from the seat and gathers the plates with an enthusiastic clatter. Telling Pa will likely see his bottom tanned.

Greta bewails her lack of breakfast. "You were playing with it," my mother says. "Lasses who play with their breakfast are not hungry either. I was going to bake some cookies today, but I'm not sure either of you has behaved well enough."

Great squeals of excitement greet this development, followed by babbled determinations as to their future goodness.

"Okay, chores time, and I will see how good you are after," my mother says decisively.

Their chores are not very hard. But it gives them a purpose. There is a vegetable plot out the back and chickens for eggs. We have a small flock of wool sheep, which are shorn once a year. My mother makes wonderful woolen blankets that are much coveted by the village. Our summers are long and warm. We mostly wear clothes fashioned from leather or hide. Still, the thick blankets will be adorning everyone's bed to supplement the pelts in the winter months. There is always something to do and plenty of smaller jobs that the children can help with.

"You look tired," my mother says.

"I did not sleep very well," I admit.

"Some of the women will be making balm over in the herb cottage. I said as you and Hazel might be able to help."

My heart flutters as I realize why we would be making balm. "I will," I say.

I meet Hazel as she is leaving her home. Sometimes, I find it hard to reconcile that she is a mate to the king. She has no airs and graces, and from the moment she arrived, has made a point of helping in whatever way she can. Long blonde hair that falls nearly to her waist, she is as pretty as she is kind. A few years older than me and yet naive to the ways of the clan, Hazel has become my best friend quicker than I thought possible.

The day passes slowly as we help the women of the clan. Finishing for the day, we pack everything away. I find I do not want to go home where I will crawl into my bedding nook and worry over Brandon. Hazel sees me hesitating. "Do you want to stay with me tonight? I would appreciate not being alone."

"Okay," I say, although my eyes dart longingly toward the forest path to the north of the king's home. A short distance along the trail is the sacred pool. But I am reserved about the suggestion, given it has bad memories for Hazel.

It was the pool where Nola engaged in mischief that saw Hazel tied to the whipping post in the square.

"What is it?" she asks.

"I would like to pray," I say. "But it must have bad memories for you."

A shadow passes over her face before her pretty hazel eyes search mine. "My memories of that day are hazy. But perhaps that is for the best. I would like to go there with you, Jessa. I would like to pray, too. I do not think Nola should sully the wonder for me. It was very beautiful and peaceful that I remember. I would love to replace that terrible memory with a better one."

With a smile and a nod, I hurry to let my mother know I will be visiting the pool before spending the night with Hazel. After, we leave together, walking the small distance from Ralston to where the pool and portal are found.

Hazel stills as we emerge through the trees. Before us is the sacred pool, surrounded by smooth, mossy rocks. A waterfall generates spray and a thrumming sound as it crashes to the pool. To the right of the waterfall is a great shimmering oval that spins and warbles, sparkling blue and golden light.

A portal. A place where the Goddess can hear our prayers.

"Has anyone ever come through?" Hazel asks.

"No," I say. "My grandma told me it was a lost one. That it goes to nowhere, and that nowhere leads here. But the Goddess listens well. I have prayed here many times."

I shiver.

Tonight, I feel the weight of all that portal is and could be.

Tonight, I truly feel the Goddess Herself is here.

Kneeling side by side, we close our eyes and pray.

I speak to the Goddess, little mumbled words of hopes and wishes for the safety of our men. It is darkening, and we should be returning, but my mind is subject to a turmoil that I dare not put into words. What do I presume to hide? The Goddess can surely see into my heart and soul, and nothing can be hidden.

So with my final prayer, I silently entreat Her to keep Gage safe. She helped me heal him for a purpose, and I cannot believe that purpose is for him to die in a war with my clan.

The sun is nearly gone when we return to the king's hall and home. A pair of the younger warriors were discreetly guarding us as we prayed. It unnerves me that these precautions need to be taken. More armed warriors patrol the village center. One instructs us to close and bolt the hall door for the night.

Hazel and I eat a cold supper.

And then we wait.

Chapter Fourteen

Brandon

Leaving the village, we travel throughout the morning, shaded from the sun by the thick forest canopy, destined for the Halket clan. A lot has happened since we returned from scouting. Fen has taken a mate...one he shares with his brother.

Shares. I can't wrap my head around the two alphas sharing a mate. I've shared plenty of lasses before, but I couldn't imagine sharing Jessa. Not now I have committed to her...nor before, if my reaction to Gage handling her is any indication.

Once this nonsense is over, we will speak our vows.

Gods, it might not be so long before we have pups on the way. I hope we have pups. It does not always happen that a mixed-race child can still shift. My mother is not a shifter. My blood comes from my father. There are many shifter families within the clans, living as we do close to the mountains where the pure shifter communities thrive. Sometimes the ability to

133

change is lost over time, and they become regular betas. But for some, the power is passed down through many generations.

Like mine.

Pups? I can't believe I am thinking about pups!

"I don't like leaving Hazel," Fen says.

It is funny how your best friend's woes can deliver a little humor. "You are a miserable bastard this morning."

He shoots me a glare. "You have no reason to talk," he says. "Aren't you and Jessa about to take your vows?"

I grunt but do not dispute the recent change in my status. Jessa fills my thoughts, both her sweetness and her lusty responses that blow my mind.

But underneath this joy, there is Gage, the bastard from the Lyon clan. I hated him before he put his hands upon Jessa. That she mentioned him yesterday only serves to further piss me off. *"He is not a monster,"* she said. *"And I won't let you say that he is."*

No, he is not a monster, but he is a bastard who stands by while members of his clan try to snatch a lass. That makes him culpable in my eyes.

We need alliances in place. I understand this. But my wolf just wants to take the bastards who hurt that Halket lass by the throat and shake them about until they are dead.

And Gage, I would end that bastard too.

An uncomfortable weight settles deep in my gut. Jessa would not like it if I killed Gage, even assuming I could. I'm no fool regarding matters of my prowess. Being a shifter raises me above beta men and even some alphas. Gage is a fucking man mountain. I would not submit easily. I know how to fight a man whether he has a sword or an ax or only his fists. I have even defeated an Orc as part of a team.

I have not killed a fucking Orc on my own. The bastard was not posturing when he said he had killed one near our lands.

No, he was calm as fuck as he announced it, and there was not a hint of lies on him.

I force Gage from my thoughts. Jack has left for more distant negotiations, while Fen and I travel with three other warriors to speak with Karry, the king of the Halket clan.

I am not expecting much of a welcome after our many altercations with Eric.

But as Jack said yesterday, Fen and I must both step up.

Our pace is brisk, but we slow the horses to a walk as we arrive at the river where a ford allows us to cross.

"What are you going to say?" I ask as we splash through the shallow water.

"I am going to talk plainly," Fen says.

"Are you going to apologize?" I ask, doing my best to hide a smirk. "For that business with you and Gwen?"

"I am not going to fucking apologize," Fen says, glaring at me. He likes to bait me. It is only fair that I bait him back. "It is Eric's own fault for being slow about it. Happen I did him a service helping the matter along."

I chuckle. "Not sure Eric will consider it in the same light."

Fen brings his horse to a sudden halt, the rest of us follow suit. "Eric?"

Lying upon the ground, peering over a low, craggy bluff, is a party of warriors from the Halket clan.

"Get down from the fucking horse," Eric hisses.

Fen bristles at Eric's tone. I brace myself in case the idiots decide to go at one another. But the rage seeps out of Fen when Gwen turns over to glare up at him. She is usually an even-tempered lass. Perhaps she is still sore about him coming all over her face?

At Fen's indication, we dismount. Tying off the horses, we creep forward to join Eric and his crew at the edge. To a man and woman, the Halket members turn back to peer over the side.

"Has he claimed you yet?" Fen asks Gwen, crouching between her and Eric. I chuckle softly. Fen does not know when to let a matter drop. Life is never dull.

"He tried," Gwen says, smirking. "But he needed a bit of help."

I snort out a laugh. Fen laughs louder. Eric punches him in the arm while shooting him a glare. "Shut the fuck up," he says. "This is not the time for fucking around. And best you move from between my mate and me, or I will finish what I started last time you got in my fucking way."

Fen raises both hands in the universal sign of surrender and squat-crawls to the other side of Eric. "About fucking time," he mutters. Then all business, adds, "Is that Danon?"

We have the vantage of higher ground since the landscape here is rocky with great crumbling boulders that form peaks and troughs.

It *is* Danon.

My heart rate surges. Danon is Gage's older brother, the firstborn and heir to the Lyon clan. I hate Gage, but I hate Danon more. Not only does he look like his warmongering father, Rand, he is also cut from the same bastard cloth.

He is not alone. Below, Lyon warriors have dismounted

"What the fuck are they doing on your lands?" Fen asks.

"I do not fucking know," Eric says. "But they're not here for diplomatic reasons, like you. And I doubt they have come to apologize."

"I also am not coming to apologize," Fen points out.

I shake my head at his diplomatic skills.

"I am not fucking delusional," Eric says. "The day you apologize for anything is the day the sky turns green. I admit I should have claimed Gwen before... I still want to fucking end you for covering her in your cum." I snicker to myself. "But I hear you have a mate now, and for her sake, I will restrain myself from such a path. Also, my father has forbidden it since we already have one war."

I should be more interested in the conversation they are having. I suppose they are starting the discussions early, and in their own way, are mending bridges. It is for the best that Fen and Eric overcome their differences. But my attention is all on the Lyon warriors in the clearing below.

"You are at war then?" Fen asks.

What do the Lyon warriors stare at on the ground? Are they arguing? I want to shift and take a closer look. The hairs on the back of my neck rise, and my buried wolf's pelt does the same.

"How many are there? Why have you not moved them on?" Fen asks.

"My father ordered us to watch and observe unless the Lyon bastards seek trouble or approach our village. He has gone to speak to the Baxters today," Eric says. "He believes Lyon are planning an attack after they sent our envoy back tied to his horse dead. My father is an honorable king. He does not seek conflict. We must live with the Lyon bastards as our neighbors. But they took a lass promised to a warrior against her will. Her intended is furious that she was taken thus, but prepared to challenge the Lyon warrior who claimed her in a fair fight. The Lyon clan's response was to send the envoy back dead."

My wolf grows restless. He hates the Lyon bastards and is ready to taste their blood.

"We have skirmished with them several times since I caught them trying to snatch the second lass," Fen says.

"What lass?" Eric asks. "One of yours?"

"No, one of yours. A few days after—" There is a long

pause where Fen is doubtless trying to find a non-inflammatory way of mentioning coming over Gwen.

"Gwen," Eric offers.

I slide a look over, worried they are about to go at one another.

"Yes, after the incident with Gwen. Four of them gave chase and caught a lass. They intended to rut and claim her there. It was not so far from your village. They slapped her to quieten her. Did no lass return with such a mark?"

"Ellen," Gwen says, anger glittering in her voice. "I thought it was her mother, who is known to have a temper. The poor lass has not had a good life. Happen she was terrified to speak lest her witchy mother beat her again. She is of age, but her mother refuses to let her mate since she uses the lass as a slave. It's time your father stepped in and found Ellen a mate who will cherish and protect her. She will come and live with us until this can be settled. That way, I may vet any male who petitions for her."

"She will not fucking live with us," Eric says hotly. "We are newly mated and have newly mated needs. Then there are your other two mates. My home is already fucking crowded!"

I raise a brow at the news that Gwen has two other mates. This is unheard of within the clans.

"She will stay with us," Gwen says, voice sharp like she is thinking of skewering Eric if he does not let the matter drop.

Fen chuckles, but I don't spare this nonsense a glance. "Fuck!" I say, scrambling to my feet.

Far below, the Lyon warriors are hoisting a wooden framework up into the trees. In the middle is a body. A freshly killed body that is dripping with blood. The dyed leather of the victim is typical of the Halket clan.

Eric roars.

I shift. Shaking out my coat and hungering for the taste of Lyon blood.

Here it is, the beginning of the war.

The Lyon warriors turn as we charge, drawing weapons and shouting to each other to ready. The two sides meet, crashing like great waves into one another. Clashing strikes of weapons, the screams of pain, and my snarls fill the air.

I take a man from behind, knocking him to the ground, teeth closing over the back of his neck.

I shake.

Under my teeth, blood pools, and bones snap.

My focus remains alert to Fen. We have fought together all our adult lives, and even before. We are honed to one another. Seamlessly, I support him, even as I take down the bastards of the Lyon clan.

Some fall.

Some scatter.

And some stand and fight.

At my side, Fen punches, cleaves, and batters any who stand in his way.

A scent fills my nose. My wolf has a good memory for those who have crossed us. I recognize the beta before me as one of those who tried to take the lass. With a savage snarl, I leap for him, taking his weapon's arm at the wrist. As his bones crunch, he drops his sword with a yowl. A heartbeat later, I have him by the throat, and he crashes to the forest floor. Blood pools in my mouth. My claws rake his chest as I tug and tug until his throat pops free.

Dead.

Turning, I find a man battling with Fen, an alpha, and his scent is also familiar.

Barry is the bastard who slapped Ellen when they tried to snatch her. Fen batters his sword away, and swinging his curving ax, hamstrings Barry as he tries to flee. Barry stumbles, gets his good leg under him, and tries to limp away.

Fen hamstrings his other leg.

My wolf growls his encouragement.

Around us, the sounds have turned from the frenzy of a skirmish to the moaning penance of dying men begging for mercy.

It is over. I shift. Chest heaving, I turn to watch Fen have his sport.

Barry begs. Dragging himself along the ground, legs limp and useless. He is bleeding, leaving a red stain over the loamy forest ground.

Fen smirks, watching the dying man.

"We should string the bastard up," I say as I come to stand beside Fen. Barry is still trying to crawl, but it is slower and weaker now.

"No," Fen says, never taking his eyes from the fallen man whose begging has turned pitiful. "He will die slower this way."

I cannot argue with that.

A call comes from behind, and we turn to find Eric has subdued Danon. The Lyon alpha snarls and curses as they bind him and set him to his knees.

"There will be retaliation," Fen says.

Eric nods, face and torso dripping with blood, although I see no obvious wound. His enemy's blood, I presume. "There will be more than retaliation," he says. Stalking forward, he punches Danon in the face, sending the bound alpha sprawling. "They wanted war. War is what they shall get."

Pivoting, he calls to a nearby warrior. "Cut my father down."

Only then do I remember the dead man strung up like a gruesome offering.

As I look up, cold sweeps my spine.

Claimed for Their Pleasure

The dead man is Karry, the Halket king.

Gwen wails, the guttural sounds of a woman in grief.

I am not in wolf form, but I still throw my head back and howl in an echo of her sorrow.

Eric, through cruel circumstances, is now the Halket king.

Chapter Fifteen

Gage

Danon has been captured.

I hate my father. I would kill the bastard in a heartbeat. But I find I cannot hold the same for Danon.

How many times have I watched on as my father chained my brother to a post and whipped or beat him to build fucking character? Too many, is the answer. These are not the whippings all men get from time to time for mischief or wrongdoing. These had no purpose and no cause that I recall.

Cruelty. It has been a part of our lives for as long as I can remember. I should leave Danon to his fate, but I find my heart does not want to. I believe there is good in him if only this tyranny can be lifted.

We all take different paths through life.

We may be brothers, but as the second born, I never suffered under the same monstrous love of my father.

"We will get him back," my father says, pacing the hall.

Outside, clouds have gathered, and lamps have been lit to offset the premature darkness.

"How the fuck are you going to do that?" I demand. "He has killed the Halket king. They will cut him up one piece at a time, send those pieces to us, and tell us to shove them up our ass!"

My father has me by the throat, slamming me against the wall.

I let him. For all he is a cruel bastard, he holds a twisted kind of love for Danon, his firstborn.

Around the hall, the clansmen and warriors grow restless. Beyond the open hall doors, the village has turned chaotic as supplies are hastily gathered before the villagers flee. Women, children, and men too old to fight are being sent into the forest for safety.

My father tightens his grip.

A tic thumps in my jaw as we eyeball each other. I want to kill the bastard. I *should* kill the bastard, but I will not start inner conflict until Danon is safe. If we fight among ourselves, we will never get him back.

With a grunt, my father steps back.

There are a dozen other men loyal to me positioned around the hall. My eyes shift to the left where Pete stands on the periphery of the room. At the slight shake of my head, I see his hand leave the hilt of his sword.

"We are taking a couple of lasses from the Halket and Ralston clan," my father says. "Both clans are weak. They will fold the moment they realize we have taken their womenfolk hostage."

My nostrils flare. "Why the fuck would you do something so stupid?"

"Don't backtalk me, whelp," he growls. Using words, he reminds me that I am lesser than him, not the king, and not even firstborn. "They will kill him if we attack. No, we need to be clever about it. A lass from the Ralston clan has a score to settle. She has already provided two lasses from the Halket clan and knows how to snatch a couple more from Ralston." He laughs softly when I reel at the news that we have already taken Halket prisoners.

"Jack gifted Nola as a slave to Halket. She was happy to help me for her freedom with us. Happen we might keep the lasses we take when this is over." Eyes settling on me, he cups his crotch. "Happen you might want to claim one."

"If I want a mate, I will claim one for myself," I say.

His dark chuckle sets my hackles rising. "Not worked out so far for you, has it, son?" he says.

Jessa

Neither Hazel nor I can sleep, so we lay together chatting on her spacious bed with too many furs. We talk about nothing important, and certainly not the war.

Night has fallen, and there is still no word.

"I met Fen a long time ago," Hazel says, piquing my curiosity. "My father is a blacksmith. Jack and Fen visited him from time to time. We sat together by the river, and while there, he stole my first kiss. I was thirteen at the time."

Giggling at this gossip, I roll onto my side to face her. She is smiling fondly.

"What happened?" I ask.

"Naught," she says. "Jack called Fen in that stern voice of his, and they left."

The Goddess was at work in their coming together again, I have no doubt.

Rolling onto my back, I stare at the ceiling. I am thinking about Gage. About how the Goddess, through me, healed him. "I kissed a lad once who was not Brandon."

Hazel gasps in shock. When I giggle at her outrage, she laughs too.

"So, Brandon is not your only love?" she asks.

Brandon is older than me by a few years. I am only just of age. Perhaps it seems strange that I have kissed another lad, although plenty of lasses get up to mischief and kissing before they are of age.

It was not even a proper kiss. I wish it had been a proper kiss.

"I have found lads handsome before," I say. Handsome does not seem adequate to describe a fearsome alpha like Gage. Brandon is handsome. Brandon is the most handsome lad I have ever met. It still makes my tummy flutter whenever I remember the things that we have done. My fantasies have gotten worse of late. The kissing and touching have awakened me to the pleasures of laying with a man. Deep in the night, I still dream about Gage.

Not only Gage. I dream of them both, of them sharing me in the way some women are shared when they wed or are claimed by two mates.

I wish I could stop dreaming about Gage, that I could settle with Brandon, as I must, and put this madness from my mind. We are at war with the Lyon clan, and my heart aches at the thought of the two men fighting.

"But he is from another clan," I add sadly, hearing the wistfulness in my own voice. I don't confess that the lad I speak of is a man and an alpha of the Lyon clan. Such details must remain forever private. "Their clan and ours do not mix so well. But I love Brandon with all my heart, and I had all but forgotten about it until you made mention of Fen."

I want to scoff at my own determination that the kiss and Gage are forgotten. If I live to be a hundred, it will be forever carved into my soul. We share a secret, Gage and I, one that hardly seems real. I am, as we all are, here by the Goddess' will. It seems cruel fate indeed that I should have these feelings and hunger for something that can never be.

"Do you know where the house for you will be built?" Hazel asks.

I'm happy for the change of subject.

"On the eastern side, next to my parents' home," I say. "Mama says she will be able to help me when I get with a child. But I also think she is anticipating me helping with all my brothers and sisters."

I will not miss the nonsense between Greta and William this morning. But when I popped over to tell Mama I was staying with Hazel, the pair of them were scoffing cookies with a grin on their faces. I love my siblings dearly. It terrifies me to think of war coming here, and of my innocent siblings being at risk.

I want Brandon to come home.

I want him to purr for me and tell me that this is over, and that we can all sleep safely now.

Only he doesn't come.

The candle has long since gone out, and we are deep into the night.

"They are very late," Hazel says softly, for we have fallen quiet.

"Aye," I agree.

A hand over my mouth stifles my scream. I struggle, but I am small for a beta, and they have me tight. Through the haze of panic, I see Hazel being subdued.

The hand over my mouth shifts, and I sink my teeth into the flesh.

My captor grunts before forcing a wad of cloth between my teeth. Another person has my wrists, swiftly binding them together. Too quickly, I am subdued, too.

I stand beside the bed, shaking, mouth gagged and hands bound, I am helpless. Mind scrambling, I try to work out what is happening. It does not seem like an attack. There is no noise or sense of anarchy. They would not need to gag and bind us were that the case.

The room is darkened, but as one shape stalks toward Hazel, the moonlight illuminates her face.

Nola.

Her arm swings, and the slap rings loud in the still night.

Goddess, she has struck Hazel.

"Leave off, bitch," a male voice says. "You can have your fun with her once we're out of Ralston."

Arm fisted by an alpha, I'm shoved roughly toward the window.

⁂

We are driven through the forest like beasts. I start every time I hear the whistle of the switch, although it rarely lands upon me. Nola is full of rage for our king's sweet mate and punishes her with a cruelty that would make the Goddess weep.

Every step takes us further from the village and hope. They allow us to remove the gags once we are too far away to make a call. I do not recognize the three men, only Nola. It seems improbable that they are from the Halket clan, yet they are with Nola, and so they must be. My stomach churns, fearing that Fen and Brandon have failed utterly in their negotiations and are even now prisoners or dead.

He cannot be dead. Surely I would sense it if that were so?

I don't know anything. The swing and fall of the switch demands we put one foot before the other.

A childhood of sleepwalking has left a legacy, and my feet only hurt a little for the lack of shoes. But Hazel is soon limping as if the switch was not bad enough.

I worry for her. I worry for us both.

We come to a stop beside the river where more men and horses wait. As I recognize the newcomers, my breath lodges in my throat.

Lyon clan.

Their murmured conversation mentions bartering the king's mate for Danon. My brows tug together. Danon is the firstborn son of the Lyon King. Has Danon been taken prisoner?

My hope lifts a little at this news. They will not kill us unless whoever holds Danon does the same.

My lips tremble as I wonder if Gage is part of this.

A fantasy explodes into my mind where Gage storms the group holding us, slays them all, and saves us both.

Hazel collapses to the floor, crushing my foolish hope under the reality of our fate. I hurry to her side. No one minds us. We are both exhausted and shoeless; running would achieve nothing besides swift capture and punishment.

"Do you know these people?" Hazel whispers.

I nod. "I recognize a warrior from the Lyon clan. Why Nola is with them, I do not know. I heard a man mention that you are to be bartered. The Lyon King's son has been taken, and they need you so that they might get him back."

"So, you are here by association," she says.

I see the pain upon her face, both the physical and the emotional kind. She is blaming herself for me being here. The only person to blame in this is witchy Nola, who conspires with our enemies.

"Our warriors will come for us," I say, voice steady although my heart is not. I cannot believe Gage would be part of this. These ruffians that hold us do not know Gage and I have met and spoken, nor that we share a secret, one that binds us before the might of the Goddess Herself.

"I wonder what has transpired for them to have captured Danon? It will not end well for them that they dared to take you as leverage." My eyes grow heavy with tears as I watch the group argue. This time, they are angry tears.

"They will be well punished." Whether it is Gage who punishes them or Jack, Fen, and Brandon, remains to be seen.

I pray that it is so.

Chapter Sixteen

Brandon

After finding the Halket king dead, we returned with Eric to his home. Danon is silent the whole journey. But when we arrive at the clan, he is taken to their village hall, the doors shut, and questioned.

Outside the hall, a funeral pyre is being built, and the king prepared for his journey to the Goddess. Inside the hall, the plaintive cries of the firstborn Lyon son are music to my ears.

A river of blood trickles over his chin and chest, his eyes are so swollen they cannot open, and his body is bruised and battered. If every rib is not cracked, it won't be for want of trying.

He laughs. I think the bastard has been beat about the head too many times.

"Why did you kill him?" Eric roars, sending the Lyon man crashing to the rough wooden floor with another savage punch.

Danon groans, rolling slowly to his side. He spits a mouthful of blood to the floor.

"I didn't kill your father," Danon says, pausing to spit out more blood. "I have said as much many times. But it seems you are not the man I thought you to be. You are too fucking drunk on revenge to care about justice."

Fen is silent; so am I.

Eric stands over the prisoner, chest heaving, knuckles raw.

"I do not trust the bastard," one of Eric's men says.

"Neither do I," Eric agrees. "The weak bastard would say anything to save his own life."

"I am already fucking dead," Danon growls. "You let one snitch escape. But even if you hadn't, I am done with the fucking clans. If you don't kill me, my father will when he learns of my actions."

"What actions?" Eric demands, grabbing a fistful of Danon's hair when the warrior remains tight-lipped.

Danon only laughs.

"You have punched his head too many times," another man says, voicing my own opinion. "He is not making a bit of sense."

A thump on the hall door interrupts proceedings before it is flung open.

"The Ralston king is here," the warrior at the door announces. "He has brought Baxter and Ross warriors with him!"

"Bind the bastard," Eric says, nudging his head to the nearest warrior. "Make sure he is put somewhere secure. He can wait until the morrow."

❧

Outside, darkness has fallen, and we find the pyre ready. The ground vibrates with the thrum of approaching horses, signifying the arrival of Jack.

As the warrior indicated, Jack does not come alone. My

wolf prowls restlessly under my skin. We have the numbers. It is time to act.

As Jack joins us, Eric orders the pyre to be lit.

Around the pyre, the Halket clan grieves as the flames rise. Jack talks to Fen, learning the details that have unfolded.

Blood and bone are turned to ashes, rising to the sky and taking the late king to the Mother of All Things.

My wolf does not understand grieving, although the man in me does. My wolf wants to act—we are aligned in this desire.

"Tomorrow," Eric says as he returns to join us. "We will take the war to them. There can be no more diplomacy. The only words will be those delivered by the sharpened steel of my sword."

Jack nods. "Tonight would be better," he boldly proposes.

My wolf stirs that our king skirts disrespect.

Eric turns to face Jack, a scowl on his face.

"They came for your father," Jack continues. "What else have they come for?"

My heart rate kicks up. My wolf is going nuts.

"Fuck! We have been away all day," Fen says. "We should question Danon."

"He is our prisoner," Eric says.

"We have left our fucking village vulnerable all day," Fen repeats, voice heating. "They killed your father. What's to say they have not attacked our home, too?"

Eric's nostrils flare. Mine is not the only temper rising as this statement settles. My wolf coils, he can sense the tension in Fen, and it amplifies our own.

Jack's hand settles on Fen's shoulder, calming him and indirectly calming us both.

"We will question him again," Eric says. "The Goddess will understand. My father will understand." Turning, he calls two of his warriors.

But as horses thunder into the village, our heads turn the other way. *Our* warriors. As they stop before us, a warrior calls, "Hazel and Jessa have been taken!"

My chest feels like it has been placed within a vice. My claws spring, my wolf fights to explode from my skin. The man in me needs to hear what will happen next, and I battle to retain control.

Jaw tight, Eric nods. "We ride!" he calls.

Chapter Seventeen

Gage

Our clan is in a state of chaos. Despite being urged to leave, many villagers remain, gathering fuck knows what. Through the open double doors of the hall, I can see the central square. A confused jumble of bellowed orders and jostling villagers, goats dragged by ropes, cages of chickens, and ragged bundles of possessions...one man is even herding pigs with a stick.

It is a calamity of the highest fucking order.

"Five more have pledged to you," Pete says as he takes the steps to meet me in the hall.

Warriors have been placed at strategic locations throughout the village. My father has left with a dozen warriors to check on them. Not that it will do us any good. He wanted to negotiate for Danon, but I cannot see that happening now. Riders returned not long ago, informing us that both Halket and Ralston are mobilizing, along with support from the Baxters.

He wanted a fucking war. Now he has gotten one.

"What are the numbers now?" I ask.

"Close to half will side with you. More will certainly fold and pledge at signs of trouble."

Dawn is creeping over the horizon. The attack will come soon. "Are the lasses safe?"

"Aye," Pete says. "Had them moved to the old lookout lodge with a couple of warriors." He spits on the dusty wooden ground. "I enjoyed slitting the throat of the bastards your father had watching them. One of the lasses was pregnant. What kind of man takes a pregnant woman as a bartering tool? No right-minded warrior hides behind a woman's skirts."

My nostrils flare. This does not get any easier to bear for discussing. "A monster," I say. "He needed to die a week ago. Had I acted then, we would not be in this mess now."

"A week ago, we did not have the numbers. You might have killed him. Or his supporters put an arrow in your back for trying, and we'd still be where we are now but with less hope. We have the numbers now."

"Danon," I say. His name is both a curse and a prayer. He is my older brother. I don't know why I suffer this desperate desire to save him.

"Has made poor choices," Pete says coldly. "If it is true that he killed the Halket king, he will be punished, and no amount of negotiating will change that. Happen we'd have to snatch the kings' mates to have any kind of credible bargaining power. That's not going to happen. Eric's mate is a warrior maiden. Jack's will be well guarded. Even that bitch Nola wouldn't dare. What you do now, you do for the clan and for yourself. If our enemies do not kill us first. Danon is gone. Let him go."

The arrival of mounted warriors curtails our discussion. Among them is Nola.

I have only met Nola on a few occasions. She's had ideas above her station for a long while. The final straw in her demise was having Jack's mate tied naked to a post while she whipped her with a switch.

My lips curl as I storm down the steps, Pete following in my wake.

My eyes widen as I notice the first lass. In the eastern clans, hair is mostly shades of brown or red. The blonde-haired, bedraggled waif is hard to forget, although I have seen her only once.

"You are fucking stupid," I roar, blood pounding so hard and fast through my veins it is a wonder I do not explode from the sheer force of it. "They will slit Danon's throat when they learn you have taken a bound mate from Jack and Fen. Then they will reign bloody revenge on every member of our clan." Hope is snatched from my fingers. My plans to confront and kill my father are because it needs to be done, but also in the hope that it might finally bring calm to the madness.

"Snatch a couple of lower-ranking women was my father's order. Not that I fucking agree with snatching a lass. Nola is bitter that she was sent away as a slave. The beta is dishonored. She has led you all for fools."

The alpha mounted behind Hazel all but drops her from the horse. Her cry of pain is sharp. Body coiling, I suck in a breath. I will kill the foolish whelp who was holding her myself.

Another lass is similarly tossed to the floor, where she rushes to aid her queen.

My nostrils flare, and my mind whites out as I recognize the tiny lass trying to comfort her injured clanswoman.

Jessa's head lifts, and she gasps as her eyes lock with mine. The two women cling to one another, shaking up a storm.

"What the fuck is the child doing here?"

"She was with their mate," Nola spits back at me. "And nothing short of their mate will have a chance to see your brother returned after what he has done."

I don't realize I have moved until Nola's bitch throat is in my fist. It feels good to squeeze. She gasps for air as I tighten my fingers, legs kicking and thrashing, fingers clawing at mine.

"I am not a child," Jessa says, her sweet voice pulling me from the brink. Her eyes flash like she is daring me to dispute that I already know this. She does seem older in ways I cannot quite pinpoint.

Nola is dropped. Falling to the ground at my feet, she heaves ragged breaths.

"Are you bonded?" I demand, stalking toward the shaking Ralston lasses. Is this the change I sense in Jessa? My gut churns and my blood rises all at once.

"No," Jessa says. Her chin tips defiantly, and her shoulders straighten.

My chest swells with both pride and joy that she is not scared of me.

"Not yet. But I soon will be."

The fuck she will. I tried to forget about her. I tried to put her from my mind. To erase the memory of her soft lips as they pressed to my forehead, her scent, her tiny, lush body that calls to the primal side of me.

I wasted my fucking time. The only way I can forget Jessa is if I am fucking dead...which might yet happen if Jack's rage for his stolen mate is anything like mine is now in seeing Jessa here.

As I continue stalking them, Hazel backs away, hissing as her right foot hits the ground. They are not wearing any fucking shoes!

Jessa thrusts her small body in front of her queen.

I stop, chest heaving with the strain as Jessa's scent floods my system.

"Kill the slave," I say, never taking my eyes from Jessa. "Snap her useless neck, slit her throat. I do not care."

The sounds of stammered pleading come from behind me. Pete does not hesitate to follow my command and Nola's begging ends abruptly.

"Well, this is a fuck up of unprecedented proportions. Between my father and my brother, it will be a wonder we have any clan left come the morrow." There is bitterness in my voice. And rage, there is also rage.

I need to do something other than stare at Jessa like a lust-drunk fool. Tearing my eyes away, I direct my attention to Jack and Fen's mate. "Are you injured?"

She nods and swallows. The poor lass is witless with her fear.

"He won't hurt us," Jessa says. Goddess, these are terrible circumstances, but her faith in me is enough to bring me to my knees.

But I need to get them both to safety. Although I don't have a fucking clue where is safe given the other clans must be almost upon us.

Taking the final step, I scoop the pair of them up. "Time to do what I should have done long ago," I say. Stalking past the hall, I head out the back for the old storage shed.

"Find out where my father is," I call to Pete.

"Where are you taking us?" Jessa demands. They are both beating me with their small fists and wriggling about.

"Quieten down, lass. I am taking you out of the way. War will be here soon, and I would not have either of you hurt when lesser men get confused in their bloodlust."

Kicking the door to the outbuilding open, I put them into the corner and draw my dagger. Grasping Jessa's wrists, I cut the binding before giving her the blade.

A great roar goes up beyond the small wooden shack. *Fuck!*

"Bar the door," I say, and pivoting, stalk out.

❧

Jessa

My heart is pounding as Gage leaves. I want to cry tears of gladness because his response on finding us taken was everything I'd hoped. Had his father been the one to greet us upon arrival, the outcome would have been very different.

Scrambling to my feet, I push the heavy bar into place before hurrying back to Hazel, where I saw through the binding at her wrists.

"You seem to know him well," she says. "He did not seem as monstrous as I expected men of his clan to be."

I sit beside her, the knife grasped within my trembling hand.

Outside the tiny shack, a battle is taking place.

Now I want to cry again, for Brandon will fight Gage once he realizes I am here.

"When I said I kissed a lad who was not Brandon," I say, my voice cracking. "Gage was that lad."

Chapter Eighteen

Gage

"Where have my prisoners gone?" my father demands as he pulls his horse to a rough stop in the village square. He doesn't come alone, a dozen men loyal to him ride with him, and all are swift to dismount. Pete takes up a position to my left, while others loyal to me similarly make subtle moves.

I don't like that Jessa and Hazel are hidden this close to the tyrant. I don't like many fucking things about this past day. With my father, I note, is one of the bastards who accompanied Nola. Probably went running the moment I had Pete end the bitch beta.

"Somewhere safe," I say. I'm not going to tell the bastard where they are.

His cold gaze lowers to the bloody stain on the floor.

"You kill Nola, whelp?"

There was a time when that word was guaranteed to get a

rise, a reminder that I'm not enough of a man in his eyes. I've been of age a while now, and it has been a long time since I was a whelp. I've more than proved myself. His insult only brings a flash of amusement that he thinks it bothers me.

"I did," I say. It wasn't me, but she died by my command.

My father takes a step closer. "You can keep Jessa. I ordered her taken for you. But I want the other three. Ralston and Halket are on their way. Along with other clans too weak to fight us on their own."

A few of the men with him grumble their support.

"I need Jack's mate. Given he lost his late mate a year ago, he'll persuade the others to let Danon go in exchange."

I laugh. The air is thick with tension, but I still fucking laugh. "Are you insane? Jack will not negotiate. He will carve this clan up. If his mate is harmed, he'll raise us from the dead so he can kill us again."

My father's nostrils flare. We have never gone head-to-head this openly before, and he doesn't like my defiance.

"Tell me where Jack's mate is," he commands.

"No."

I see the blow coming, but I don't try to avoid it. The pain as he backhands me across the face is nothing compared to the pent-up emotions coursing through me. I relish the pain.

I welcome it.

It reminds me that I am alive but prepared to die rather than suffer his darkness a moment longer.

"Search for them!" my father calls.

The blow I will take gladly, but Jessa and Hazel are too fucking close, and I cannot let him have them.

With a roar, I draw my sword. The cry is taken up by my men.

I have the pleasure of watching disbelief flash across my

father's face. It is gone as quickly as it arrives. His lips lift in a sneer as he draws his sword.

The metal clashes with a mighty ring as we take the first strike. All around the village square are cries and clangs of clashing weapons as we battle among ourselves.

Brandon

My wolf wants to run, but I force myself to mount my horse and ride. When I get Jessa back, it will be with me that she rides home.

The journey takes hours of hard riding, and my inner beast howls at every turn. I think of my sweet Jessa taken in the night, stolen away from our clan. If that bastard Gage is behind this, I will rip his throat out.

A call comes from ahead that we have hit the first resistance.

As we follow through, we find more bodies. The scent of blood permeates the air, making my wolf growl.

Then we arrive at the village, and confusion fills my mind.

They are already under attack, only not by us. They appear to be fighting among themselves.

Good. That just makes it easier for us.

Fen and Jack jump down from their horses, axes flashing.

I shift, leaping from the horse and transforming in a single fluid motion. We fight together, teeth and blade, claws, and ax. Carving through those who dare to stand in our way. I taste blood. It covers me until I am bathed in the sticky, coppery evidence of the violence we have wrought.

As the time between engagements slows, I sense the battle draws to a close.

Fen and Jack are facing one another, talking. My wolf does not understand human words. Sometimes he can infer meaning by the body language. Today, I cannot.

I shift.

Jack's chest is sawing with harsh breaths. Blood from our enemies spatters his chest and face.

I do not linger on the two brothers for long. Beyond them, directly before the great hall, the Lyon king, Rend, and his second son, Gage, fight.

A vicious, bloody fight.

A fight that I sense only one will survive.

"Fuck!" I say. Jack and Fen turn toward me before pivoting to see what has arrested my attention.

What we have witnessed here suddenly makes sense. They are at war with themselves, and our arrival is coincidental to the bloodshed. It is only now that I notice many of the Lyon clan members have tossed their weapons to the ground rather than fight with us.

"He is not a monster, and I won't let you say that he is," Jessa said. *"If these men from his clan hurt a lass, then they did it without his permission."*

She believes in him, my sweet Jessa. It leaves a taste of bitterness in my mouth, yet I suspect Gage fights because Jessa was taken.

"Gage is not a bad man," she said.

She is too fucking sweet to know a good man from a bad one. I reserve judgment on whether Gage is good or simply not wholly bad. The bastard wants her. I saw the look on his face when she stood between us, the way his arm had curled protectively around her when she sat before him on the horse.

I fucking hate him.

I hate that his scent was all fucking over her.

I hate that she scented of lust more strongly with both of us than she has ever done for me alone.

But he is not his father, and Jessa is right. He is not a monster.

I feel sick.

But I am also grateful that he is neither bad nor a monster, for I know he would die before he would allow harm to come to Jessa. Acknowledging this is like a second kick in the gut.

Our continuing conflict with this clan balances on the outcome of Gage's battle with his father.

All other fighting has stopped. We are caught watching to see which way the final blade shall fall.

Blood splatters, blades ring, and fists fly amid snarls and growls of rage.

But the Goddess is watching this village deep in the eastern Hinterlands. With a roar so visceral it springs hairs on the back of my neck, Gage slays his father.

"Fuck!" I snarl. My wolf wants to spring and go at him, even knowing he is wounded and it would not be a fair fight. Now he has slain his father, he is a different kind of threat.

Perhaps he hears my growl, for his head swings, and his eyes meet mine.

He knows everything I have been thinking because he is also thinking it himself.

Gage

My sword arm is heavy, but years of suppressed rage carries me through. I can sense the Goddess weeping that it has come to me battling my own father and blood.

He needs to die.

I have strength and youth over him, but he has experience.

"You think you can kill me, whelp?" he growls as our swords clash and hold.

I don't answer him. I know I can.

With our weapons locked, we battle for dominance. Neither of us will yield. I sense the fighting around us has declined, but I don't dare to check. No one has put an arrow in my back yet, and until then, I will fight on.

We shove apart, swords swinging, clashing together with such force that it reverberates the length of my arm. I am tiring, but I think he is tiring more. With every strike, the balance tips subtly in my favor. Confidence can kill a man as quickly as doubt, and I do not wallow in either, keeping my focus tight upon each blow.

I will win.

I must win.

For my brother, if by a miracle he still lives.

For my clan, who have long lost the way of the Goddess.

And for Jessa.

Our swords clash once more. My fist rises in an uppercut that connects with his jaw. He staggers, sword dropping momentarily.

That is all the opening I need.

With a feral roar, my blade stabs up into the opening. I slice through his belly, behind his ribs, and into his chest. There is so much force behind it, it sinks clear through the other side.

Chest heaving, I yank my sword out. His face goes slack, and surprised eyes lock with mine. His mouth opens and closes. Blood bubbles out, and the only noise he emits is a wet wheeze as he tries and fails to draw breath.

Good. I do not want any last fucking words to taint me. The bastard has tainted my life enough.

He sinks, crashing to his knees. Not yet dead, but on the wrong side of living.

I step back, sword lowering. He is no longer a threat.

Eyes wide open, he topples to the ground. I have seen enough dead men in my life and recognize the signs.

Gone. My father is really gone.

I heave another breath, one that tastes pure despite the blood saturating the lands. I become aware of my surroundings, of the weight of my body, and, in particular, my sword arm.

My head lifts from the dead man who was once my king and father. All around, more killing continues as my supporters find and slay those who once followed my father. The clans are never afraid of war, living as close to the Blighten bastards as we do, but the Lyon clan has long been the bloodiest of them all.

Today, we are broken.

Tomorrow, we will be remade into something better. If necessary, I will slay every man who would get in my way.

A feral roar arrests my attention, and my face swings to my left.

Brandon, the bastard who would take Jessa from me. Although human, he is shimmering like he's about to shift and attack.

I don't know what I would do if he did.

"Find our mates!" Jack roars, and the impasse is broken.

My eyes find Pete, ever close, and watchful of my back. I nod my head at him. He will show them where they are.

Chapter Nineteen

Jessa

We cling together within the darkened shack as the sounds of battling grow louder and more frenzied.

"I do not think this is so safe?" Hazel says. We are alone in here, but she holds a sturdy plank of wood with the same determination with which I grasp Gage's knife.

The door rattles suddenly. We both cling tighter, respective weapons shaking in our hands.

A cracking crash follows as an ax slams into the door. A second blow disintegrates the wood, and the shattered door swings open.

"Found them!" he calls. Lowering the ax, he stalks inside.

I do not lower my blade. Were the man sent by Gage, he would not need to search.

Tightening my fingers, I prepare myself. I will not be taken willingly.

"I'm not going to hurt you," he says, eying the knife I hold out.

"He is Lyon," I hiss, and lunge for him with my knife.

He laughs as he batters my strike away, fat fingers closing painfully around my wrist. They bite into the bone, making me cry out and drop the weapon.

Hazel swings her plank, hitting the side of his head with a dull thud.

"Uff!" he grunts, releasing me when Hazel beats him over the head again.

He tries to snatch the wood from her, but she is savage and beats him once again. The knife has fallen too far away for me to reach. Instead, I leap for his back just as he rips the wood from Hazel's hand. I sink my teeth into his ear. He roars and spins around. I taste his foul blood, but I cling and bite harder.

Another great crash sounds behind me as the shattered door is slammed open.

Jack!

The world spins as the Lyon warrior flings me from his back. Jack swings his arm, striking the Lyon warrior's head with his ax. It makes a sickening popping sound as it enters the skull and another as Jack yanks it back out. Blood arcs in a great spray. The warrior drops to his knees before crashing to the side, dead.

Dazed, I try to pick myself up only to feel strong, familiar arms surrounding me.

"Brandon," I sob. Pressing wild kisses all over his face as I cling to him. He is naked and tastes of blood, but I do not care.

He purrs for me. Finally, I am safe.

On the other side of the tiny shack, I hear growling as Jack and Fen discover all the terrible suffering done to Hazel.

"It was Nola," I say.

"I will fucking kill her," Fen growls.

"She is dead," I say. "Gage ordered her death for taking us."

"Fuck!" Brandon growls. He does not like me mentioning Gage. Suddenly, I am not feeling safe anymore. Now I am terrified that Gage has been killed.

"Is he...is he okay? Do you know?" I shouldn't ask, but I *must* know. Inside my chest, it feels like a tiny fist is crushing my heart.

"He was alive, last I saw," Brandon says. "More's the pity."

Trembling with relief, I sink into Brandon. Beyond the broken door, the sounds are no longer those of battle. Another Lyon warrior stands in the broken doorway. He was the one who killed Nola when we first arrived. He is Gage's man and is watching me with interest.

"Can we go home now?" I ask.

"Aye," Brandon says. "We will go home."

His hands tighten. Something has changed between us. "I don't want you to leave me," I say. "When we get home. I don't want to be in a different home. I want to be with you—always."

His arms make a strong cage around me. My ribs creak a little, so tightly does he hold me. It is the best kind of hold. I never want him to let go.

"We will work something out," he says. "I don't want to be parted from you either, Jessa."

Tears spill down my cheeks, but they are tears of release as the tension leaves my body. I am not a child anymore. I want to be with him, wholly, as a woman is with a man. To lay with him. To feel him inside me, completing me in the way I sense it will.

Hazel is similarly complaining that she wishes to go home, which puts a smile on my face.

On the dirty floor, I spot the knife, *Gage's* knife. I snag it just in time as Brandon rises, lifting me into his arms. "What is that?" he asks.

"Mine," I say. "I am taking it with me."

"You are not taking a filthy Lyon knife with you. It doesn't even have a sheath. You will cut yourself!"

"It's mine." My defiance wells up. "I am keeping it."

He sighs. "I am too fucking tired for this, Jessa. Drop it to the floor."

"No!"

Suddenly, he chuckles. "You are a fucking brat. Fine, keep your war-prize, but it will be going in the saddlebag when we reach the horse and a proper sheath when we are home."

"Agreed," I say.

Brandon carries me out in his arms, Gage's knife clasped tightly within my fist.

Gage

My head turns, catching movement behind me. Jack and Fen. Hazel is in Jack's arms, head pressed into the crook of his neck. I meet Jack's steady gaze. I nod. We will need to talk soon. But not today while he has an injured mate to care for and there is death and dying in every direction.

As they pass, I suck breath in, bracing as Brandon—still fucking naked—brings Jessa out. The mutt eyeballs me. The sight of her in his arms is a greater blow than any my late father dealt. He is taking her away from me, and the bastard is gloating about it.

My fist tightens on the hilt of my bloody sword. *Damn mutt!* The primal side of me wants to slay him, take Jessa, and fuck her in a pool of his blood.

But I am not my father. So instead, I watch them leave, feeling like I am being gutted and flayed all at once.

As they pass me, Jessa's eyes lock with mine. In her hand is a knife—*my* knife. I smile. If she wanted something of mine, I would give her something better than a well-worn blade.

I feel the pull between us, a thread binding us together. One that cannot be denied.

She is mine.

And she knows it.

Brandon is the only one who does not realize yet.

Jessa

Brandon tosses me up into the saddle. Grabbing pants from a saddlebag, he drags them on. There is a small battle when he insists that I put the blade in the saddlebag.

I don't want to let it go.

"Jessa, put the fucking blade in the bag." Voice stern and brows bunched, he brooks no discussion. My tummy ties in knots. This is not the best time for defiance, but my body still responds to his dominance and the danger by heating with arousal.

He growls.

I thrust the blade into the open, waiting bag. He snaps the flap shut and mounts swiftly behind me.

"You are a fucking test," he mutters. Gathering the reins, he nudges the horse, turning us away from the village square.

I shouldn't look back. But I can't help myself.

The fighting is over and the fallen litter the ground. Men move with purpose through the decimation. Gage is still there, standing over the body of a fallen warrior, and staring directly at me. I have only seen his father Rand once, and that was a long time ago when he visited our clan. But I think the fallen man is Gage's father.

I think Gage just killed him.

And I don't know what any of this means.

The Lyon clan has been well punished by our warriors, but also by themselves.

"We ride!" Jack calls, and the hoots of victorious warriors fill the air.

Chapter Twenty

Brandon

We ride through the night, every beat of the hooves taking us closer to home.

Inside, my wolf is restless. My mind and body are in a state of flux that neither time nor the proximity of Jessa can bring down. Her sweet scent fills my nose, her tiny, lush body pressed to mine, is a source of comfort and arousal.

I have been patient for many days since I first set myself to woo her. We have pledged to one another. Our wedding vows are all but a formality.

I want her. I want her in the way a man wants a woman, to rut her, to fill her with my seed and mark her as mine. A tendril of Gage's scent lingers on her skin, and it drives my wolf fucking nuts.

I saved her.

But Gage saved her first.

Gage. I fucking hate that alpha bastard. He will be sorely disappointed if he thinks slaying his bastard father will win him charity or respect. He should have killed the monster long ago.

I am not entirely rational, I recognize this. Killing your own father, even a monster like Rand Lyon, is a task I wish on no man. It is done now. Things will change. How much depends on how he handles the fallout with his clan. They are rotten, and the rot goes deeper than a single man.

If the infighting we witnessed is any indication, they have given a fair go to culling the disease.

I hope the Lyon clan takes a turn for the better. We have enough problems to deal with as winter will soon approach. It would be better for everyone if Lyon would stop their warring ways. But that does not mean we are friends. It doesn't mean *he* can look at Jessa like he wants to claim her for himself.

My wolf recognizes the threat he represents. I'm convinced the knife Jessa is determined to keep was once Gage's. I can't see Jack striking an alliance with the Lyon clan any time soon. But that he might is a risk neither the man nor wolf in me is prepared to accept.

I need to claim Jessa. Once that is done, there will be nothing Gage can do.

Better yet, I get her with a pup in her belly, then the matter will be well and truly done.

The sun climbs the closer we draw to Ralston. It has been a long day and night since we left, and as we emerge through the trees and onto the shore of the loch, I suffer a sense of relief in being home and in seeing all appears well. The loch glistens, reflecting the pine-covered slopes of the mountain. The little jetty poking out into the water is surrounded by fishing boats.

As soon as we are spotted, a cry goes up, and villagers hasten from tasks to welcome us home. We have lost a few men, not as many as the Lyon clan, but any loss is too many.

Soon, some villagers will be holding returned loved ones close, and others will be grieving.

I never thought much about the fragility of life before today, about the way those you love can be snatched from you in an instant. My hands tighten around Jessa, and I lean in to draw her scent into my lungs, letting it calm me.

Her small hand closes over mine where I grasp the reins.

Inside, my wolf howls. He wants to claim our mate. It is the way of the clans that a beta would usually wed, but my wolf does not care for such intricacies.

As we draw closer still, I see familiar faces among the crowd. My mother and father. Jessa's parents, her siblings dancing about and squealing with excitement when they see their big sister returned.

As we come to a stop and I dismount, I hear the first wails of grief.

Fen carries Hazel inside. His little mate is badly hurt after Nola's cruelty, bearing far more welt marks than Jessa. Jack takes a position on the steps of the hall to address the village.

I lift Jessa to the ground only to have her snatched from me. Her mother, father, and all five siblings crowd around in a giant hug full of tears and mumbled words of relief.

Then my mother and father are there with me. It has been many years since I have been hugged, but my ma does not hesitate to draw me into her arms. "We were terrified when we learned Jessa and Hazel had been taken," she says. "Your father said you would not come home without them."

On my periphery, I see Jessa talking to her mother. A clanswoman brings over supplies, and they head together for the steps to the hall.

"I need to go," I say. "My wolf needs to be close."

My father nods. He is a wolf, too, and he understands. "There is a home waiting for you," he says. "We were hoping to make it a surprise. Well, things don't always work to a plan. It's not finished yet, but I dare say you can fix the rest in your own time now. Ed and I will help you with the bigger jobs."

I frown in confusion. "What home?"

"The old cottage that belonged to the Bennets afore they left," my mother says. "Jack was keeping it for Fen. He won't be needing it anymore since he will be living with Jack and their mate."

I rock back on my heels. The old Bennets' place is beautiful, if a little unloved. It comes with a decent size vegetable plot and a small sheep paddock.

"A newly bonded couple need a place of their own," my father says gruffly.

"There are fresh bedding and blankets there," my mother adds. "We all knew you would not want to be separated from Jessa after you returned. And well, it gave Betty and me something purposeful to do while we were worrying."

I glance across to see Ed doing his best to contain his brats with the aid of the older ones. "You brought her back, son. You have my blessings. Happen it's time you had somewhere with a bed rather than sneaking off into the woods all the time," Ed says...and is that a smile?

Fuck! I have gotten Ed to crack a smile!

"Thank you. Thank you so much," I say. But my eyes shift to the hall entrance where Jessa and her mother have disappeared from my view. "I need to go."

Not waiting for a reply, I shift to my wolf and push my way through the crowd listening to Jack.

Chapter Twenty-One

Jessa

As my mother and I treat Hazel's injuries, Brandon paces restlessly in wolf form near the bedding chamber entrance. He does not like to be separated so soon after the harrowing events. I do not want to be separated either, but I take comfort in him being there.

I am exhausted, but I will not rest easy until I see Hazel has been treated.

My focus is on the wickedness done by Nola, but my heart is with Brandon as he paces by the door.

Hazel's right foot is cut, and dirt has been ground into the wound. After bathing it, we apply a salve and carefully wrap it in a bandage.

"You should not walk until it has a chance to heal," my mother says as she gathers the supplies before wrapping an arm around me.

"That won't be a problem," Jack says from the entrance to

189

the chamber. "Our mate will be busy for the next few days while we tend to her."

I smile. It feels like I have not smiled in a long while. Leaning in, I press a gentle kiss to Hazel's forehead. "May the Goddess bless you with a child," I whisper before leaving with my mother.

Brandon stops his pacing seeing me approach. The moment I near, he comes at me, nearly bowling me over. Is he... herding me?

My mother chuckles. "Ah, lass, it feels good to chuckle at his nonsense. Happen he doesn't trust himself to shift afore he has gotten you home."

"Home?" I cannot bear the thought of being parted from Brandon. I run my fingers through his thick coat. Goddess, he is so soft. I don't remember ever touching him in wolf form before.

"Let him take you, lass," she says with a wink. "Happen he knows where to go, and we will talk on the morrow." She hugs me swiftly before letting me go.

Brandon, taking this as a cue, all but knocks me over again.

"Goddess!" I mutter. "I am coming. Show me the way."

I don't think wolves can understand human words, but he lets me know what he wants, nudging me out of the great hall. I follow him all the way down the lane to a part of the village I don't visit often. Here, he comes to a stop outside a rickety gate.

I blink a few times in confusion. This is the old Bennets' place. It looks different...like someone has been in here. The ramshackle cottage is covered in Jasmine and creeping ivy. A picket fence, weather-worn and broken in places, surrounds the property and garden.

Before I can turn and demand answers from the wolf, the air crackles behind me. Strong arms surround me, one slipping under my legs and lifting me up.

"I believe it is tradition to carry the bride over the threshold," he says, a huge grin on his handsome face.

"Brandon! What is going on?"

Ignoring me, he pushes the gate open and carries me along the little brick path someone has cleared of weeds. At the door, he pauses. "This is our home, Jessa," he says. "Our parents have been readying it in secret. They thought we might not want to be apart tonight and gave their blessing to have it early. I don't want to be apart, Jessa, not for a single minute. It nearly killed me waiting while you tended to Hazel. Do you want this? Do you want to spend the night with me in the way of a husband and wife?"

My mouth opens, but no words come out. Tears spring from my eyes. Leaning up, I press a kiss to his soft, bearded cheek.

"Yes. Goddess yes." I manage to croak the words out past the tightness in my throat. "I want that more than anything."

With a grin, he shoulders the door open, steps through, and kicks it shut again.

Inside, it is clean and furnished with a wooden table and two mismatched chairs. The fire is cold but stocked with wood. A cloth-covered jug and bowl are resting upon the table. Sure of foot, he strides through the living area, through another open door, and into a bedroom.

Here, he gently lays me upon a bed.

A bed?

A proper bed in a bedroom and not a bedding nook!

"I can't believe they did this in secret," I say. "This is the most beautiful home I have seen!"

"And you are the most beautiful woman I have ever seen," he says.

My breath catches at the seriousness in his tone. His dark, too-long hair has fallen forward over his forehead. I have watched him grow from a boy into a man and his features are familiar to me. I have seen them so many times over the years living as we do on opposite sides of the lane.

Today, I have been confronted by my own mortality.

Suddenly, I am on the verge of tears.

"Hush, lass," he says. Settling beside me, he takes me in his arms.

I sob. It is like a dam breaking, and all the tears pour out. I have been frightened for my life, and now, I am safe again.

He holds me. And we lay like that together for the longest time. Outside the shuttered window, I can hear the distant sounds of the clan as folks go about their lives. Some will be grieving, and my heart aches for them. But the passing of their loved ones must also be rejoiced. They have died bravely and will be with the Goddess now.

My sorrow feels endless. But nothing is forever, and it loses sharpness with time. The tears slow. Under my cheek is the warm, hair-roughened skin of Brandon's chest. He purrs, and it comforts me. I have always loved his purring, even though many women don't. I cannot think of anything more soothing than that sweet rumbly sound against my ear.

As my awareness returns, I become conscious of the softness beneath my body—one of my mother's best woolen blankets is adorning the bed, I'm sure. But I am also aware of Brandon. Of his hot flesh, of the heavy thud of his strong heart beating under my ear.

"Do you want something to drink?" he asks, rolling onto his back and tucking me against his side. "I don't know what was wrong with me bringing you straight to bed like an animal. My wolf is impatient."

"Just your wolf?" I ask, sneaking a little kiss against his chest.

"Aye, the rest of me, too," he admits, chuckling. "I feared I might rut you before your family and the village in the king's hall."

Rising, I look down at him through tear-dampened lashes. "I wouldn't care if you did. I don't want to wait anymore, Brandon. I have been scared. But I am alive."

My hand rests against his chest, but my gaze trails the over ridges of his firm abdominals to where his cock nestles against dark curls.

"Jessa," he says, the word holding a warning.

But my hand moves of its own accord. He is glorious like this, naked, cock bobbing simply because I have feasted my eyes upon it.

My hand is captured before I can snag my prize, and I am tumbled onto my back.

"You are wearing too many fucking clothes," he growls. Hands at the hem of my hide top, he tugs it up and over my head. It lands on the floor behind him even as he attacks the fastenings of my skirt. I help, both our hands getting in the way. I wriggle, and together, we push it over my hips until it follows my top and lands upon the floor.

"Don't move," he says, gaze roaming over my body. "Goddess, you are so beautiful."

My breath catches, and I wonder at the hunger I see in his eyes. I am small for a beta in every way, from my breasts to the gentle swell at my belly and hips. But I see no disappointment in Brandon's face, only love and lust.

Gathering my hands, he places them above my head.

Holding my eyes, he says, "Keep them there, Jessa. I will lose my mind if you touch me. I am so fucking close."

I nod, chest rising and falling unsteadily. My skin feels hot and extra sensitive as Brandon places one hand against my hip and slowly, so slowly, skims it up to cup my breast. He watches his hand, biting his lip as he squeezes, testing the weight.

I suck a sharp breath in as his thumb brushes over my nipple, sending all the nerves there springing to life.

"More," I beg.

"When I'm ready," he says.

I groan, wanting everything all at once. Between my thighs, slick gathers as my body prepares for him.

Catching my taut nipple between his finger and thumb, he rolls it first gently and then harder.

"Goddess, yes!"

"Is that what you want, Jessa?" he says. "Or do you want me to kiss you there?"

"Yes," I gasp. "All of it. Kiss me there, pinch it. I don't care. I want it all."

His head lowers. But not to the breast he is teasing with rough tugs. No, his head lowers to the other side, where he sucks the hardened tip into his mouth.

My fingers are in his hair, grasping, pulling him closer as all the sensations hit me with the ferocity of a winter storm. I squeeze my legs together, trying to ease the ache.

With a growl, he peels my hands away and slams them back to the bed. Goddess, that sound and his handling of me sets me on fire. His mouth shifts to the other breast, the one he has teased until it is a hot kind of sore. He trails the tip of his tongue all around the peak before sucking it into his warm, wet mouth.

My hands make fists. I want to grab him closer. I want to pet all the glorious flesh of his beautiful body. But I don't dare move lest he stop this wondrous exploration.

I am torn between obedience to his request and rebelliousness. What will he do if I disobey him? Will he spank me? Will it push him to subdue me and thrust his hard cock inside me where I am desperate for his touch?

I battle with the two sides of me as he squeezes my breasts

together and teases me to the point of madness with his fingers and mouth.

"Brandon, please," I whine. "I cannot wait. You have made me wait too many times, and I do not want to wait today."

His head lifts, eyes crashing to meet mine. His lips are a little swollen and glisten where he has been sucking against my breasts. Shifting, he rises above me onto all fours, giving me a perfect view of his glorious rippling flesh. Lower, his thick cock juts from the dark curls. The tip glistens, and a thin trail of clear stickiness connects it to the soft swell of my stomach.

Hand lowering, he cups me intimately, warm fingers over the entrance to my pussy, the heel of his palm teasing my clit. My hips lift, seeking more of his touch.

"Please," I say.

Slowly, too slowly, he pushes two thick fingers inside.

"Gods, you are drenched," he says, pumping in and out with maddening slowness. As he watches my face, I wonder what I look like with my mouth open as I gasp with pleasure. "Come for me, Jessa. Come all over my fingers, then I will give you everything you need. Will rut you and claim you forever as mine."

His thumb swipes over my clit, back and forth, each stroke lifting the pleasure, bringing the quickening to my breath until it all tumbles over into a glorious release.

I lay panting after, satisfied and yet needy for more.

There is no more waiting. I am barely recovering from the climax when the tip of his cock snags the entrance...and sinks slowly in.

"Goddess!" I gasp. It is far thicker than his fingers, silken smooth and yet deliciously hard as it slides into me.

"You feel so fucking good, Jessa," he says, voice low and rough. "Tell me if I'm hurting you. Tell me if you need me to stop."

"Don't stop," I plead. My hands find the back of his neck, pulling him closer, demanding a kiss. "All of it, Brandon. I want it all."

Pulling almost out, he surges deep, filling me completely, driving a gasp from my lips as he breaks through my hymen. There is only a slight pinchy-sting before it flares to a heated fullness.

"Are you okay?" he asks, lips close to mine, holding himself still.

"Yes," I gasp. "Yes, it feels so good. Full of soft, hot, hardness. A perfect kind of full."

With a groan, his lips lower to capture mine in a feverish kiss as his hips begin to rock. It felt nice when he was deep inside me, but this is a thousand times better. Each glorious stroke flares inner nerves to life. My hands tangle in his hair, holding him close. His kisses and the sweet, heavenly sensations of his cock surging into my pussy become the center of my world. My legs wrap around him, making a cradle for his thrusting hips. I feel alive in ways I have never done before, complete, whole, full of his love and his cock.

Drawing his lips from mine, he stares down at me, his handsome face flushed. "Tell me if you need me to slow... If I'm too rough. You feel so fucking good, hot, wet... Your pussy keeps clenching... Sucking me in like it doesn't want to let me go... I am going to lose my mind."

"Don't stop," I repeat. "Don't slow. Harder. Make it harder. I need more."

"Fuck," he growls. Shifting to his knees, he takes my hips in his hands and begins to rut me harder, slamming our bodies together, making the wet sounds as my pussy gushes out the slick.

"Yes!" I'm going to come again. I can feel it building. The change in position hits somewhere deep inside that melds all the sensations into a great wave that finally crashes, taking me into another glorious climax.

Nonsense pours from my lips before he slants his lips over mine, slamming his hips harder, filling me over and over. I open to the kiss, tangling my tongue with his. My body keeps rising higher while the kiss drives me deeper underwater until I am drowning in Brandon and the pleasure he wrests from me.

I let go, surrendering to the sensations, letting them take me where they will.

Where they take me is to another heart-pounding climax. This time Brandon is with me, and the pleasure is twice as wild and intense. His cock seems to grow as he thrusts deep and holds.

I feel him coming, a hot flood inside, filling me until there is nowhere for it to go, and it pulses out around his cock.

"Are you okay?" he asks on a gusty breath.

"Yes," I say. "I have never felt so good. Why are you stopping? Can we go again?"

Chuckling, he eases out, sending a great gush of stickiness all over the beautiful bed. This rutting business is very messy, but I am too sated to care. He collapses on the bed beside me, drawing me into the crook of his arm, and purrs.

"A man needs some time between rutting," he says. He peeks at me through a crack in his eyes. "Are you sure you're not sore?"

I am a little sore, but I'm not telling him this in case he decides we must abstain from the next rutting, whenever that is.

"I am not sore," I announce. "How long does it take?"

His cock is soft now, but it jerks at my words.

"Not long if you keep staring at it like you want to gobble it up," he says dryly.

My eyes flash to meet his. I smile. On my periphery, his cock begins bobbing enthusiastically. It is still sticky, covered in his cum and mine. Now, I can't stop thinking about how it tasted, how it made me needy. The sensation of his thick flesh sliding into my mouth, especially when it went deeply, all the way to the back of my throat, was sublime.

He curses as I scramble to my knees.

"Jessa," he warns.

I have heard that warning voice before, and I am not scared of it. His cock is hard and ruddy-looking. He likes it when I take it into my mouth. He likes the thought of me doing it now.

My smirk is ripe with naughtiness as I grasp his length at the base, tilting it as I lower my lips to kiss the crown.

We both groan as I lap at the sticky tip. It pulses under my hand and tongue, getting harder, growing with every swipe of my tongue.

"Gods!" he says as I suck half of it into my mouth until it hits the back of my throat and surges a little way inside. That I can weaken this man with pleasure, enthralls and empowers me to drive him wilder still.

"Fuck!" he growls. Grasping a handful of my hair, he pulls me off and tips me onto my back. There is no tentativeness this time. This time, he lines his cock and surges deep.

I gasp, he feels harder, or perhaps I am sensitive after the vigorous first rutting.

"Did I hurt you?" he asks. Capturing my chin in his hand, he tips my face toward his.

I shake my head.

"Jessa?"

The warning is back. It stung a small amount, and I think I might have winced. He is not moving, but at least he has not pulled out. I wrap my arms and legs around him just to be sure.

"It only stung a little," I say.

"I think you need to rest," he says. "Your mother, in all her wisdom, is bound to have left some oils as might ease the soreness."

My pussy grips, and my arms and legs tighten when he tries to pull out.

"Don't," I beg. "It was only a little sore when you first pushed in. It does not even hurt now."

"I don't fucking believe you," he says on a groan. "But your clenching pussy is a test. I will go slowly if you promise to tell me if you need me to stop."

"Okay," I agree. I dare not tell him that I like the soreness in the same way I like the sting when he spanks my bottom. Goddess, thinking about him spanking me while his hard length is inside me, deep and so intimate, is enough to make me... I come. It sideswipes me out of nowhere.

His lips crash over mine in a hungry kiss that makes the pleasure twist higher still. His hips begin to move, his hot flesh surging in over and over.

He purr-growls as he ruts me with agonizing gentleness. My body is in a state of euphoria. His lips, his hands, his hot male flesh, his growly sounds of pleasure, they belong to me and me alone. I sink into the sensations and into him. I feel his love wrap around me. I sense his devotion and caring with every tempered stroke. He is a strong male capable of rutting me harder and being rougher, but he puts my newness above his own pleasure.

I wish he wouldn't. But I love him all the deeper that he does.

The next climax takes us both, dizzying, blissful. It sweeps my whole body up. Deep inside, he fills me again.

Tears spring from my eyes, and he presses kisses to my cheeks, begging me to tell him what is wrong.

"Nothing," I say, fighting to stop the torrent, for I know I am upsetting him. "I am so Goddess-blessed to be here with you, Brandon. I'm just overwhelmed with joy and love."

"I too, Jessa," he says. "I have been through hell this last night and day since I found out you were taken. The thought of losing you, too painful to bear. You disarm me with your ways, both the lusty ones that make my cock hard and the sweet loving ones that care deeply for those lucky enough to have you within their circle. The man in me wants to wed you before our village and family. But the wolf in me has already claimed you as a mate."

Nestling his face into the crook of my shoulder, he presses a kiss. "Right here, I will mark you. Not today, but soon." Lifting his head, he meets my eyes. "If it fades, I shall mark you again. You are mine, Jessa. My wolf has claimed you. I have claimed you. Until the Goddess takes one of us into the afterworld, you are mine."

Chapter Twenty-Two

Gage

"What is that?" I ask, frowning at the cloth-covered basket Pete has placed upon the great oak table of the hall.

Beyond the open double doors, the villagers return in a rag-tag procession, complete with goats, chickens, and...a herd of pigs. The village is decimated. Half the buildings will need substantial repairs. While others are ruined and will need to be torn down.

I dare say we are less in number now and will not need so many homes.

"A kitten," Pete says. "Last of the litter. The rest have been homed."

"And this is the pressing issue of the moment?" I ask, wondering if Pete has taken a blow to the head.

"My mate gave it to me," he says, face coloring even as he scowls. "You know the ways of womenfolk at times. She thought it might give you something to..." he trails off under my censorious glare. "Its mother is a good mouser. It'll keep the rats and mice at bay."

Now I am a fucking charity case. The womenfolk will be fussing over me and seeking to find me a mate before the stain of my father's blood can be washed away.

A small white paw pokes out from under the cloth, and tiny claws rake the top of the basket.

I sigh and nudge my head toward the basket in indication for Pete to show me. "Won't it run off?"

Why am I discussing this?

"Not once it bonds to you." Grinning, he reaches in to pull out a scrap of ginger fur.

Ginger, of all the fucking colors. The one white paw was there to throw me off the scent.

It makes a cute, squeaked mewling sound at being liberated from confinement.

"I dare say it wouldn't hurt to have it around," I say, motioning him to hand it over.

"What are you going to call it?" he asks.

"Cat," I say, holding it up to eye level by the scruff of its neck. Its tiny mouth opens like a gate to emit another high, elongated squeak. I make the mistake of bringing it closer. The little paws shoot out, grasping my beard and throat with needle-sharp claws. "Fuck!"

I try to peel it off. It clings tighter. A few paces away, Pete emits a deep guffaw at my expense.

The demon-possessed fur-ball is having none of my attempts to remove it. The moment I stop trying to peel it off, it eases the claws and burrows into the crook of my neck with its head in my hair.

It purrs.

I find myself petting its silken fur. I am soothing it so I can take it off without losing skin, nothing more.

"It has bonded to you already," Pete says, nodding his head approvingly. "Keep it inside for a few days. Put some sawdust in a box, and it will go in there."

Great! Now I must make a place for it to shit!

A warrior stomping up the steps to enter the hall brings an end to the discussion. Simon does a double-take as he notices the small bundle of fur I'm petting like a fucking sap.

"He is bonding," Pete says to Simon.

"Aye," Simon says, giving me a similar approving nod. "Little mite has taken to you. My sister took two from the last litter. They have not had any bother from rodents since. Kids love 'em. Niece sleeps with 'em on her bed. Better than a guard dog."

It is not sleeping on my fucking bed.

"Did you come here for a reason?" I ask.

"Aye, sire," Simon says. "Rounded the last of them up. You said as you wished to talk to them."

My new title is jolting. It will take some getting used to.

Wise to the tiny demon clinging to my neck, I peel its paws off first before putting it back into the basket. The cloth is heavy, but I can't see that holding it for long. "I'll see them now," I say.

I put the basket in my bedding chamber, ensuring the shutter is secure before closing the door. This business will not take long. I'll stop by the workshop on the way back and have a lad make a box with sawdust for it.

Turning back to the room, I find the two men waiting, expressions solemn. This is not a pleasant kind of business that I must tend to. We have been ripped asunder by my conflict with my father. Clansfolk, who were once neighbors, are now enemies depending upon how their loyalty fell.

Men are dead. Some have fled.

They will need to adapt to the change if they want to stay here.

We have retrieved most who fled, but I expect a few escaped in the chaos last night.

"Let's go," I say.

I find them in the hay barn that is yet empty at this time of year, thirty, maybe fifty men, some alone, some with women and children. I will not turn women and children away, but if their men cannot adjust, it is their choice whether to go or stay.

A hushed quiet falls over them as they notice my arrival.

"I know some of you think yourselves loyal to my father, and through him, Danon," I say. "But Danon will never be king. Not without killing me, and he will never defeat me. So, you have a choice. You can go, or you can stay. But know that if you go and take to raiding, I'll be the one who hunts you down, and your dead body will be making food for the crows when I string you up as a warning to others."

"Know, too, if you stay and I hear any word of plotting, I'll also cut you down and string you up. I won't ask you questions. I won't discuss it. You'll be dead, and your family will be without a husband or mate."

I don't shy away from the words or the message that I must deliver. The clan needs to heal, and it can't do that while any man is plotting revenge.

"I want Danon back. If I can negotiate for his release, I will. But he killed the Halket king, and our chances are small."

"Danon would not do that!" a man at the back calls. "It is not his way."

Danon has done many things that I do not believe to be his way under the direction of my late father. But I don't point this out. This discussion is about whether they go or stay, and that is about them and me.

"That remains to be determined," I say. "But Danon still

won't be the king even should by a miracle we bring him home because I am the fucking king. If he wants to dispute that, it'll be between him and me as such a challenge should be."

"I am not my father. I disagree with his ways. Winter is approaching—the time of year when Orcs raid. We need alliances, not war. Our chances of alliances are small, but they are better than they were when my father was still alive."

"You have heard my words. Now, you must choose. Stay or go. I hope you will stay and help me to rebuild the Lyon clan."

As I turn and leave the barn, I hear the murmurs of conversation. Warriors are on guard, and those within will not be allowed to leave until they decide.

"Anyone I need to worry about?" I ask Pete as we make our way to my home and hall.

"Aye, a few of them," he says. "But I'm expecting them to leave. I'm also expecting them to get up to mischief, so I have a couple of shifters ready to follow them and make sure they quit the Lyon lands. If they hole up nearby with a mind to raiding, I'll slit their throats myself. Got a family who'll be safer under your watch. And not prepared to let worthless bastards threaten us again."

We pass by a carpenter busy at work repairing a busted door. "Hey, Milt!" Pete calls out. "Can you make one of those sawdust boxes?"

"Who's it for?" Milt asks, pausing his hammering.

Pete thumbs toward me.

Milt's face splits in a grin. "The last one from the litter, I take it? The missus will be disappointed. She was hoping you wouldn't find a home for it so we could have another one. I'll get right on it as soon as I finish this door."

What the fuck is happening to my life?

Today, I am a clan king.

Today, everyone is talking about the fact I have a cat.

Chapter Twenty-Three

Jessa

Brandon woke me with a gentle kiss this morning. Still tired after spending an afternoon and night learning about each other, I had murmured demands for his purr.

He purred as he kissed me, but when I woke up again, he was gone.

I feel different today. The whole world feels different, truth be told.

Rising from the bed, I wash in cool water, grateful to find the jug and bowl waiting together with a new block of soap and a soft woolen towel. There is a dresser opposite the bed, and when I open the top drawer, I find my clothes neatly tucked inside.

I smile.

Dressing swiftly, I open the shutter to let the morning sunshine in. Outside is a small vegetable patch. I can't believe that all this is mine.

My smile fades as recent events come crashing back. The terrible swishing sound of the switch and Hazel's cries of pain.

The fear.

The hope.

Gage when he found we had been snatched.

Gage as he carried Hazel and me to the outbuilding for safety.

Gage as he stood, bloody, over the body of his father.

I shiver.

He is a fearsome alpha, and yet he has only ever been gentle with me.

I wonder where the knife is? I think Brandon knows whose it is. Will he throw it away? He might. He probably should. I still want to keep it, the most ridiculous reminder, yet it once belonged to Gage, and I want it.

I sigh.

This is not over nor settled. Deep in my belly is the fluttering, the nervousness, and the anticipation of something *more*.

"You're up!"

Spinning, I find Brandon in the entrance to the bedroom. Well-worn boots adorn his feet, leather pants molded to his muscular thighs, and leather jerkin that does nothing to disguise his beautiful body. He is mine, I realize, and I, his.

"I don't want to be wedded," I blurt out. Goddess, I am a tactless lass.

He frowns. "You don't?"

I feel my face flush. I need to explain myself before he comes to the wrong conclusion. Where this wanton side of me comes from, I cannot say. But every moment with Brandon brings it closer to the surface. "I want you to claim me," I say, the words tumbling out in a rush. "Like you spoke of yesterday. I want you to bite me as you rut me and to mark me for all to see. Some shifters still do this, even if they are a beta. It would be acceptable."

"Fuck!" he mutters roughly. His eyes darken and nostrils flare in a way that tells me he likes the sound of this.

My pussy clenches. It is a little sore, but I like the soreness. I like it in a way that feels improper for a good beta lass. The slickness begins to pulse. His gaze drops to the crux of my thighs, hidden from his view by my skirt.

"Are you sore?"

My lips tug up. "Not enough to stop."

"Good," he says, stepping up to me. Arm clasping around my waist, he takes my lips in a searing kiss full of hunger like he wants to devour me whole.

My hands fumble with the ties on his leather jerkin. He takes over, breaking the kiss long enough to tug his jerkin up and off. My top follows it to the floor. We kiss, my hands roaming over the muscular plains of his chest, shoulders, and back as his hands make light work of the ties on my skirt.

As it drops to the floor, he kicks his boots off, even as we chase the next kiss.

"Bed, now," he growls, shoving pants down his muscular thighs and taking his cock in hand.

But I don't do as he says. Instead, I drop to my knees. I have heard lasses talking about sucking a man. Some liked it, and some didn't. But all agreed that cum did not taste very nice.

I am greedy for it. I cannot get enough. From the first taste that evening in the woods before the great oak tree, I was addicted. When it hits my belly, it is like a swarm of butterflies settling low. Like moon berries, only better.

"Please," I say. "I want to taste you. It needs to be part of the claiming."

His cheeks flush. "Taste all you want, Jessa. Afterward, I

will taste you. Then I will fill you and claim you in the way of a wolf."

His cock is long, thick, and ruddy. It leaks in anticipation. Closing my hand around the base, I gently lap the offering from the crown.

We both groan. His hands tangle in my hair, holding me gently as I enclose the tip in my mouth. My tongue lashes the head, swirling all around the leaking tip. It tastes a little salty, and of him. My belly tumbles in anticipation as I begin to bob my head, sucking him as deeply as I can.

His groan dips to a growl that makes my pussy quiver. Fingers tightening, he encourages me to go deeper until the head of his cock brushes the back of my throat.

I want more. I always want more, deeper, harder—*more*.

My other hand skims over his thigh until it reaches the sacs of his balls. The rough hair is springy under my fingers; they tighten as I gently play.

"I'm going to come," he says, voice low and growly.

I suck deeper still, taking the head down my throat a little way. My throat and jaw aches, air becomes a luxury to my starved lungs, but I don't care. His cock pulses and his hands tighten. Enthralled by the feel and scent of him, slick begins to trickle down my thighs. Moving both hands to his thighs, I score my nails down the flesh, wild for tasting him.

With a ragged groan, he comes, shooting thick cum into my throat, and filling me. I choke a little, gulping as much as I can. I keep sucking and licking until there is no more, and his legs begin to tremble.

As my lips pop off, I find him watching me with a dark expression that sets a fire under my skin. Hands under my arms, he lifts me, scooping me up and placing me upon the bed as if I were the most precious thing.

"I love you," he says. "I love you more than I thought it was possible to love a person. Now, I am going to love your body to show you. Afterward, I will claim you, exactly as you have asked."

❧

Brandon

I had much I intended to talk to Jessa about when I returned to the house. I forgot all of it the moment I saw her face. Her bold announcement that she wished to be claimed has put me in a spin.

Then she sank to her knees.

I am obsessed with her, I realize. Everything about her tiny, lush body, her sweetness, and her carnal awakening bewitch me until I am utterly lost. We came together so many times last night, but I am addicted to her and cannot get enough.

On her back, legs spread wide, I feast upon her slick pussy. Nothing about Jessa is ordinary, not her ways, and not her body. She tastes different, or perhaps it is only that I experience this all-encompassing love. I have never been this addicted to eating pussy in my life. My cock is hard, pulsing and leaking all over the bed in anticipation of sinking into her welcoming tightness.

"Goddess! I am going to come!" Her small hands make a fist in my hair, tugging enough to bring a sting that urges me on. Swiping my tongue back and forth over her clit, I curve my fingers in her drenched pussy, finding the spot that drives her wild.

She comes, inner walls squeezing and juices flooding around my fingers, hips rocking as she rides my face.

I wrench away, knowing if I don't stop now, I will never fucking stop. There is no more waiting. My wolf is restless and close to the surface of my skin, demanding we claim our mate. Rising, I crawl over her, feeling my chest swell with pride in seeing the aroused flush covering her face, neck, and upper swell of her tits. Leaning in, I suck her pretty nipple into my mouth, drawing a groan from her lips. My mouth pops off, trailing kisses up over her collarbone until I settle at the side of her throat.

Taking my aching cock in hand, I line up with her weeping pussy and thrust.

"Brandon, please. I need it all!"

I have no idea what she mumbles about, but I set up a hot, fast pace that sees her small nails scoring my back. Her tightly clenching sheath is both heaven and hell. Heaven because it feels so fucking good as it sucks me in, and hell because I want to come, but I also want this to last.

"Do you like that, Jessa? Like it when I fill your slick little pussy up?"

"Yes!" Her breathy answer is accompanied by her hot passage clenching tighter around my thrusting rod. Filthy, wet, slapping noises accompany our vigorous rutting. Gods, that sound is near enough to take me over the edge.

"I'm going to bite you when I come...when we both come. My gums are aching; my wolf wants to push his fangs out so that I might claim you properly and to his satisfaction. Do you want that, Jessa? Do you want my wolf to claim you?"

Her words turn to mumbled nonsense and encouragements to rut her harder and deeper. My rutting takes an edge of brutality. She goes fucking wild, slamming her hips up to meet every stroke. This tiny, sweet lass was Goddess-sent to take cock.

I pause to grind deeply. "I could take you deeper if I rut you from behind," I say softly, lips skimming the shell of her ear.

Her nails dig into my shoulder, and her hot inner walls clamp over my length. "Please, Brandon, I want you to do that."

I can deny her nothing. I want to see her pretty face contorting with pleasure, but my wolf also wants to claim her in *his* way.

Pulling out, I catch hold of her thigh to tumble her over onto her front.

Her outraged gasp brings a smile to my lips. "Stop fussing, lass. You like it when I'm a little rough."

Ass lifting, she throws a look over her shoulder that is ripe with challenge.

Taking my cock in hand, I tease her clit with the tip, smirking as she starts the sweet begging to be filled. "When I'm ready," I say, knowing it will drive her crazy.

It is driving me crazy too.

Inside my chest, my heart pounds. I want to wait, to draw out the beauty of this moment, but I need to claim her now. As the tip breaches the entrance of her pussy, I take her waist and slowly fuck in. I grit my teeth as she clamps around me.

"Oh Goddess," she says with a groan. "I can't. I'm going to come again."

"Hold it, Jessa," I say. "Not until I'm all the way in."

She groans.

I keep my thrusts shallow, making her beg and plead for more, slowly rutting her deeper until my body is flush to hers. Then I take her, hard and fast, driving as deeply as I can. She flutters around me, gripping me, setting my climax rushing. I can't possibly hold off.

"Come for me, Jessa. Come all over my cock." My head lowers, mouth watering, gums tingling and shifting as my canines spring. She throws her ass back wildly, pussy rippling. My world empties to everything but Jessa and the bliss of filling her with my seed. I bite, tasting blood, growling, sucking harder, biting harder. Her groans turn to a jumble as I slam one last time and hold deep. The jets of my cum pulse, trickling out around my length and coating my balls.

Sanity is slow to return. My teeth are locked on her throat in a way that brings panic surging to the fore. I ease my jaw open, cursing myself when she whimpers. I pull out, sending a gush of stickiness between us. Gently, I turn her over so that I can see her face.

I expect to see horror.

I find her hooded eyes gazing up at me and a smile upon her lips.

"Are you well?" I ask. My attention is torn between her rapturous expression and the weeping wound at her throat. "Gods, I am an animal!"

"You are," she says, chuckling. "Goddess, I want to do that again. Will it leave a mark?"

I heave out a great breath and collapse beside her on the bed. Everything inside me is conflicted. "Aye, it will leave a mark."

"Good," she says decisively, and rolling onto her side, she nestles into my side.

My arm comes around her, drawing her a little tighter as I press a kiss to her silken hair. "You might not say that when you see it," I say.

"It stings," she says. "I like that it stings. I like that your wolf claimed me too. It makes me feel happy deep inside because you are mine."

216

Mine.

Her breath tickling my chest brings a sense of completion and joy, but it is soon tempered by the dark thoughts that I can never wholly keep at bay. I am hers completely, but I wonder if she is also mine...only mine.

Gage.

After leaving the bed this morning, I found the saddlebag where I'd told her to put the knife. It is *his* fucking knife. I don't like that she seeks to keep it. I should throw the fucking thing away. Maybe this will be over if only I can get her with child. "When did you last bleed?" I ask.

"I have not yet bled."

A cold, sickly sensation settles low in my belly. "You haven't?"

"No, my ma says it is natural for a lass who is small like me not to bleed until later."

My brows draw together. Not this late, surely? I don't want to alarm her, so I press a kiss to her forehead and force my body to relax. But I am not feeling relaxed. The only time a woman does not bleed is when she is with child. Jessa was a virgin when I claimed her. She must know a lass should have bled by now.

Perhaps her mother is right. She seems wise in other ways.

I feel like I want to ask someone about it, but I don't have a clue who to ask.

Maybe Jessa will never have a child.

My chest saws unsteadily as I let that settle in. I roll, gathering Jessa closer, pressing a kiss against her silken hair to try and hide the devastation rushing through me. I force myself to let her barren nature settle in. I'd imagined a future with a whole brood of brats running around up to mischief. Fatherhood was once a distant consideration, but it has filled my thoughts since I first committed to wooing Jessa.

"Are you sore?" I ask.

"A little," she says, then she giggles, and that sound turns my heart to mush. "But mostly hungry. I am going to make some food."

Wriggling from the bed, she pads naked toward the door. Here she pauses, to look back with a smile on her pretty face. "Are you hungry too? Would you like me to bring the food here, and we can eat it in bed?"

Goddess, she is beautiful in ways and looks. I want nothing more than to have a dozen little Jessa's running around wrapping me around their finger the way their mother does. I shove up in the ruined bedding, planting my back against the headboard. "Aye, lass, this rutting business is hungry work."

I wiggle my eyebrows at her. She disappears through the doorway, her sweet giggle following her.

I wanted it all with Jessa, all the highs and lows, the brats, and the noise and nonsense that goes with them. Only now, I wonder if Jessa will ever be a mother.

If I will ever be a father.

My chest squeezes as I come to terms with her strange determination that she has not bled.

I want to say I am overreacting, but I do not believe I am.

Perhaps Jessa and I will grow old together just like this, the two of us.

If that is all we shall have, I will cherish it because it is with Jessa. Some men take a second mate if their first cannot bear a child. I love Jessa with all my heart and soul. I have marked and claimed her. I do not want anyone else. I do not want a child with anyone else. If we two are all that the Goddess shall give, I will be blessed to receive that much.

But Goddess help me, I sense she wants children, she has spoken thus about her longing even as she bemoans her sibling brats. I have seen how she is with them, patient, caring, and always telling me the tales of their mischief with a smile upon her face.

It will break her heart if she cannot bear children, I know it. I must be strong for both of us if that should be the case.

Chapter Twenty-Four

Gage

Evening is closing in as I toss the reins of my horse to a stable lad. Together with a dozen warriors, I have been patrolling after some sheep went missing. We didn't find the culprits, more's the pity. We are still licking our wounds, clearing the mess we have made, repairing, and recuperating. Although every time I leave for patrol and return, I feel the sense of community growing as folks work together to ready homes for winter and complete the harvesting. Our grain stocks are reasonable, and the orchard yielded a bumper crop of apples, so we won't starve, at least.

The mated warriors head home to their families, while those unmated follow me up the steps to the great hall where servants bustle about fetching beer and warming stew. We are closing in on winter, and the great fire has been lit, emitting warmth and a cheery glow.

The dais where the king and queen chairs sit empty draws

my attention. But I don't linger on the unsettling notion that there will never be a queen to share it with me.

I know I need to put Jessa from my mind and find myself a woman and mate for the good of the clan.

Not yet. I do not need to do it yet.

The cat sprints over, darting in front of my feet and nearly tripping me up.

"Aye, look at how he has grown!" Simon says. "Have you named him yet?"

"He is a cat," I say, scowling as I take the seat at the head of the table.

A server places a beer before me, which I accept with a nod of thanks.

"Well, I dare say your mate will pick a name for him in no time," Simon says, lifting his beer in a salute. "Women like to think of them as pets."

The other men laugh, sharing stories of pet naming and other nonsense.

The quiet conversations and good-humored banter around the table is nothing like the drunken revelry that happened all too regularly during my father's reign. I would be happier if the number of men joining me was less because they had women and brats to go home to. They are rough men and warriors, but they are also good men. And I can tell from the wistfulness in their teasing that they would like nothing more than to have a mate or wife fussing over the naming of a pet cat.

The problem of the lack of women is one that never goes away, but I have been talking over some possibilities with Pete. Namely, the Orc slaver trains.

Ridding the lands of the Orc slavers is in everyone's best interest. If we happen to collect a few of the beta lasses the Orcs favor for their house servants, it would be a bonus. If those lasses should happen to want to make a home here with the brave warriors who liberated them, better yet.

There are many holes yet in this plan, but any dead Orc is a blessing for the clans.

I accept my bowl of stew with a nod of thanks, rip a hand-sized chunk of bread from the nearby platter, and tuck into my food.

In the weeks since the fateful night when I slayed my father, tentative alliances are forming. I am still no closer to Danon's release. He is not yet dead, though, as I heard when I traveled to the Halket clan last week to begin the long negotiation. A dozen of our best-quality deer hides were accepted with a nod. That their king spoke to me at all, I consider it a positive sign.

I have also met with Jack and Fen of the Ralston clan on a few occasions. Theirs has been an easier undertaking. No one killed their former king for a start, and their leader, Jack, has time and maturity on his side. Not that I consider Eric a fool, but he is young and still grieving the loss of his late father.

I'm confident I can find a way to peace with the Halket given time. I tell myself that I can weather their treatment of Danon, and that if his fate is to join the Goddess, I can accept that, too.

The truth is, I don't know if I can.

Maybe he is dead, and they are stringing me along?

I pause my eating to drink deeply from my beer.

No, I don't believe that. Eric is plain talking and unafraid. The bastard would tell me to my face if Danon were already gone.

As I place the tankard back on the table, Mara quickly brings a jug to top it up. The lass has long been trying to catch my eye even before I became the clan king.

My heart is not in a quick tumble with a lass. Although it

might help ease the rage I suffer knowing Brandon has claimed Jessa. Not even wedded the lass, no, he has claimed her as a shifter does, marking her throat for all to see. My temper flares every time I think of his mark on her flawless skin. The mutt is probably rutting her every chance he gets.

I know I would be.

The conversation washes over me. The servants clear the dinner plates and fetch more beers. I sup slowly. Tomorrow, I have been invited to join the Ralston clan for their annual feast.

I am yet undecided on whether to go. I know what happens at such feasts, the drinking and rutting in celebration to the Goddess.

Jessa will be there.

So too, Brandon.

It will be Jessa's first year as a bonded woman. It seems likely she would honor the Goddess.

Rutting.

I should leave it well alone. Only a fool would go.

Can I bear to watch her being rutted by Brandon? Is it any worse than when I torment myself imagining it?

I swallow hard. I would take any pain to see her once again. Even watching her with the mutt would be better than not seeing her at all.

As the last two warriors finish their beer and take their leave, I stare after them.

Mara gathers their empty tankards. "Is there ought I can do for you, sire?"

My eyes regain focus as I turn to the pretty serving lass. Were I a sensible man, I would take her up on her offer—the lass is good with her mouth.

"Nay, lass," I say. "Head on home."

With a swift bob of her head, she follows the warriors out.

I frown. Where the fuck is the cat? Normally, he hangs

around for scraps. The little furred beast is growing and has even caught a few mice. I might not have named the tiny bastard, but he sneaks onto my bed in the early hours of the morning when he has finished his hunting. When not on my bed, he loves basking before the fire.

I'm about to go and push the doors shut when the tiny scrap of ginger fur trots through. Turning, I stare after him.

"Little hellion," I mutter, pushing the door shut. He is dragging a dead rat bigger than he is! "What the fuck are you going to do with that?" Thank fuck my bedding chamber door is shut so he can't try to take it to my bed.

He comes to a stop before the fire, drops the rat, and proceeds to play-wrestle with it.

I take a seat at the table, where I can watch his macabre sport while finishing my beer.

The dead rat is tossed, bitten, growled over, and savaged with his small teeth. "It's already dead," I point out. He doesn't appear to care. Finally, he tires of these antics and sets about chowing it down. Starting with the head... Why does he begin with the head? Why not the belly? Surely the belly is soft and gives easy access to nutrient-rich innards?

No, the cat eats the head. I am on the other side of the room, but I can still hear the crunching noises. I don't consider myself a squeamish man, but I am nevertheless disturbed by my furred monster tucking into his feast.

The cat is small, the rat is massive, but he still manages to eat half of it before he's done. Sated, he sits over his kill, using paws to clean the blood from around his mouth.

As I finish off my beer, he flops onto his side, belly proudly swollen.

Sighing, I go and pick up the half-rat by the tail and toss it out the door. Head lifting, the cat watches me with haughty disgust.

"Your belly is fit to burst," I say. "You do not need more, you little heathen."

Tired, I head for bed. I am barely settled when the fanged monster jumps onto the bed and makes a nest for himself by my side. "I guess you don't need to go out hunting tonight."

I don't know what to do tomorrow, whether to go to the festival or not. It is the right thing to mend bridges. It is the worst thing to mend bridges if I go into a fucking rampage, beat the shit out of Brandon, and steal his mate away.

I sigh.

I can do this. I can see Jessa happy with Brandon and then let my anger go. I am not my fucking father. I have a clan and responsibilities to think of.

But as I close my eyes, a familiar dream plays out.

Jessa underneath me, face flushed, mouth parted on groans of pleasure as I rut her roughly.

🐾

The following day when I rise, the remainder of the dead rat is being tossed around the floor. "You are a black-hearted heathen," I say.

Pete raises a brow as he enters the hall and sees a cat with the rat. "What happened to the top half?" he asks, indicating my tiny killer and his prey.

"Aye," I say. "He ate the other half last night. Now, he's slaying the corpse again. You did not warn me they were such macabre beasts."

Pete chuckles. "Told you he would make a good mouser. One less rat in the stores."

Then he nudges his head at me. "Are you heading for the Ralston clan today?"

"Aye," I agree.

"You are worried," he surmises. My interest in Jessa is of no surprise to anyone close to me. I'm sure it is the talk of the fucking clan after I killed my father because he'd threatened to search for Jessa that fateful night.

"Aye," I say.

"Some lasses need more than one mate," he says. "Have you considered the civilized approach? I was there that night, remember. I saw the way she looked at you."

I huff out a breath. At times, I convince myself her feelings toward me are a figment of my imagination. "We have barely started negotiations," I say. "There is yet more bridging needed... Years of fucking bridging. And even so, the two mates would need to tolerate each other with a mind to becoming brothers through bonding. Can you see me and the mutt forming a bond?"

His lips tug up. "No, but if you want the lass, that is the only way. I share a mate. In this clan and with so few women-folk, it is more common than most clans. There are some that have gone on to take a third mate. It is rarely easy unless the men are firm friends. It is more natural for an alpha to take two beta mates. But you learn to accept, and given enough time, you even come to enjoy it. A beta will respond to alpha pheromones. It makes them lustier than they might have been wedded to a beta male. Or so I have heard from beta males who have gone on to share their partner with an alpha. It might even be a preferred coupling, alpha and beta male with a beta lass. Never thought I would say this, but I enjoy watching her with Karl. I enjoy dominating them both."

I suck a breath in. I'd like to dominate Brandon and put the cocky fucker in his place. Watching him rut Jessa? Not so much.

"Do you believe in the Goddess?" I ask.

"For certain," Pete replies.

227

I wrestle with what happened in the woods when I was gravely wounded, possibly on the path toward death.

"I met her in the woods," I say. "It was after I had battled with the Orc. My ribs were busted, and I was coughing up blood. My chest was black with bruises."

There is a brief widening of Pete's eyes before his brows tug together in a frown.

"Injuries like that take many weeks to recover from, if you recover at all. Jessa found me sitting on my ass by the river, pain near debilitating me. It makes no sense how it happened. But she healed me with nothing more than some mashed root and herbs. She healed me with a kiss. We agreed to keep the matter private. And who would believe us, either way? I asked her if it had happened before. She said it had not. She healed me from injuries enough to put a man in the ground. Why would the Goddess, through Jessa, heal me if we were not meant to be?"

"The work of the Goddess," he agrees. "What will you do?"

He doesn't question the truth of it nor dismiss what this means.

"I don't want to start a fucking war," I say.

"Aye, we are barely recovering from the last. Whatever comes next is by the Goddess' design, and she is as cruel as she is gracious. I was surprised when you mentioned the invite. But in this new light, I cannot help but see Her hand at play. You need to go and let whatever will be, play out."

I nod. I have realized this myself the more we have talked. Impatient, I am ready to see Jessa, who is now with Brandon, even though it will be like a fucking knife in the chest.

Chapter Twenty-Five

Jessa

Today is the day of the festival, and I should be feeling happy as I visit with my family. I sit at the old oak table where I have sat a thousand times, watching my mother fold washing. This is not my home anymore, but I still come here most days.

Not long ago, Hazel left to get ready for the feast. I should be doing the same.

I want to talk to my mother, yet I don't know where to start.

Through the open door I can hear my siblings excited squeals of laughter. Finishing work early, my father has just chased all the brats outside.

For once, their laughter does not warm me, and the weight of melancholy comes crashing in.

"Are you okay, love?" my mother asks, pausing her work folding the last of the washing.

My eyes meet hers, and I see the caring there. But it is suddenly like there is a gulf between us as I remember the whispered conversation she had with my father late one evening.

"Brandon asked me when I last bled," I blurt out.

Face softening, she puts the clothes aside and goes to the door. I experience a strange pang thinking she is about to leave. But she calls out to my father to watch the brats for a while in a no-nonsense way all mothers seem to have. Closing the door, she comes over and sits opposite me.

"I heard you talking about me late one night. Talking about how I hadn't yet bled." I want to say the other things, but they get stuck in my throat.

Her hand reaches across the table to take mine.

"You heard us talking about you being an omega?"

My eyes widen, and for a stretched moment I forget to breathe. They did not use that word as they talked, and it never crossed my mind. I know very little about omegas other than whispered conversations. They do not bleed monthly like a beta lass might, and they also make nests. I don't remember all the details of their late-night conversation. Still, I remember them talking about me changing and about me nesting.

How did I not realize?

Omega. Can I be an omega? Is this why I am so strangely drawn to both men?

"I don't know why you haven't bled. I didn't want to frighten you at first. Then after, when you didn't reveal, I assumed you had started your monthlies but didn't mention it. You have long done your own washing. You would not be the first lass who doesn't talk to her mother about such things."

My thoughts are like leaves in the wind, tumbling about and settling nowhere for long. I might have been an omega, but I have not revealed thus. I do not know if it is true, but I heard they have an enticing scent that can send weak alphas into a rut such that they end up claiming a lass without her papa's permission. Assuredly, I have not provoked such a reaction, thank the Goddess.

But now I am even more confused.

When Brandon first asked me about my moon blood, the words my mother told me had rolled off my tongue. Only after, as I lay snuggled against his side listening to the wild beating of his heart, did the dread begin to bloom.

"Hazel is already with child," I say. To my own ears, I sound small and lost. I always foresaw a future with children, a whole brood of the noisy monsters, truth be told. Now, I don't know anything. I watch Hazel with her mates. I see the pride on their faces as they hold Hazel near, resting their hands upon her belly that has yet to even show.

I am so happy for Hazel, but there is also a wound that feels raw when I realize that she has a child growing inside her, and I...and I may never have.

My mother's hand rests over mine.

"We should arrange to travel to the Baxter clan," she says decisively. "Molly has recently visited and may not be back until the spring."

"How can Molly help?" I ask. "I have not revealed, thus."

"She said that she thought you were a latent. That it might need an alpha to claim you before you revealed. Omegas are rare in the clans. They are usually born to an alpha-beta pairing. The parents know the child will be an omega even before she is born. How, I don't know, but Molly was certain of this."

"There are connections between alphas and omegas." Her hand presses to the center of her chest over her heart. "Here, inside. Like a thread tying them together for all their lives. Perhaps that is how the father senses his omega child. Your papa and I are betas. We have no sense of such a thing. But from the first time Molly met you when you were still a babe, she was certain you would be an omega."

My mind reels.

Can I really be a latent omega who needs an alpha to claim her?

I see the distress on my mother's face.

I know what it means.

I have bonded to Brandon, a beta. And a beta is not enough to force my body to reveal.

"What if it is not that?" I say. "What if I am barren?"

"Ah, lass," she says softly. "Even barren women still have moon blood. They just do not catch with child."

Gage. His name crashes through my mind along with our fateful first encounter.

"Do you believe in the Goddess?" I ask.

My mother nods. "Aye, lass, I do."

"I met a warrior once," I say. "I was in the forest gathering blackroot."

My mother stills.

"When I came upon him, he was badly injured after slaying an Orc. His ribs were black, his body battered. I have only seen a man once with ribs that color, and he died of the wet lung. I didn't think about the nonsense of trying to apply a balm to someone so injured. I did it anyway, like I was compelled."

It is all tumbling out now, and I don't have the will to stop.

"I went to the river many times to prepare the balm. I said a prayer to the Goddess after every one. Then when I was finished, I pressed a kiss to his temple and begged the Goddess to make him well."

"Gage, the king of the Lyon clan," my mother says.

"Gage," I agree.

"He was hail enough to stand, by all accounts, before Brandon carried you off," she says dryly. For the first time since we started this discussion, there is a small smile on her lips.

"I healed him," I say. "We agreed to keep it a secret."

She raises a brow.

We both turn as a thump sounds upon the door. "Can we come in yet?" my father calls.

"Not yet!" we say in unison.

"The brats are a test!" my father mutters. "How do you manage them all day?"

His complaints fade away.

"How many times have you met with him?" my mother asks, all business once again.

My cheeks flush. "Gage came to see me...after Brandon carried me off, to make sure I was well. Then I saw him when we were taken by Nola. He was furious at finding us snatched. He hid us out of the way knowing the other clans were coming to war with them. He ordered Nola's death."

"I thought you loved Brandon," she says. Her face softens as she looks at me. "Aye, you love them both. They have been at loggerheads long before you entered the picture. And both are aware of your dual interest if Brandon's reaction to Gage bringing you back that day is any indication."

She huffs out a laugh. "My love, if the Goddess should venture to heal a man through you, I have every faith in Her divine wisdom to see the matter resolved. One way or another."

"They hate each other," I point out sadly, hardly daring to hope.

"But they love you," my mother counters. "Their actions speak as much. Have faith, Jessa, for a little longer. You will find your place and the joy you deserve. I have long understood you were different. Even when you were a child."

Her smile grows, and tears shine in her eyes. "My sweet, firstborn is an omega no less."

She seems so sure. I am yet to feel the same.

"What should I do?" I ask. "Should I...should I talk to Brandon about it?"

"Aye," she agrees. "Find a time when you are both clear of head and talk to him. He will be shocked, I'm sure. But he loves you so very deeply that I'm sure Brandon and Gage will find a way. There will be bumps in your path. Of that, I have no doubt. Now, since you denied your mother a wedding, the least you can do is enjoy tonight to the fullest. The Goddess will be close, and She will be listening. Do not waste such an opportunity on tears. This is your first festival as a woman. Embrace it, my love."

Chapter Twenty-Six

Brandon

"What the fuck is he doing here?" I say, nudging my head at Gage, the former second-born son who is now the king of the Lyon clan. The big bastard is on the other side of the village square talking to Jack. Between us is the industry as Ralston prepares for the coming feast. It will start this afternoon, allowing the children and older clansfolks to enjoy the fun. As the sun sets fully and darkness falls, the children will be sent home under the watch of older siblings and those not inclined toward the carnal side of Goddess worshipping.

"We are building alliances," Fen says, scratching his short beard and frowning like this should be obvious.

I want to say something snarky, but it is not my fucking place. Winter is approaching, and everyone is talking about raiding. I am thankful that we are not at war with the Lyon clan anymore, but that doesn't mean we need to invite them to our festivals.

A man hastens past, straining under the weight of lanterns. Another follows, carrying the poles.

"We don't have to be friends to make alliances," Fen says, tone serious.

I turn toward him. He has changed since he acquired a sweet mate, and more so since Hazel has gotten with child. He is also right. We do not need to be friends. We also don't need to invite former enemies to our festival like they are our best fucking friends.

"Cart coming through!"

We both shift to the side as old Mike drives a laden cart full of wood for the bonfire toward the shore of the loch.

"I know it is difficult for you," Fen continues. "With Gage because of Jessa."

It is like twisting the blade she brought back in my gut. She keeps the bastard thing tucked in the lower dresser drawer. A reminder, as if I need one, that it was Gage who saved her that night and put her somewhere safe. I am even grateful that he did and that he is not the monster I accused him of being. But none of this makes her interest in him any easier to bear.

Now we are making alliances with his clan.

He is no longer the enemy.

It would even be acceptable for us to bond in the eyes of the clan, even if it would be a shock at first. Yet the sharp pain in my chest wants nothing to do with it.

Other men share lasses. Fen and Jack share a mate, and I have never seen them happier. I tell myself if I loved Jessa enough, I could put my prejudices and pride aside and talk to her about it.

A horde of children skip past, whooping with excitement.

The girls all have flower garlands in their hair and around their necks.

Brats. That is another quagmire that is too tender even to put to voice.

"Why would she care about a beta shifter if she had an alpha mate?" I regret the words the moment they spill out. They are churlish and self-centered. As a beta wolf used to following, these feelings are foreign to me.

Fen's face softens. "It does not work like that, Brandon. If a lass loves two men, she loves them equally, or she would not choose to be with two. And if the first cannot accept the second, then there is no second."

"I know that," I say. "I know all of it. And I want to make her happy. I think I would manage were it with anyone but Gage."

That is a lie, and I know it. Six months ago, she was just a shy lass who blushed prettily whenever I was near. Now she is the center of my world, and I don't know how to manage this complexity of feelings.

"Have you talked to her about it?" he asks.

I shake my head.

"Then you don't know anything yet. Maybe it is only a rutting interest Jessa has in him. Maybe she would be happy if he shared the furs once in a while. Some couples do that, and it is not the same as love and committing to being together in a menage."

I growl at the thought of sharing Jessa in the furs. I know it was only a figure of speech, but it reminds me that furs are for alphas. I'm a beta, and when I'm not in wolf form, I prefer the more civilized setting of a nook or bed.

Fen chuckles as he notes my sour expression. "Don't knock what you have yet to try. I love watching Jack rut Hazel. He is rougher with her than I am and has a stern way that drives her fucking wild. Sometimes when I watch him with her, I imagine it is me and what I look like when rutting her. And sometimes, I just get lost in the pleasure on her face. Then there are yet more times when we take her together. We have shared lasses before, you and I, you are no stranger to such pleasures. Besides, none of this even matters yet. You have not spoken to her about it. Maybe Jessa will laugh when you ask her and say that is not what she wants."

"Maybe," I say, but that is more about the beta in me agreeing with the alpha I have followed all my life. As I remember the way Jessa's aroused scent exploded when she was standing between Gage and me, a growl escapes my lips.

"Maybe not," Fen says, chuckling again.

"I will talk to her after the festival," I say. My heart knows that this matter needs to be broached and that no amount of denial will make it go away.

Over the tops of the cottages, smoke rises. They have lit the bonfire.

"Come on, best go and prepare yourself for the feast." He winks. "It is both of our mates' first time at the festival as bound women. I do not want to miss any of it."

We part ways. Fen heads to join Jack, and I head to my new home.

As I push open the rickety wooden gate, I hear Jessa's singing. The lass is Goddess blessed in her sweet voice. Inside I find her threading flowers in her dark hair. She is wearing a forest-green linen dress that reaches her knees, ornately embroidered with flowers and vines. It is fine material...and see-through in places. The swirling embroidery is the only thing between her being naked. Bows clinch the fabric together at her right shoulder and right hip, with a little of her skin flashing between.

A vow dress, the prettiest vow dress I have seen on the prettiest lass in all the lands.

"I thought you did not want to say the words?" I croak out past the tightness in my throat.

"I don't," she says, selecting a flower from the collection on the table and threading it through her hair. She smiles, but there is a slight puffiness around her eyes like she has been crying.

Taking the steps to her, I tip her chin and search her face.

"All the excitement," she says. Stepping back, she runs a hand down her dress, face shining with joy. "My mother made this dress for me thinking I would wed. She asked me if I would wear it today. I feel like a princess. It seems fitting I should wear it today for my first festival to the Goddess."

"Aye, it is perfect." Capturing her face between my hands, I claim her lips in a kiss. She opens sweetly, and our tongues tangle. That fast, blood surges through my body straight to my dick as I anticipate rutting her under the stars. This vow dress will be a crumpled mess underneath us, and all the pretty flowers scattered as I fist her hair and fill her. Wrenching my mouth away, I press my forehead to hers. "You are perfect," I whisper.

Her eyes glisten with fresh tears, and I don't have a clue what it means.

"It is nothing," she says, dashing the dampness from her cheeks. "Tomorrow, we will talk. But today and tonight, I want to worship the Goddess with you."

Chapter Twenty-Seven

Jessa

A great fire blazes on the shore of the loch by the time we arrive, and the clan are gathered around on the grassy banks.

My parents have laid out their blankets and fare on a perfect spot beside the forest with the perfect view of the bonfire and loch. Nearby, my younger sibling brats play at rumbustious games. Amos is not far off being a man and has gone to hang out with his friends.

Joining them, we lay out our own blankets and a few soft furs.

Greta squeals with excitement and makes a beeline for Brandon, flower garland in her hand.

Brandon laughs and dutifully kneels so she can place it around his neck.

"When Jessa dies, you can marry me," she earnestly informs him.

"Eh, lass," my father says, laughing. "You shouldn't wish your sister dead!"

"What if Orcs eat her?" Greta demands. "Brandon will need a new lass to collect their eggs. I'm best at finding the eggs!"

"You are best at finding eggs," my mother agrees. "But let's not make Jessa Orc food. Don't you want to be an aunty when she has a baby?"

I sense Brandon still behind me, although the nuances of his reaction are lost when Greta squeals with excitement. She is as obsessed with babies as she is with finding the eggs the chickens hide.

My mother passes me a loaded platter and a jug of honeyed wine as Greta toddles off to join the other children.

We laze upon the furs eating, supping the sweet wine, and laughing at the children's antics. Villagers come and go, stopping to chat with my parents, and sharing food and drinks. On the far side, musicians play a lively tune on pipes and drums. Greta dances out of beat, her little body bouncing and swaying, her foot-stomping a few times before she completes a twirl.

I have been to the festival every year, but it is the first time I will not be sent home with the children.

It is the first time I have had a bonded mate with me.

Brandon never leaves my side, always touching me somewhere even as we enjoy the delicious feast.

I catch him watching me, and I know he is thinking about what I said before we left home. I smile. He returns a lazy one, and leaning in, steals a kiss.

"The sun is sinking," he says. "Let's walk around the village before everyone has other things on their minds."

Standing, he grabs my hand and hauls me to my feet. With the light fading, the lanterns are lit, giving the feast a magical feel. People lay, sit, and stand in groups to chat, watching children play games of chase. We stop to talk to Brandon's parents, then Hazel, Fen, and Jack. We share a few words here and there, sampling delicious food offered as we pass through. It hardly seems possible we were at war not so long ago.

I have just spotted a friend when Brandon does an abrupt about-face, his arm around my waist. "The children are heading off," he says.

I have an odd notion that it was not the children leaving that prompted Brandon to turn.

I peer over my shoulder, but all I can see are the crowds.

The music picks up a different kind of beat that sets the flutter rising in my belly.

When we reach my parents, they are busy packing up and corralling the younger brats. Greta is in my father's right arm, a packed basket in the other. My remaining siblings are being loaded up by my mother, except for William, who has thrown a fur over his head and is pretending to be a bear.

"Brats will never sleep!" my father says, shaking his head even as he chuckles at their antics.

My mother laughs as she places the wine jug and basket with some food beside our furs. Standing, she draws me in for a hug. "Enjoy your night, love. I'll see you both on the morrow."

Then they are leaving, William running ahead, still growling and making pretend claws with his hands. Barely are they gone when Brandon kicks off his boots, scoops me up, and takes me down onto the furs. "Thank fuck for that," he says. "I love your family like my own, but I couldn't wait to have you all to myself."

I giggle. Gazing up at Brandon, my chest swells as all the love I feel for him hits me in a rush. My mother is right. There will be bumps in the road before we find happiness. Tonight, though I will show Brandon how much I care, I will demonstrate my love for him through the pleasure we will share.

My smile fades as we gaze upon one another. The place within my heart that belongs to Brandon blazes. I feel the Goddess's love wrap around us, setting the tiny hairs on the back of my neck rising.

There is more, I realize. Another presence is reaching for me, weaving together with the thread that connects me to Brandon.

My eyes shift, as I am *drawn*.

The air leaves my lungs, and my pulse begins to throb at my throat.

It feels like forever since I have seen him. The last image I have was of him standing over the slain body of his father. He was the second-born son then. Now he is the king of a clan.

His upper body is bare, revealing the great slabs of muscle to his chest, shoulders, and arms. Hide pants, tucked into soft leather boots, encase his muscular thighs. A silver pendant hangs around his neck, nestling into the dip of his throat. Goddess, he is a breathtaking man and alpha.

He looks like the king of a clan.

He looks like the missing piece that my heart and body yearn for.

Only he is not missing anymore, for the Goddess has sent him to me.

"There are connections between alphas and omegas." My mother said, pressing a hand to the center of her chest over her heart. *"Here, inside. Like a thread tying them together for all their lives."*

There has ever been a connection between Brandon and me. It bloomed long ago when he saved me as a child from wolves, and even though he is a beta. But another thread budded when I found a brave warrior gravely wounded in the woods.

The Goddess is here. I shiver as the cooling breeze skitters over my hot skin.

She will expect me to show her my love and gratitude through the pleasure I give and receive.

🕭

Brandon

I don't need to turn to know exactly who it is that steals Jessa's attention.

Gage.

The bastard couldn't fucking wait and let us have this night. I have had her all to myself for these weeks past, I reason, knowing he wanted her too. Yet, it does not temper my aggression toward him.

He sits as if I were in any confusion about why he is fucking here.

It is not necessarily acceptable to stare at other people rutting

But many people do.

And many people enjoy being watched.

The weight of his stare sets a fire under my skin. My hands find the ties of Jessa's pretty dress. One...two, and it slips open, giving me access to her soft feminine curves. Her flower-strewn hair makes a fan around her face as I lower my head to take her lips. Her wildness infects me as her tongue meets mine. There is desperation, too, in the way her small fists tangle in my hair to hold me close.

Perhaps, she has forgotten that Gage watches.

Perhaps, she can think of nothing else.

Heat pools in my belly as my hand skims over her trim waist to cup her tit. I swallow her groan of pleasure as I brush my thumb back and forth over the engorged tip. Her fingers tighten on my hair, and the scent of her arousal permeates the air, and just like last time when she was between us, it is twice as heady. My cock thickens and lengthens, pressing painfully against the constriction of my leather pants.

My lips make a trail over her throat, over her collarbone, all the way down to enclose her stiff nipple within my mouth.

"Goddess, yes!"

Her back arches, her fingers are so tight on my hair, it burns my scalp.

I bend my knees, forcing her to spread her thighs to accommodate me. My dick wants inside her hot channel; the man and wolf in me wants that too.

Gage's low growl catches my ears as I suck bites against the soft flesh of her tits, marking her as mine. Fuck him for forcing himself into the situation. Fuck him for sitting there and watching. If he doesn't like what he sees, he can leave any fucking time.

Her sweet scent fogs my mind. Hand lowering, I cup her intimately feeling her slickness leaking out. Gods, she is drenched, and I have barely started yet.

Dragging my mouth from her pretty tits, I pause to admire my work. Her face and chest are flushed, eyes bright, and her lips parted. "Let's get this out of the way," I say, drawing her dress off her shoulders and tossing it aside. I need to rut her, but I also need to taste.

Another growl reminds me of our voyeur, but I don't let that deter me. If anything, it drives me to further assert my claim.

"Oh, muuunnn!" Nonsense pours from her lips as I feast on the plump folds.

My wolf goes nuts for the taste of her. The man in me wants her to come hard and fast. I want her to gasp with pleasure. I want her screaming my fucking name. My fingers curve inside as I tongue her swollen clit. She is so slippery, but something is different. The front wall feels rough...like a little puckered bud. As I rub my fingers over it, slick gushes out, and she strains, thrashing and panting.

Clamping an arm over her hips, I hold the wriggling bundle of woman still and pet the sensitive spot until she comes apart, gasping and groaning and trying to hump her hips.

I think she has another one in her, so I don't fucking stop. She tastes different, sweeter, and it is pouring from this little rough patch, this *gland* in the wall of her pussy. A flush spreads through my body when she comes, breath stuttering, and gushing her sweetness over my waiting tongue.

Groggy, I lift my head and shake it to try and clear the fog. I feel drunk, although I only supped a little honeyed wine.

Chapter Twenty-Eight

Jessa

I am drunk on the pleasure Brandon has wrested from my body. My chest rises and falls unsteadily. Deep inside, that place where he petted me throbs and pulses. It is too intense, and yet I need and want more. Through hooded eyes, I watch my mate as he heaves gusty breaths.

His handsome face is unusually stern, and it is fanning the flames of my ardor. The music has taken on a sensual beat that thrums in time with my pulse. Around us, hidden by the cover of darkness, men and women meet in pleasure as they worship the Goddess, their low groans blending into the music.

In a swift and sudden motion, Brandon tips me over onto my hands and knees. The head of his cock snags the entrance to my pussy, and he surges deep. I squeal out in joy, head tipped back, and ass pushing back for more. Goddess, it feels so good. Wild and a little rough. But I always want more.

Amid the pounding of the rough coupling, my eyes flutter open.

Gage.

My pussy squeezes sharply, and a deep moan escapes my lips. The alpha is no more than a few paces away, sat leaning against the trunk of a great oak tree. His pants are shucked down and his cock is in his hand. He pumps it slowly, eyes locked on my face.

I groan again. My body rises to a fever pitch. I can smell the salty, tangy scent of the pre-cum leaking from the tip, and it sets flames rising under my skin. We are so close that I could take him into my mouth if I were to crawl forward a few paces. Desperate for the taste of him, I lick my dry lips. Goddess save me. His cock is huge, thick, long, and tipped by a fat bulbous head. It is obscene, monstrous, and beautiful all in one.

The wet slapping sounds as Brandon ruts me is a debauched testament to how much I enjoy this. Brandon takes me with powerful thrusts from behind. Gage watches us as he pleasures himself. My groans turn guttural as I push back, encouraging Brandon to go deeper, harder, rougher. The sound of our flesh slapping together sends me spiraling higher and higher, yet I cannot find the sweet release.

Does Brandon see that Gage and I stare at one another?

Is that why he takes me with this barely tempered savagery?

Gage's lips tug up in a lazy smirk, his hand jacking up and down faster. Then he tears his gaze away to look over me. His grin turns wicked. He is staring at Brandon now. If the bruising hold on my hips and brutal strokes are any indication, Brandon is staring back at Gage. It is like all three of us are caught in a spell of madness that none of us can break.

Heat flashes over my body, and I climb higher still. Sweat pops along my spine. The coil tightens yet again. I am so close to bliss, desperate to tip over, hanging onto the carnal cliff and yet never falling. I feel like my heart and soul are being torn apart, and I can't quite grasp what I need.

I *need* more.

As my breath stutters and my groans turn to incoherent sobbing and begging, both men growl. Through bleary, tear-ravaged eyes, I see Gage, once more watching me.

That is all it takes.

I come, hot, wild, groaning out my rapture, never looking from Gage. His face twists, and cum shoots in thick ropy arcs. The scent hits me, and my eyes roll into the back of my head. Brandon is still rutting me deeply, and it rips another tumultuous climax from me. His cock seems to grow. Thick, so thick, enough to bring a surge of panic when it doesn't seem to fit. Hands bruising, he surges deeper and stills.

I feel the flood deep inside my pussy stuffed by his great girth.

I feel...stretched in a dark and twisty way.

Goddess! has he knotted me?

Gage's growl deepens. His cock still spits more cum. I have never seen so much. It forms a sticky pool all over the thick ridges of his belly.

My mouth waters for the taste even as my pussy grips Brandon's iron-hard length. I groan as yet another climax rips me up and spits me out. "Brandon," I say, voice slurred. Weak, my head falls until my forehead and cheek mash against the furs. "Have you knotted me?"

Gage growls. This is not the growl of pleasure I have heard thus far, but a fierce sound of aggression that sets hairs rising on my nape. I sense he has risen, but my vision is coming through a tunnel, and I cannot see. Scents hit me; rich, complex, they enter my nose and lungs and set off a dizzy chain reaction that goes all the way to my pussy and the engorged tips of my nipples until they throb in tandem.

The knot softens, and I collapse, sending a great gush of cum splattering over the furs. Savage growling follows, penetrating the fog holding my mind.

They fight, but it does not fully reach the cognizant part of my mind.

I hug myself, cold and disorientated, trying to pick myself up as the snarls of fighting assault my ears.

I need to stop them.

I need to calm them. But I cannot see through the tears, and my body feels like it has been broken under a supernatural storm.

Getting my hands under me, I heave myself up.

Blinking, I try to see, pushing up until I am on my hands and knees.

Gage has Brandon in a headlock. He pulls him into the shadow of the trees.

❦

Brandon

"You know what happens now," Gage growls. His arms bulge as his muscles strain to hold me—to prevent me from shifting. "Your body recognizes that scent, even if your mind refuses to accept it."

"Get the fuck off me, asshole," I growl.

"An omega," Gage continues. "And now that she is an omega, she will be handed over to an alpha."

"Let me fucking go!"

"Not a fucking chance," Gage says. "You are not listening to reason as a man. If I release you, you will shift, and your wolf will try to rip my throat out."

"There will be no *trying*," I say, straining harder. The bastard is as strong as a fucking ox, and I cannot budge him.

"Do you want Jack to give your sweet little mate over to someone else?" Gage demands. "Don't be an idiot, *mutt*. You cannot keep an omega. They will never allow it."

"Jack wouldn't take her from me."

"Jack won't have a fucking choice."

An omega. My mind is in a state of chaos. Her aroused scent clogs my nose and lungs, making me dizzy and hard for her. Distantly, I recognize that I am no longer rational. I had planned to talk to her about Gage to see how I might navigate sharing her with another mate. But that he dared to rip me from her has my wolf clawing at my skin.

On my fucking terms. Not on his.

I shake my head, but it does not clear her potent scent from my nose. She watches, face flushed, naked body resplendent as she kneels, captivated by our deadly struggle. Her knees are parted, offering a view of her weeping pussy and the shiny slickness coating her upper thighs. Her hand lowers, and her lips part on a breathy moan as she spears her fingers into her pussy. The other hand rises to cup her breast, where she pinches and tugs her nipple roughly.

Gods, she is aroused to the point of delirium.

I am not far behind.

"A beta will never be enough for her," Gage says. "Never change her sweet, ripe fuck-me scent. She would never be safe. Every alpha in the village is going to want her. Jack and Fen are mated to a beta, but the scent of an unmated omega would drive them, too. They aren't weak men. Maybe the other alphas could control themselves as well. Either way, her scent would be like a drug, arousing them to the point of madness until finally, someone broke. No, you need me to claim you both. It is the only way."

The air lodges in my lungs. My cock is stone-hard watching Jessa finger herself, but it also jerks at Gage's determination that he will claim us both. He would have complete mastery over me. He would dictate how and when I could rut her. He would have ultimate power. My mind rails against it, even as my wolf wants to submit to the dominant alpha *if* he is worthy and can prove himself.

"You can't fucking claim me," I snarl. "I'm not your fucking bitch!"

"But you will be mine. Mine to command, mine to control, just like Fen is your master now."

Every word growled against my ear is like a prophecy of my doom.

"She is an omega. Her scent drove your wolf to knot her, but it still wasn't enough. I have just watched you rut her. Watch her begging you for more. She needs more than you alone can give her. I bet she's been demanding your cock every chance she gets."

He speaks the truth. Yet I strain still, determined not to show weakness and prove that I am a worthy second.

"She needs us both," Gage says. "She has always needed us both. Right from that day when she stood between us, her aroused scent enough to make every shifter and alpha in the village square hard. You want that for the rest of her life? With me, her scent will change. With me, you will both have an alpha. You will be complete."

"I belong to Fen," I say, yet I know in my heart that connection is slipping, and another, more profound bond is shifting into place. "If you take us, there will be a fucking war."

"Take? Aye, there would be a war for sure. But I'm not taking you. I'm claiming you."

Jessa

"Help me bind him, Jessa."

Gage's voice pulls me from the darkest part of my daze. I shouldn't help him bind Brandon. Brandon is my mate, yet I understand on a primitive level that Gage is the dominant alpha and must be obeyed. He has tried to reason with Brandon, but my first mate is beyond reach.

As I stare down, I realize how I touch myself. I am horrified and yet reluctant to stop.

Taking a deep breath, I let my hands fall away, although my body craves more.

"Please, don't hurt him," I whisper.

"He is a beta, lass," Gage says. "But he is also a wolf. Your newly awakened scent, combined with my presence, has driven him mad. He cannot be reasoned with, not until I assert dominance over him. And I cannot do that here."

"Where then?" I ask. I don't like seeing Brandon like this, hurting, crazed. He needs to be dominated. Only then will he find balance and peace.

"Jessa." The warning in Gage's tone penetrates the fog threatening to recapture my mind. "Brandon is not the only male who will be affected by your sweet omega scent. Other alphas will scent it too. I cannot fight them all. Find something I can use to bind him before we have a blood bath on our hands."

I lick my lips. I like the thought of Gage fighting for me.

"Don't," Brandon says.

"Jessa!" Gage demands. The crack of his voice makes me tremble, and I scurry to do his bidding. My eyes search the ground, settling on my beautiful vow dress crumpled among the furs. The fine gauze-like material will be easy to tear.

"Don't do it," Brandon growls. "Don't fucking help the bastard to tie me up!"

I hesitate for only a moment before ripping the pretty garment in half.

"Gods, that is a tragedy," Gage mutters as I hand him the strips of cloth.

Brandon glares at me, growling and straining as Gage sets about binding his wrists.

"Get a fur to cover yourself, Jessa," Gage says.

Brandon eyeballs me as I collect the softest fur before returning to where they struggle. There is a little of Brandon's cum on it, and it smells absolutely divine. My lips tug up. I like seeing Brandon like this, mastered by a more dominant male. It is the most arousing sight I have ever seen, truth be told. I step closer still, the fur all but forgotten as I become riveted by Brandon's hard cock. The thick length juts out from the dark curls. It weeps copiously, bobbing.

He is overpowered and helpless.

I grasp his cock. "Fuck!" Brandon hisses as I suck the weeping tip into my mouth.

It's like a jolt of lightning passing through Brandon. He jerks and growls trying to thrust toward me.

"Jessa!" Gage jerks Brandon from my hold. Kicking the beta's legs out, he drops him to the ground. "Gods, you are as drunk on my pheromones as he is on yours. How shall I ever get the two of you to safety!"

Brandon grunts and thrashes. With his hands bound, he cannot gain his feet.

A little of his pre-cum has gotten smeared over my chin when Gage snatched him away. I wipe my fingers through it before stuffing them into my mouth. Eyes closed, I sigh contentedly.

When I open my eyes, I see Gage storming toward me.

With a squeak, I about-face and try to run only to be snagged around the waist. "You are a fucking test," he says. "Now is not the time to be a brat. You're halfway into your heat. If I don't get you home before it breaks, we will be fucked in ways none of us will enjoy!"

Chapter Twenty-Nine

Gage

Brandon is still snarling on the forest floor, but at least he is partially hidden within the trees.

The tiny waif doesn't struggle once I snag her waist. Thank fuck because I am holding myself by a thread.

Jessa couldn't keep her eyes off me earlier when she was putting on a show. Not only her. Brandon was also posturing, not that I can blame the mutt for claiming her before me, claiming her for *his* pleasure. I knew what they were about but elected to let it play out. Her sweet innocence had shone through when I met her by the river. Now I barely recognize this lusty lass who has turned our lives upside down.

The three of us are connected, a deep connection that will bind us irrevocably for the rest of our lives. The mutt doesn't have a hope of satisfying our sweet little mate alone. She needs more than he could possibly give.

I need to talk to her. To reason with her, if that is possible. Reluctantly, I ease my hold on her waist.

She turns, gazing up at me like she has never seen me before. Her scent is shocking in its potency. With a hand under her chin, I tip her to face me.

"Jessa, look at me," I say, waiting until her glazed eyes settle upon me. "Do you understand what is happening?"

"I...I feel funny. Urgent. Everything smells divine."

"You have revealed, lass."

Naked, as she is before me, it pleases me that she shows no shame or fear. Slick smears the tops of her thighs. His cum is there, but it pisses me off less than it ought to.

"We need to leave. If you stay, Jack will have no choice but to insist you accept an alpha. You understand this, Jessa. A beta is not enough and cannot give an omega what she needs. Even so, you are valuable. You will draw others to try and snatch or claim you should they allow you to stay with Brandon."

"You are frightening her, asshole!" Brandon snarls.

The bastard has a point, given tears begin spilling down her pretty cheeks.

"Do you want me, Jessa? Do you want me in the same way that I want you? I cannot bear to leave you like this with all this uncertainty and pain, but I will if you tell me to. But if I take you, Jessa, make no mistake, I will claim you as my mate."

"I cannot be apart from Brandon," she says.

The mutt offers a low growl.

"I am not asking you to. Brandon is part of your bond. Even a fool can see it is so. If I take you, then you will be a mate to us both."

A shiver ripples through her, although I do not think it is from the cool night air.

"I want that," she says. "I have wanted that from the start. Since the changes first began in me, and even before. I desire you both." She looks to where Brandon has thrashed about so he can see Jessa. "I think the Goddess always intended this to happen. I think... I don't know what to think. I only know that I must be with you both. And I need to be somewhere safe. Somewhere that I cannot be found by anyone except you."

Nest. She is talking about a nest. As a newly awakened omega, her first rutting by an alpha will likely take her straight into heat. My control snaps. There is no more time for discussion. She has said she wants me—that she wants us both. The need to find her a safe place where I can rut her is an imperative that cannot be ignored.

Taking her chin in hand again, I demand her attention. "We are leaving now. I will need to carry Brandon until we reach my horse. You will stay close to me and obey me at all times. Understood?"

"Yes," she says.

I have her trust. Brandon is another matter.

I use the remainder of Jessa's pretty vow dress to gag Brandon before hauling the heavy bastard over my shoulder. A beta shifter is small compared to an alpha, but it is all fucking muscle. Also, he is fighting and thrashing, which makes carrying him a challenge. I contemplate choking the mutt out. Only the sure knowledge that his dead weight would be harder to carry stays my hand.

Thanking the Goddess that everyone is either home or too busy rutting to notice, we skirt the forest border, working our way to where my horse is stabled. Jessa stays close to me. She is in shock, docile now...and naked. I have a cloak on my horse, which will cover the temptation. It won't help with her lush scent. Nor will it erase memories of her on her hands and knees taking Brandon's cock. But it will help temper my urge to throw her to the ground and rut her into heat.

Once inside the stable, I lower Brandon to the ground and use a rope I find to bind his ankles. Then I tie that to his bound wrists so he can't kick the horse. I tug the rope a few times to be sure. Two horses would be better. There is no way mine can carry all three of us. But we will need to manage. Taking another horse would raise an alarm. Brandon and Jessa are unlikely to be noticed for a good while. Most likely, they will be assumed to be sleeping off the festivities of the night.

I drag Brandon up. "Give me any trouble, and I will knock you out," I tell him. His eyes spit fire. He has not calmed down any.

I put him over the horse, bracing in case he does ought to harm it. A grunt is all I get.

Taking the cloak from my bag, I cover Jessa before lifting her into the saddle.

We exit the village by the least conspicuous route.

My heart is pounding within my chest. Brandon struggles but is bound tight and stays where I have laid him.

Leading the horse, I don't breathe easy until we are clear of the village. Then I set a brisk walk that takes us clear of the houses and into the forest.

Once we are about a mile away, I stop and drag Brandon from the saddle. I do not take much care, and Brandon hits the ground with a thud.

"What are you doing?" Jessa asks.

"We need to travel fast, lass," I say. "And the horse cannot carry all three of us."

"Why are you putting Brandon on the ground? You said you would not take me from him." There is anxiety in her voice, and the mutt begins thrashing in earnest again as her words stoke his anger.

"We cannot linger here," I repeat. "You are on the cusp of your heat. I need to get you to safety. I have a place where we can go, but it will take the night and then some to reach, even if we travel swiftly. If you go into heat this close to the village... I don't like to dwell on what might happen. But they may take you away from Brandon and me. They may have another alpha tend to you. You will be insensible and will not even care by that point. While I'm not knowledgeable about omegas, happen I know more than most. My mother was an omega, and she told me things about them. I think in the hope that I would be a better man than my father."

I point to Brandon. "When I cut the ropes, he will follow in wolf form, and he will catch up."

She looks doubtful. I *am* leaving gaps in this story.

"Won't he attack the horse?"

"Not if we have a head start."

She looks like she wants to argue. But I don't give her any chance. Taking the blade from my belt, I flip it handle outward, and rap Brandon over the back of the head. Finally, the bastard goes still.

"Oh! What have you done?"

"What I needed to do," I say.

I cut his bindings swiftly from his wrists and ankles. Shifters are fucking hardy, and I expect he will rouse faster than I would prefer.

Tucking the blade back in its sheath, I mount behind Jessa, wrapping the cloak tightly around her.

"I do not like to leave him," she says.

"He will follow us, I promise."

Sooner than I would probably like. With a nudge to the horse's flanks, we take off at a fast canter.

We ride throughout the night. As we near the outskirts of the Lyon clan, I hear the distant howl that tells me Brandon is closing in.

An old outpost we use as a lookout for Blighten during the winter months is situated to the north of the clan. It is kept stocked with wood and has fresh water via a well. But we will need more things if we are to get through Jessa's heat. Stopping is a risk. I don't want Brandon to confront me in the village, not while Jessa is close to her heat. I trust Pete and a few others I consider higher ranking, but certainly not all the alphas within my clan. I cannot protect her from the weaker alphas and fight Brandon at the same time. If I linger in the village, it will trigger the same carnage that would have unfolded at Ralston.

Omegas also prefer a quiet place where they can feel safe to nest when they go into heat. The old lookout will be perfect, nestled as it is among the trees far from man. When the leaves drop with the turn to winter, it offers views all the way to the distant mountain passes, thus allowing us early warning when the Orc trains are sighted.

As I come to a thundering stop in the village square, Pete is the first to greet me.

"I need supplies gathered swiftly," I say. "Get a couple of younger beta lads on fast horses to ride ahead to the lookout lodge with them. Enough food to last a week. Pelts and furs from the stores. If there are any of the softer blankets, take those as well."

Pete's eyes shift to Jessa. He takes a step back before returning his attention to me.

"Omega?"

"Aye."

Jessa wraps the cloak tightly around her, and I feel the tension enter her small body.

"I will see to it," Pete says. He doesn't ask more. I have an omega, and he will know what that means. Lads are sent scurrying, and horses are brought out. Seamlessly, alphas are positioned around the square to keep the area around us clear.

As the lads hasten to load horses with supplies, Pete returns to me.

"There will be a shifter coming through shortly," I say. "Tell the villagers to keep out of his way. He wants Jessa. He will follow after us as long as no one tries to stop him."

Pete raises a brow. "Is that advisable? Shifters can be ferocious when their mate is taken. You might be injured."

"Advisable? Big word there, Pete. Since when have I done anything advisable?" Now it is my turn to raise a fucking brow.

Pete's smile is wry.

"I will handle the damn mutt." If I kill the bastard, Jessa will be pissed, and a pissed mate is not congenial toward rutting. I will handle him, and then I will handle her. And then I will handle them fucking both. "Tell the villagers to keep out of his fucking way."

"I will," Pete says with a nod. "You are going to give him the run around while the lads prepare the lodge?"

"Aye," I say. I hear the unmistakable howl of a wolf. He is no longer far away. "Tell them to be quick about it. I do not want to be caught before I can get Jessa settled there."

Pete tips his head. "We shall get it done."

Gathering the reins in hand, we ride on for the lookout.

Chapter Thirty

Jessa

I am tired and yet, full of nervous energy.

We ride through the night and into the morning, stopping briefly at the village where Gage ordered his men to gather supplies. He said he was giving Brandon the run around while they delivered them. This is the farthest I have traveled from home, and I recognize nothing.

Brandon has been running all this time as a wolf. I worry for him, although I know wolves have great stamina.

I also worry about what will happen when we arrive at the lookout lodge.

We have walked the horse a little for this last part, only rising to a canter when we hear Brandon's call.

"We are nearly there," Gage says. "Drink some more water, lass." He hands me the waterskin.

I don't want any water. "No!" I say, pushing the waterskin back into his hands.

He growls as he hooks the waterskin onto the saddle. It is not the aroused growl like the one he made while watching Brandon rut me at the festival. No, this is dark and rattles with menace. It still makes my pussy weep. Everything about Gage has the same effect upon me. His scent fills my nose and lungs. It is like a blanket covering the surface of my skin, saturating me, penetrating deep to the core of my body until I tingle everywhere. With only his cloak to protect me, I ought to feel cold, but I am hot, burning with a sickly fever that fills my mind with images of debauchery.

My slick constantly weeps, saturating his beautiful fur-trimmed cloak.

His big, powerful body cages me as we ride. I have napped on occasion when exhaustion pulled me under. Neither Brandon nor Gage have taken any rest.

And now, they will fight.

I don't want them to fight.

Yet I cannot deny that it aroused me when they struggled as Gage held Brandon after I revealed.

I am an omega. How strange is this day? How strange are these new feelings that tear through my body?

As we crest the next rise, a small clearing comes into view. There, nestled between trees, is a two-story log cabin. It is pretty in its rustic setting, *isolated,* and I find that I like that.

As we draw the horse up into the stable attached to the right, Gage is swift to dismount and lift me from the horse.

He does not put me down. I'm not sure my legs would work if I tried to stand after all the riding, so it is for the best that he carries me.

A howl shatters the quiet forest, setting the hairs on the back of my neck rising.

"He is close," I whisper.

"Aye," Gage agrees. "And you are going into heat if your petulance is anything to go by."

I don't know what he means by that. Is he cross because I refused to drink the water?

He heads straight in, taking the stairs upward into an open loft...leaving the front door wide open.

The loft is spacious. A fire has been stocked but remains unlit on the right. On the left, shutters are drawn closed. Beneath the shutters is a great table bearing bundles, sacks, and jugs. But directly ahead, straw has been strewn deeply to make a low platform of sorts, covered by thick blankets.

A nest? The beginnings of a nest, I correct.

Gage strides for the table with me still in his arms. Hot and restless, I try to wriggle down.

My eyes remain on the nest. I helped Hazel create one once. Although Hazel is a beta, it still helps her bonding with her mates, Jack and Fen. Hazel loves her mates well and was eager to try. She made it on the bed, forming a border with pelts and drawing a soft blanket over the top to create an intimate space.

This is nothing like that civilized nest. It feels different.

Animalistic.

There is a thin rope among the supplies, which Gage selects. I frown for only a moment before Gage carries me to the giant nest, lowers my feet to the floor, and sets about binding my wrists.

"What? No!"

I struggle in earnest now. The heat coursing through my body does not like this development.

"I don't trust you not to interfere," he says. "It would devastate the both of us, should you be injured."

Another howl, close, kicks off a thud in the base of my skull.

I feel woozy and a little disconnected from reality as my hands are drawn over my head, pulling me onto my feet. My head rolls back against the rough wooden wall. Above me is a great iron ring, and the rope is passed through.

I kick out. "Ow!" I only succeed in hurting my toe and drawing Gage's thunderous glare.

"Brat," he growls. Spinning me around, he lands a sharp spank to my bottom that hurts twice as much as my toes.

Goddess, his hands are big. I groan as my slick pulses out to join the other stickiness.

His head lowers, and I know he is looking at the mess I have made—the evidence of my arousal. He sucks a sharp breath in through his teeth, head lifting, shoulders straightening, he rises to his full height. My chest heaves. I shake my head, trying to rouse myself from the foolish desire I suffer to spread my legs. Left hand planting against the wall beside my face, he leans into me, his broad, naked chest inches from my lips. I can't stop myself from pressing forward within the confines of the rope, stretching my tongue out to the limit of my reach to lick his glistening skin.

I groan as the taste hits my tongue.

He shifts slightly away so that I can no longer touch him. Writhing against the wall, I tug on the rope in the futile hope that it might release me so that I can feast upon the god taunting me. His fingers tip my chin up, and even that light touch feels like heaven.

"Drunk on pheromones," he mutters. "It will not take much to tip you into full heat."

A thud rattles the floor, followed by a savage growl.

He is here. Brandon has come.

Gage

I turn just in time as a snarling mass of fur bounds into the room. I spring to meet Brandon's leap, taking him by the throat and sending us both crashing to the floor. We roll, each of us seeking a position of dominance. His claws rake my chest, drawing a little blood. I keep my fist locked around his throat. If I release him, the bastard is crazed enough to try and rip me apart.

I squeeze harder. The wolf whines, claws raking me again.

Brandon will not make this easy for me. Both the wolf and the man need to be mastered or there will never be peace. Rising above him, I heave him from the ground and toss him against the wall. Behind me, Jessa squeals. I'm glad I had the foresight to bind her lest she interfere.

The wolf scrambles up, shaking his head before facing off to me. Lips curled, he issues a savage growl.

Arms spread wide, muscles flexed, I growl right back.

He leaps again. This time I swing my fist, knocking him sideways into a tumble of fur and skittering claws as he tries to gain purchase.

We clash again and again.

I could end this. I could end him. But that is not my desire.

What I desire is his submission, and I will have it before we are done.

Jessa

The crazed sounds of snarling and growling fill my ears.

The scent of blood and pheromones fill my nose.

Shivers wrack my body. My slick weeps so copiously that it trickles and drips all the way to the floor. I'm on fire, yet I am deeply cold.

I just want them to stop.

I beg, and I plead, but they are both lost to me.

My eyes have grown swollen with tears, but I am also empty of the love and attention my body needs.

Gage is covered in blood where Brandon's claws and teeth have found their mark. My beautiful shifter is less bloody, but he limps and carries himself in a way that suggests deep internal hurt.

In a move that speaks of impossible strength, Gage takes Brandon by the throat, lifting and pinning the snarling wolf to the wall.

"Shift mutt," Gage roars, chest heaving. "Or I will end you here and rut her over your bloody pelt."

"He can't hear you in wolf form," I whisper. The place in my heart that belongs to Brandon is aching and raw. "Brandon, I am begging you, please, shift back. Please, end this madness."

The air crackles and Brandon stands where the wolf was, his body glistening and chest heaving.

Gage releases him and steps back. Only to send his fist smashing into Brandon's face. Body and head rattle as Brandon bounces off the wall.

Gage does not stop there. Whatever the shifting healed, Gage revisits upon Brandon's human form. They go at one another, filling the air with grunts and growls and the meaty thuds of fists connecting with flesh. Blow after blow, Gage demands Brandon's submission.

Finally, when I am sure my heart can stand no more, Brandon raises his hand and says the words, "I am yours."

Gage fists Brandon's throat and drags him up, only to toss him to my feet. "Release her."

Growling, Gage begins pacing on the other side of the room. "Let her make her nest to her satisfaction. Once she is done, you are going to clean her up."

Chapter Thirty-One

Brandon

You are going to clean her up.

I throw a look over my shoulder at the alpha who has mastered me. I swallow. My cock is rising, blood rushing and pulsing as her heady scent fills me.

Turning back to Jessa, I ignore the temptation of her weeping slick and stagger to my feet. Fingers clumsy, I free the rope binding her to a heavy metal ring attached to the wall.

"Oh! It hurts," she says as her arms lower.

"There," I say, working my fingers and thumbs into her sore muscles. "Does that feel better?"

My nose is dripping blood, and I pause to wipe it away with the back of my hand. I sway a little on my feet, destroyed, battered, and bruised. But that is on me. I entered the challenge recklessly, and I will pay my dues.

But I don't like that Jessa is in pain, although I understand why he did it. My wolf could have hurt her in the rough and tumble of our battle. I was not much better as a man.

I am clear of thought now that a change has happened inside me. Gage has broken me down to my raw components and remade me. I am his now. My wolf is submissive to his dominance, as is the man. I will follow his lead.

Jessa leans into me the moment her arms recover. Plastering her lush body to mine, she peppers kisses over my chest and throat, grasping my hair in her fierce grip as she seeks more.

Gage's growl is a warning. He watches us as he paces. I have no doubt he will beat me again should I not follow his orders swiftly. Taking her by her arms, I set her aside. "The nest, Jessa. How do you want the nest?"

Her head swings toward the bed. It is little more than straw covered by rough blankets. It is not fit for a sweet omega who is succumbing to her heat.

"Yes," she says. Eyes puffy from the tears, she regards the bed. I hate that she has been crying over me. I hate that I needed so much before I could accept my place. "Yes, it needs more."

More. That is a word I have heard from Jessa often since we first committed to one another. She needs more than I can give her.

She needs Gage.

She wants Gage.

No, that is not the whole truth.

She wants and needs us both to claim her for our pleasure.

Our pleasure and hers.

I feel foolish, selfish, and relieved all over again that finally, the lass I have come to love more than life will get what she desires.

"More what, Jessa?" I release her arms, allowing her to sink to her knees beside the coarse bed. "Shall I get you some blankets and pelts, so you can make it to your liking?"

"Yes," she says, petting the bed with a grimace of distaste.

My lips tug up. Our little mate is soaring high. On the table, there are supplies enough to last many days. My wolf sensed we were being taken on a convoluted route after passing through the Lyon community. Gage had the foresight to arrange provisions and to select a private place for her heat, it would seem.

Gathering an armful of the soft pelts and blankets, I return to Jessa.

"Yes!" she says. Pulling the pelts from my arms, she sends them tumbling to the floor. Taking the first pelt, she rubs it against her cheek, a soft little rattle emanating from her chest.

Was that a purr?

My eyes flash to Gage, who has frozen his pacing. As he looks from Jessa to me, a smile blooms on his face. In that shared moment of joy, we are no longer enemies. We are brothers bound more tightly than blood brothers could ever be.

We are three.

He purrs. It has a deeper timbre than mine and is a little rattly. I take up the song, mine more of a contented hum.

Jessa is industrious. The straw is patted down in the middle and left thicker at the edges. Pelts and furs are layered among the softer blankets. I fetch her more, and those go in as well.

A *nest*.

Goddess, I never thought myself to be bound to such a sweet, disarming omega. I take in the gentle curves of her petite body, the light blush to her soft skin, and the rich scent that permeates the room. Her nipples are hard points, and her thighs are coated with slick. There is a sensual grace to her movements. The soft things she selects are drawn over her body, brushed against her breasts, and sometimes between her thighs to coat them with her scent.

On the other side of the room, Gage strips his clothes before resuming his pacing.

"Oh?" Jessa says. On her knees before me, she looks at the empty place where the pelts were.

"They are all gone, Jessa," I say. "You have used them. The nest is done."

She turns back to her creation. I know nothing of omega nests, but it is beautiful to my eyes.

Crawling forward, she finds the center of the nest. Here she lays on her back, opens her legs, and stuffs her fingers into her pussy with a groan. "Please," she says. "I'm so hot. I need you inside me. Both of you."

"Fuck!" I mutter. I didn't think I could get any harder, but my dick jerks at her words.

"I gave you an order," Gage growls on the other side of the chamber, still pacing, monster cock jutting out and making me twitchy on Jessa's behalf.

I turn back to Jessa. There is no hesitation as I clamber into the nest. I don't even care that every inch of my body is aching like a bastard. Taking hold of her wrists, I tug her fingers from her wet pussy.

I don't expect her to fight.

"Uff!" Her small feet plant in the center of my chest, and she strains to kick me off.

"I want Gage!"

Gage chuckles, the bastard. "She is going into heat, mutt," he says. "She won't let you claim her unless you show her who is in charge."

He doesn't need to tell me fucking twice. Grasping her ankle, I tug her closer and open her legs. With a wrist in each hand, I pin her still and bury my head between her slim thighs. She struggles until I get my tongue all up into her drenched pussy.

I feel like I've been starved for the taste of her, and I can never get enough. She tastes fucking delicious, and I dive in and feast. Shifting her wrists to one hand, I slide two fingers in to find the little rough spot that gushes her slick.

"Mnnnn!"

Twitching wildly, she strains to escape, but I keep working that spot as I suck on her clit.

She comes, squirting a great gush all over my fingers and the nest.

"That didn't work out so well," Gage mutters. "She needs to be fucked."

❧

Jessa

The red haze consumes me. Everything is coming through a tunnel, and I feel like my skin is on fire.

Brandon has stopped. Why has he stopped?

Maybe it is because I tried to kick him?

Maybe it is because I demanded Gage?

Maybe Brandon will spank me again if I misbehave?

I buck, putting all my small strength into it, giggling when I manage to escape Brandon's hold.

He curses and tries to grab my ankle.

I'm too nimble.

"Jessa!" There is a warning in his voice that I like very much.

"She needs to be dominated," Gage says. "Just like you did."

Brandon growls at that, snagging my waist from behind. I claw at his arm, determined to make him prove himself before he can have me.

Fisting my hair, he shoves me face first into the furs, lines up, and fills me in a single thrust.

Wildness rushes through my body. "Goddess, yes!" I groan, struggling harder, feeling everything clench blissfully inside when I cannot escape.

"You are a very naughty girl, Jessa," he growls, rutting me roughly and making all the nerves inside my pussy flare to life. He pauses to spank my ass before taking my hips and pounding into me again.

A low growl on the other side of the room tells me Gage likes what he sees.

But I don't want him watching. I want my dues.

❧

Gage

She goes wild as Brandon ruts her. I don't remember seeing a more alluring sight. I wanted Jessa when I thought she was a sweet beta who could not possibly handle my rough ways. Now she is an omega, she is impossibly more perfect.

"Take her harder," I say. Rolling my shoulders as I pace, I try to retain wits enough to control them both. My cock inflames to the point of madness, the glands beginning to swell at the base, although we have barely started yet. I know the moment I enter her weeping cunt, the last of my sanity will flee.

I want to ruin her.

I want her pretty pussy gaping after I have stuffed her with my cock and knot. Growling, I realize that with thoughts like that, I am already gone.

On the makeshift nest, Brandon uses her for his pleasure. Naturally far gentler with her, the mutt is deep into his rut.

Conflict consumes Jessa. She tests Brandon constantly,

bucking and growling her displeasure if he does not rut her to her liking.

I expect she will want to test me too.

I hope that she will.

She comes with a squeal, mouth open, humping herself backward onto Brandon.

He stills, fingers pressed deeply into the flesh of her hips, growling as he follows her through.

I nearly fucking come all over the floor watching the rapture on Jessa's face.

"Work the knot in and out," I demand.

"The fuck!" Brandon turns to glare at me.

"Do I need to tell you everything twice, mutt?"

"It's a fucking knot!" Brandon growls.

"No!" Jessa wails.

I ignore the bratty omega.

"It's a small one," I say, eyes narrowing. "She is about to be ruined when I get my cock and knot inside her. Now, do what you are fucking told."

He turns to the beauty in the nest. He is mine now. Mine to command, and mine to control, and in no position to challenge me. It is a heady thing to dominate a lass, but it is no less enticing to dominate a male. Brandon is no weak beta. He is a shifter, powerful, and that makes his submission all the more arousing.

As he grasps her slim hips, Jessa snarls at him, knowing what is to come.

"In and out," I repeat. I have resisted taking my cock in hand thus far, but I can no longer hold back. The first rough tug on my shaft coincides with Brandon pulling his knot out.

"Fuck!" he mutters. A great gush of frothy cum spews out. "Gods, the knot is sensitive."

He presses forward again, groaning. From where I stand, I

can see the swollen glands forcing their way into her cunt before his hips snap to hers.

"Again," I growl. My cock has flushed deep red with pleasure. The knot at the base is a purple lumpy mess of interconnected glands. I work my fingers over it from root to tip, mesmerized by the omega panting on the bed. Her arms collapse, and small hands fist into the furs beside her pretty face.

Her hooded, heated eyes stare directly at me.

"I'm going to come," Brandon says. "I—I can't keep doing this. It's too fucking intense."

He is asking my permission. Asking *me* if he can come.

"Come then," I say.

He comes, growling out his pleasure, as Jessa snarls her complaints.

"Now, I want her on her back. There, you will use your fingers, hand, and fist to open her some more."

"I don't want you," she snarls. "I want Gage!"

Little brat.

I take the steps to the bed just as Brandon tumbles her over. The beta has her measure now and doesn't hesitate to force her submission. Gathering her wrists in one hand, I pin them to the nest above her head.

"Goddess," she gasps as I close my other hand over the front of her throat. Her glazed eyes stare up at me as Brandon eats her out, working his fingers deeply.

She strains, growling when she finds herself thoroughly trapped.

"Does that feel good, Jessa?" I ask.

"Yes," she says. "It feels so good. And better now that you are both holding me. I dreamed of being between you. Of being safe when you both pressed tightly against me."

Her words are slurred, and her skin is hot under my hands. Just holding her is enough to send me to my limit and beyond.

"I want to taste you," she whines. "Please, Gage, let me taste you."

My dick jerks. A long trail of pre-cum hangs all the way to the furs. I take my cock in hand, lean over her, and tease her lips with the bulbous tip. Her tongue comes out, chasing it, lapping up all the stickiness. I give her only a little, sliding it in and out of her mouth. She groans, eyes never leaving mine as she lavishes it with her hot tongue.

I sink slowly in. *Bliss.*

"Fuck!" Brandon mutters, but I don't spare a thought for whatever the mutt is up to as I slide deep into Jessa's willing mouth. I rut her mouth, trailing my fingers over her soft cheeks and all around her stretched lips. "I'm going to pour a river down your throat, mate," I say. "And you're going to swallow every drop."

"Fuck!" Brandon says again. This time I tear my eyes away from Jessa to see half his hand disappearing into her cunt. Growling my encouragement, I surge deep and come.

Chapter Thirty-Two

Jessa

Lost in a sensual cloud, I gulp and choke as Gage comes down my throat. As the taste hits my belly, it sets off an explosion of pleasure deep inside my womb. My pussy spasms. I can't breathe around the monstrous rod filling my throat. My pussy spasms harder still. I struggle. The cock filling my mouth and throat pops out, and I gasp for air.

Goddess!

I groan like an animal, deep, guttural. I can't work out what is happening to me, but I can't stop coming as something that feels like a tree trunk is lodged inside my most intimate place.

"Fuck! Fuck! Fuck!" Brandon mutters. Gage growls, the low, animalistic one that makes me pant and writhe.

I squeal as my pussy flutters around the giant intrusion.

I blink, but I still can't see. Gage is still holding my hands. His cock jerks against my cheek—it is not him filling me.

"Fuck! I am all the way up inside her."

Tears stream down my cheeks. I shudder. My pussy spasms yet again as I come, gasping and groaning.

What are they doing to me?

"Good," Gages says. "She is limber with her heat. My knot is bigger yet than your fist when fully formed. This will open her up well."

Another groan is torn from my lips when I realize what is being done. A tongue laps gently at my clit even as Brandon fills my pussy with his fist.

"Good girl," Gage says, stroking his fingers down my cheek. "You were made for this. Your hot little cunt will be gaping by the time Brandon is done. Then I will ruin you further when I fill you with my cock and knot."

I wail out my complaint, but Brandon begins to move his fist inside me with tiny in and out movements. So tiny, yet they drag my mind and body underwater, drowning me in a sensual high, the likes of which I have never known.

Gage pushes his fingers into my mouth, opening it up, filling me. Then his fingers slip out, and his cock surges in.

I groan around him, grateful for the distraction from the strain that courts the fine line between pleasure and pain.

My tongue lashes the length and head with every deep surge.

Then Gage is coming, and the taste, scent, and sensations set my pussy convulsing again.

Lips suckle my clit, making it throb just as the thick intrusion filling me slips out.

Gage's cock pops from my mouth, leaving a trail of sticky cum over my chin and throat.

My lips are sore, my pussy more so. "Goddess!"

Gage moves to stand beside Brandon, who kneels between my splayed legs. I lay panting, trying to work out where I am. Trying to temper the urgency running through my blood that impossibly wants more. Their fingers probe me gently, purr-growling as they explore the terrible openness.

I blink again, trying to crawl from the darkness that has me in its hold. I sense movement, but I am deaf and blind to the world.

I *feel*. Silken thickness filling the entrance to my pussy, forcing aching muscles to give. My heart rate surges, pounding at the base of my skull.

Then Gage's thick cock surges in, and my external senses come rushing back.

"Open your eyes," Gage commands. "See what I'm about to do to your needy omega cunt."

My eyes flutter open, my chest heaves like I'm running for my life.

There, between my spread thighs, is a great beast of an alpha. A bruise mars his right cheekbone and a dried cut, his swollen lower lip. Dark, tousled hair, dark eyes, and a rough beard. His face is a picture of determination as he thrusts slowly in and out. Not all of it. There is still much outside, along with the lumpy mutilation of his knot at the base. My gaze skitters upward. Over the thick, corded muscles of his arms, shoulders, and chest. While lower, his abdominals ripple as he ruts me with his big hands braced around my waist.

My gaze shifts to the side, landing unerringly upon Brandon, who sits slumped against the wall, watching what we do. Cuts and mottled black and purple bruises cover his face and body. He is well punished for daring to challenge Gage.

I groan. The thick rod filling me surges a little deeper.

A broad hand cups my cheek drawing my focus back to Gage. "I'm going to knot you," he says. "I'm going to breed you."

His words are like a trigger. The blood pounds harder

through my veins, twisting the pleasure up and bringing a surge of hot rebelliousness spilling out.

I buck, dislodging his cock, hissing as he tries to take me in hand. My nails find flesh, raking, tearing into his skin. He grasps my wrists, shaking me roughly, but that only drives me on. I sink teeth into his forearm, heady on the taste of his blood. His growl is aggressive, and I like that well. With a fist in my hair, my teeth are ripped off. I lick my lips, glaring at the male who dares to try and master me.

I am an omega. Only the worthiest may breed me.

My hands are thrust against the furs over my head, pinned there by one huge hand.

I hiss, bucking my hips again, daring him to try and rut me. He leans over me, massive, powerful, his broad hand collaring my throat, pressing me to the bed as his mouth lowers toward mine.

I growl, teeth snapping as he draws near. But he doesn't take my lips even though they part in anticipation. Instead, his lips trail over my cheeks, toward my ear, tongue circling the shell and setting goosebumps springing all over my skin. My hips rise, straining to escape this torturous blissful, shivery delirium. His lips blaze a trail down my throat, sucking kisses that bring sweet anticipation of him filling me again.

I want his lips on mine now. I struggle weakly, but I am no longer sure I am trying to get away.

His kisses trail over my jaw until his mouth hovers over mine.

Featherlight kisses are pressed to each corner of my mouth. "Tell me to rut you," he says. "Tell me to further ruin your filthy little pussy that is gaping and needy for my knot."

More kisses torment me, bringing a stuttering to my breath.

"Tell me to breed you," he growls.

I sob, arms moving weakly, while my wrists are still shackled within his fist.

"Tell me to rut you."

Groaning, I chase his lips. Lifting my hips and feeling a frisson of heat rush through me as I brush against the silken length of his cock. His fingers sink into my cheeks roughly, holding my jaw open as he plunders my mouth. I suck down on his tongue, maddened by my need to be filled as my body fights my mind's desire to submit. My chest heaves with frustrated sobs.

"Submit to me," he demands. "Give me what I want, and I will give you what you need."

I don't care that my jaw aches where he holds it. I don't care about anything but the desperate need to be filled.

I want to fight, but I want this all-consuming ache to be assuaged more.

Frustration consumes me. I want Gage to take. I don't want to beg for it. "Please," I whisper, hating my weakness.

His nostrils flare before he leans in to capture my lips in a drugging kiss. The hold on my jaw gentles. He knows he has won. He is taunting me now, daring me to bite.

His hand slides down my throat, over my collarbone. His mouth follows his hand. Cupping my breast, he sucks hungrily, marking the plump flesh before drawing my nipple into the hot wetness of his mouth.

I'm on fire. No longer trying to escape, I arch my back, encouraging Gage to suck harder, to mark me. He takes what he wants, in his own time, eyes glittering with primal possession. He torments me to the point of desperation, and then he taunts me some more. When he finally lines his cock with my pussy and surges deeply, a shudder ripples through me. Nerves spark and tingle so powerfully deep inside that I'm already hanging on the edge of a climax.

"It's going to hurt some," he says.

By then, I'm too far gone to understand or care about what that means.

ঌঌ

Gage

I hold myself in check by the slimmest of threads. By mastering Jessa, I have driven my own control to breaking point.

An omega is different from a beta in many ways. The clenching hotness of her pussy encourages me to spill my seed, although I have not yet penetrated her fully. I feel resistance blocking my way. Omegas have a second hymen close to the womb. Even after Brandon fisted her, I can still feel the rubbery flap of skin blocking me. Until I tear through this, she will likely never get with child.

I need to breed her, claim her, and make her mine.

Brandon has already bitten her and marked her as his.

"This will hurt some," I growl, and bracing her hip in my hands, I surge all the way in.

She screams. I feel her pussy give, and my cock sinks to the root. The bliss is white-hot as my knot is welcomed into her gripping cunt.

Beneath me the tiny omega now writhes with fresh need.

My fingers bite deep into her skin as I begin to work my knot in and out. Our bodies slap together wetly, slick and cum splattering out over the furs. I like the thought of pushing Brandon's cum out, of emptying her so that mine can fill her anew. I rut her faster and deeper. My knot bulges obscenely until the point where I must battle to force it into her hot slippery channel. Sweat bathes my body, springing from pores across the surface of my skin. My spine tingles, and my balls clench and rise before my cum spews deep.

Bliss.

Head back, she squeals and gasps as she grinds her pussy against me, muscles squeezing over me, encouraging me to come again.

Filling her with another hot flood, I grasp her body to mine, lips finding the juncture of her throat where Brandon marked her. I taste coppery blood as I meld my mark with his.

My balls clench, and another flood gushes out.

I hear the blood rushing through my ears.

Yet more cum jets the entrance to her womb.

My chest tingles, like a delicate flower opening, and an awareness unfurls.

Her fingers are in my hair, kisses peppering over my cheek as she cleaves me to her.

My cock jerks again, balls straining on the cusp of pain as yet more cum floods out.

The awareness blooms.

Three entities.

Three hearts.

A perfect menage of three.

Brandon

Rocked by the connection, I rise to a crouch. Gage has knotted her, bitten her, and now he is rutting her again.

Gage has beaten me half to death.

I have gone down on Jessa until my face and tongue are numb.

I have fucked her until my dick is raw, have forced my fist into her cunt, and still, she needed more.

Gage is a savage. I have never met a more savage alpha in my life. But even as he ruins her with his monstrous cock and knot, she is begging him for more.

I don't know how she takes it.

I can't work out where or how it even fits in her tiny little body. But I also understand that he gives her exactly what she needs and what I alone could not.

But I still want Jessa, raw dick notwithstanding, I will go at her a-fucking-gain and again until her heat is done with.

My entire body throbs. I could shift to heal, but I carry my wounds like a twisted badge of honor.

He comes with a roar, triggering a climax in Jessa that has her screaming with pleasure. Gods, the sounds make my raw dick jerk and spit as I watch them.

With her legs spread wide, I can see where he is buried in her pussy, see the pulsing seed gushing around his knot and further ruining her hastily prepared nest.

Rolling onto his side, knot still deep, he thrusts a finger in her ass. Her cry is sharp and guttural, and she instantly begins to writhe. My heart rate kicks up as he begins to finger her ass. She is slick with cum, and his finger makes wet sticky noises as he pumps it in and out.

Does he intend to take her in that way?

Why the fuck does my dick turn stone hard at the thought of him doing that to sweet Jessa?

Only she is not so sweet today. Today, she is all screeching demands and sexual hunger.

I know nothing of omegas save the occasional rumor I have heard. Gage's mother was an omega, so perhaps he knows more.

Or perhaps this is instinctive to an alpha. Everything I have seen so far suggests this is true.

"Does that feel good, Jessa?" he demands as he fingers her ass.

"Yes! Goddess yes! More, Gage. Please, I need more."

Rolling onto his back, he pulls her over him, spreading her legs wide around his much greater bulk. One hand fists her hair, eliciting a needy, approving whimper from the heat-drunk lass. "If I choose," he growls, his finger still pumping into her tight virgin ass. "You may get more. Now, be a good little omega for me, and squeeze your alpha's knot."

She whimpers, and I see her ass clenching and hips rolling as she does as she is told.

I close my fist around my cock, hissing at how sensitive it is.

Gage's eyes shift to me, and a smirk lights his lips. He enjoys his domination over me as much as he enjoys his domination over Jessa.

I always presumed I would be tied to Fen for all my life. But I am surprised by how right this feels. I will have her only by his will. I should rail at such control, but instead, it makes me even harder when I realize my pleasure is no longer mine to command.

I am in the fucking corner, cock in hand while he enjoys the lusty omega who has taken possession of my heart.

I want her. I want to push his finger away and fill her ass with my cock. She is limber, as Gage has mentioned. An omega was sent by the Goddess to take cock in all the ways. Not only can she take it, but she is fucking greedy for it.

"There, my knot has softened," he says. "Ride me. Get yourself off. Use me how you need to."

His finger slips from her ass, and I see the little hole wink at me before he takes her hips between his massive hands.

"Oh! It has not softened much," she complains, although

her hips are moving as she pushes up from his chest.

"You can take it," he growls. "Work your hot little cunt up and down."

"No!"

Fist tightening, I begin to jack my hand.

His fingers tighten on her ass, and he lifts her off to her squeal of protest. A great slew of frothy cum gushes out. He scoops it up and feeds it to her. Eyes closed in bliss as she sucks it down.

"Ride me," he repeats. "Let yourself drop all the way down onto my knot."

Hand collaring her throat, he watches her gasp and groan as she struggles to take the partially formed knot.

He growls when she lifts before sinking onto the knot.

"All of it," he demands.

Jessa sinks lower, emitting a deep guttural moan as the knot sinks inside, and a gasp as she rises. Her arms and thighs begin to tremble, but like me, she is caught under his dominant spell.

He lets her do the work riding him before grasping her hips and slamming up into her roughly. Head back, she moans with pleasure.

She is so beautiful in her heat.

Their bodies slap together wetly. His powerful thrusts send a judder through her. As he takes her faster and rougher, nonsense begins to pour from her lips, and I know she is close.

I am so caught under a spell watching them that I don't immediately notice he is staring at me.

"What are you waiting for, mutt?" His words are lust-roughed and pushed out between ragged breaths. "Our mate has needs."

Reaching lower, he grasps her hips and pulls out, sending a gush of cum splattering. He holds her up, presenting me with a perfect view of her waiting pussy.

Mutt, I fucking hate that word, but I don't linger on it when he just called her our mate.

Ours.

Both of ours.

Inside, my wolf howls his agreement. He will follow this alpha who has mastered our sweet omega and us.

All of ours.

"Please!" Jessa begs. Her head hangs limp, thighs trembling and hot pussy open. She tries to rock her hips, but he has her pinned, body quivering with the strain.

Nostrils flared, I surge from where I crouch in the corner.

Gods, this is a lot for her to take, a young lass new to rutting. But her heat does things to her, makes her body limber even as it makes her mind crave. Instinctively I know she needs this.

Crawling into the nest behind her, I take a fistful of hair and arch her neck back. The kiss is dark and aggressive from the tension coursing through me. She opens to it, and her tongue tangles with mine. My other hand closes over the front of her throat, squeezing gently before I skim my hand down, over lush tits all the way to her pussy where I gently strum her clit. She groans into my mouth as I rub my aching shaft against her plump ass.

With a growl, I wrench my lips from hers, pushing her forward onto her hands and knees so she is braced over Gage. She is slippery with cum and slick, and my cock breaches her with an ease that is shocking.

"Gods," I say, pumping into her wet heat. I don't even care that Gage is lying under her, playing with her tits and kissing her deeply as I rut her from behind. "What have you done to her?"

Gage doesn't answer me, and I don't really care about the answer.

We fall into debauchery that knows no bounds. Taking turns to rut Jessa, filling her mouth and pussy with cum over and over.

As her heat rises, she demands ever more.

I lose track of time and place. Darkness falls, light rises, and still her heat is not done.

⁂

The nest is ruined. The straw scattered, the soft furs and pelts crusted with cum. Gage offers her food and drink, but she wants none of it. The most she tolerates is a few sips of water.

"Drink some more," he says, holding the waterskin to her lips.

Even as he tries to get her to drink, I am sprawled out between her thighs, inspecting her ruined pussy.

"Gods, her poor pussy is puffy and open." My finger slips in and out easily. "Clench," I say.

"No!"

She might be talking about the water or my determination that she should clench. I am so fucking high, I wouldn't know either way.

"Clean her up," Gage says.

When my eyes flash to meet his, I find a stone-cold expression. I'm a happy drunk on her pheromones. Gage is fierce and unwavering in his domination.

At my hesitation, he fists my hair and presses my head between her parted thighs. From the first taste, I am gone. Sweet mewling sounds begin pouring from her lips as I lap at her slick folds.

Gage holds me pressed so close that I can barely fucking breathe. I don't care about it. He has told me to do this, and he will enforce that decision. He dominates me as easily as he dominates her. And Gods, I have never been so fucking hard. His hand remains on the back of my neck, and my complete lack of free will is like a shot of raw lust skittering down my spine, burrowing into my dick.

My balls tighten. I am going to fucking come against the furs, and I don't care about that either.

"Come if you need to," he says like he can read my fucking mind. "You are deep into your rut. We both are. Give yourself over to it fully."

I come, balls tightening to the point of pain as I hump the ruined nest, hot cum gushing out. I groan against her pussy, barely conscious as my climax takes me.

His fingers rub the nape of my neck, gentling.

"I need to rut her again," he says.

Somehow, I rise before collapsing to her side, panting. I swipe my hand down my face. It is covered in cum, and every breath drives the scent deeper into my lungs.

Her hips lift, encouraging Gage to rut her. But instead, he scoops up the cum I spilled over the furs and swipes it over her throat and down to her tit, cupping it roughly.

Her eyes roll back. She is high, just like me.

He flips her onto her belly. Dragging her ass up, he lines his cock and fills her with a savage growl.

When she growls back, his big hand connects with a crack against her ass.

He ruts her and knots her. Then I drag myself up and do the same.

Time is lost under the haze of her heat. Our rutting grows ever wilder, as does our mate. She tears into us with her nails, bites, and demands more.

But every storm must end. Exhaustion pulls us under, and we collapse with our little omega squished between us limp and sated.

Chapter Thirty-Three

Jessa

I wake up convinced I have passed into the afterlife. Only, I am not with the Goddess. No, assuredly, I am in hell. My entire body aches from my toes all the way to the roots of my hair.

A weak groan is all I can manage. The hot, hair-roughened flesh under my cheek shifts.

"Get the lass some water," Gage says.

Another grunt comes from behind, and the warm body I only now realize is blanketing my back shifts away.

"No," I croak, hand fumbling behind.

"I'm here, Jessa," Brandon says. "What is it?"

"Nothing," I say. "I am just happy." I can't speak further as the words catch in my parched throat. I have dreamed of being like this, laying between them, for the longest time. The soreness and deep aches of my body are of little consequence besides my joy.

They purr. The one before me is deeper and has a slight

rattle. The one behind is softer and rumbly. I sob as I cling, holding them both tightly. They are inside me, in the little deeply tucked place I can sense both their anxiety and tenderness for me. Goddess, it is the most incredible sensation, and more tears leak from my poor swollen eyes.

"You do not look very fucking happy," Gage grumbles. "Maybe I should beat the mutt some more for how slow he has been about this."

"I am not fucking slow," Brandon growls. "Given you're the kind of man who stands by while his clan brothers snatch a lass, happen anyone would be slow. At least Barry won't be taking any more lasses after Fen killed him. I ripped his worthless companion's throat out, so he's gone as well."

The purring has stopped. I try to work out where this went wrong.

"Aye, and I beat two of their accomplices to death when I found out what they had done," Gage says. "They weren't my brothers afore, and they weren't my brothers after."

Silence settles, and confusion floods Brandon's side of the bond. Gage is all seething rage.

Gage huffs out a breath. "You have me painted as a spineless bastard who would rape a lass against her will?"

"You have just stolen Jessa!" Brandon snarls.

"Aye, and she fucking wanted me to. You both needed me to."

"Please, don't argue," I whisper.

They still, and the anger churning through the bond implodes.

"I'm going to get you some water," Brandon says. "It is only on the table. I will not be away for long."

"Okay," I say.

I miss his warmth the moment he slips from the ruined nest. My eyes won't open more than a crack, but I look up into

Gage's stern face. The lines soften as he takes me in. With gentle fingers, he brushes the ratty hair from my face. "Are you happy, too?" I ask, suddenly unsure of myself.

He gathers my small hand within his. Drawing it to his lips, he presses a kiss to my palm before placing it over his chest where his heart is. "The bond does not lie, lass."

The nest is displaced as Brandon surges back in. He has far more than a waterskin in his hands. There is also a tied cloth bundle that he opens to reveal a small flatbread, wrapped cheese, and jerky. I sip a little, peeping at Brandon out of the corner of my eye. "Why don't you shift?" I ask, brushing my fingers over the bruise that lines his jaw. Even without shifting, shifters heal faster than humans. That he is still bruised thus speaks of the terrible damage done by their fighting. My memories are hazy, but I could weep looking now.

He shakes his head, capturing my hand, and mirroring Gage, presses a kiss to the surface. "I will heal soon enough," he says gruffly.

"I will light the fire and put some water on," Gage says. "You will feel better for being clean."

The bond tingles with a slight discord as Gage pulls away. But Brandon tucks me against his side and encourages me to sip some more. Within Brandon's arms, I watch Gage move about the room, gloriously naked. Taking tinder from the nearby shelf, he lights the fire before heading down the stairs.

"Eat a little if you can," Brandon says. "Gods, I could gnaw my own arm off, I am so hungry!"

I chuckle as he tucks into a stick of jerky. When he holds it out to me, I instinctively take a bite. A smile spreads across his face. He is pleased with himself for that sneak attack.

It takes a bit of chewing before I can swallow it, but it settles a comfortable weight in my empty belly.

"I was going to tell you the day after the feast," I say quietly. "About Gage... About how I feel... About all of it."

At his stillness, I lift my eyes to meet his. I see hurt, but also understanding.

"Most omegas reveal when they are a child. But my mother told me on the day of the feast that there was a chance I was a latent. She thought because I had chosen you, that I had bled and become a beta. I never bled. I didn't realize that was because I was an omega. Nor that I couldn't get with a child unless an alpha rutted me."

My cheeks heat.

He nods, discarding his half-eaten jerky on the cloth.

"We are connected, Gage and I. That day when you were so cross because he brought me home, a miracle happened. I healed him, Brandon. His injuries were grave, perhaps fatal, after he fought with the Orc. The Goddess blessed me to heal him. She would not have done so without reason. I felt a spark inside me bloom that day. It was the same spark that bloomed for you the day wolves cornered me after my sleepwalk. We are tied. All of us have long been tied."

He presses his lips to mine.

"I know, Jessa," he says. "Not that you healed him, but that you needed him too. It was hard for me to accept. I was angry that I could not have you to myself. Were it anyone but Gage, it would have been easier. Not easy, but easier. But it is hard for me with Gage, Jessa. I have been at loggerheads with him for as long as I can remember. But he is not a monster. I didn't believe you when you said that at first. But I believe it now, for the bond does not lie. And without him, I would not feel this Goddess-blessed connection to you."

He presses another kiss to my lips, this one longer, full of all the love that we share.

"I was going to talk to you, too, after the festival. To tell you that I would find a way if you wanted to be with us both."

"You did not seem like a man ready to accept," I say, smiling tentatively.

"Aye, well, happen it might have gone better had he not turned into a fucking caveman."

A blush creeps over my cheeks. "I quite like that about him," I say before I can think how that might come across as inflammatory.

Rolling his eyes, Brandon snatches up the jerky and holds it to my mouth.

Dutifully, I open and take a bite.

Overly loud thudding signifies Gage's return with a wooden bucket in his hands. He cuts a glare toward the nest. Also, he is still naked, and my poor sore pussy clenches at the arresting sight.

"You will not be getting any of that today," he says gruffly, filling the great iron pot over the fire from the bucket and setting it to warm.

"Goddess," I mutter weakly when his stern alpha voice makes my pussy clench twice as hard. It is bad enough that they can scent my arousal without them also sensing it through the bond.

Gage stomps back down the stairs.

"I think I saw some apples in another bag," Brandon says. "Would you like an apple to eat while the water warms?"

"Yes, please," I say. I try to sit up, wincing when my intimate places throb.

"Let me help you," Brandon says. He makes a roll with a nearby pelt, and lifting me forward, tucks it behind me.

"Thank you," I say. The throb in my temples eases now that I am sitting. My hand trembles as I brush my hair back. Tentatively, I touch my throat, finding a crusty residue there. I smile at a hazy memory of how it came to be there.

Brandon halts when he turns back to see me smirking. His eyes narrow, and he shakes his head. But he is also grinning as he leans down to present me with an apple. Standing, he runs a hand over his messy hair. My eyes track his activity, watching the play of muscles under the skin of his arms, shoulders, and chest as they bunch, flex, and stretch skin taut. Even bruised, battered, and filthy from all the rutting, he is still the most beautiful man I have ever met.

Heavy footsteps signify Gage's return.

He enters the room, clean and dripping water everywhere.

Goddess, my eyes do not know where to look first with the two of them standing so gloriously naked.

"River?" Brandon asks.

"River," Gage agrees. "It is fucking freezing. I thought my balls had dropped off!"

Brandon chuckles, and it warms my heart that they are not growling at one another. "I will go and clean up too."

He heads down the stairs.

In Brandon's absence, I feel suddenly shy. I do not know Gage well, although my heart has claimed him as mine. He is a huge, stern alpha in some ways, yet he is also gentle with me. Turning, he tests the water temperature before pouring some back into the bucket.

I am trying to heave my weak body out of the nest when he turns and levels me with a glare.

"Stay there," he says. Striding over, he puts the bucket down beside me. "We will get you a proper bath once home, but this will help some."

He heads over to the table, returning with a soft washing cloth. Dipping it in the warm water, he leans over me.

"What? Oh!" He wipes it over my face, growling when I try to take it from him.

"I wish to do this," he says, voice brokering no discussion. Meekly, I let him clean me up, feeling my cheeks heat from shyness all over again. He purrs, and it is like a soft, comforting blanket settling over me, taking my concerns from my grasp and leaving a sense of peace.

"Where is home?" I ask. My cheeks are hot, but my body soothed as the cloth is dipped, wrung, and wiped over me from fingers to shoulder. He repeats on the other side.

"With my clan," he says. "I am the king now, lass. My late father did a piss-poor job of leading them. My brother is a prisoner of the Halket clan. I must accept that he is unlikely to return home alive."

He stills before dipping and wringing the cloth again, this time brushing my hair aside and cleaning my chin. "I would not abandon them again. It would not be the right thing to do."

I feel like a great cloud has passed over me, and he stills again, pausing to tip my chin. "It is not so far from your family. You can visit them as often as you like."

"I always imagined I would take a home in Ralston close to my ma and pa where I could still see them every day." Moving from the people I have known all my life is daunting.

"I can see you would need to be a true king to your people who have been troubled for so long. But I am also nervous," I admit. "About meeting them...and about what will happen when Jack finds out that I am gone. I do not want to start a war."

"It will not start a fucking war unless Jack acts like an ass. He is a level-headed leader. He will not start a war. Happen he might be a bit pissed about how it came about, but he will see sense." He goes back to cleaning me, down my throat, lifting me forward, and sliding the soothing cloth from my nape to the base of my spine before settling me back to rest.

It feels intimate and tender.

"I did not expect you to clean me, thus," I say.

"Well, I am partly to blame for you being in this state. It seems reasonable that I should help to make you as comfortable as I can. It feels natural for me to do this. You are small and weak compared to me. A mate should be cherished. But you are an omega and smaller and weaker than most."

I don't like that I am small and weak compared to a beta lass, although I have never let my size stop me from doing anything I wanted to, nor would I be lazy and expect to be coddled. But he is my mate now, and his actions do indeed make me feel cherished.

He dabs gently at the claiming mark. It throbs and makes me wince.

"The womenfolk of the clan will have some balms as will help with this and the other soreness you have."

My cheeks turn to flames again, just as Brandon enters the room...dripping. He could have shifted to dry, but he wears his battle scars from his conflict with Gage proudly.

"Oh!" I say as Gage rips the pelt covering me away, snapping my attention back to what he is doing. "I can clean there myself!"

"You will lay fucking still like a good lass and let me do this, or you will get your naughty bottom spanked."

Brandon chuckles as he comes to stand beside Gage. "That is a poor threat. She likes her bottom spanked too well."

"Aye," Gage says, returning to his task of applying the cloth gently to the outer petals of my pussy. "I noticed as much when I gave her a spank for backtalk when we first arrived."

Brandon's face darkens. He is staring at the apex of my thighs as Gage pushes my legs wide, exposing me to their lustful gaze. I squirm as Gage carefully parts my pussy lips to inspect me. I try not to look at Brandon's cock, which is bobbing as it rises to attention.

There is no hope for me. I am torn between Gage's enrapt expression and Brandon's cock. All I can think about is how good it felt when one of them thrusts a hardened length inside me.

Brandon's swallow sounds loud.

"Please," I say. Both sets of eyes turn on me. "You can't just look at me thus, without tending to me."

The cloth is tossed aside and they both surge into the filthy nest, purring, strong bodies crowding me in their eagerness.

"We will be gentle," Gage says before taking my mouth in a drugging kiss that steals my breath.

"We will be careful," Brandon says before his lips enclose the stiff peak of my nipple.

That quickly, I am soaring. Their clean male scent, the glorious sensation of firm flesh against mine, the lips, the hands, and the delicious awakening, fill my every sense.

"I am going first," Brandon mumbles against my breast, fingers skittering down to circle my throbbing clit.

"You are not going fucking first," Gage growls, lifting his head and glaring at Brandon.

"I *am* going first," Brandon says, lifting his head and glaring back. My pussy squeezes in excitement at being caught between these two warring males. "Much as I'm deeply aroused by her openness after you have impaled her on that monster rod, sometimes I'd like not to get lost in there."

That assuredly should not make my pussy weep, but nevertheless, it does. My fingers slip into my wet pussy.

"I don't care who goes first," I say on a groan. "Just so long as it is soon."

"You can go first," Gage concedes. Snatching my fingers

from their mischief, he pins them to the bed. "I do not think the lass is as sore as she was making out."

Brandon's fingertips pet my slick folds before pressing two thick fingers up inside me. Watching my face, he pumps them in and out. "She feels hot, wet, and tight," he says.

"Please," I say.

With my thigh in his hand, Brandon tugs me down the nest. I groan as he takes his position between my spread legs.

"Fuck!" Brandon growls as he surges deeply, filling me. "How does a pussy feel this good? Clench for me, Jessa. Make it nice and tight."

I squeeze. It stings a little, aches more, but it also feels a blissful kind of good as Brandon begins to power in and out.

Taking my chin in hand, Gage draws my face to his, kissing me deeply and setting all the glorious sensations twisting up. He cups my breast, squeezing it roughly as our tongues tangle in a heated kiss. The two sets of stimulation split my focus, and it makes everything twice as hot. When Gage captures my nipple between his fingers and thumb, the pleasure explodes all the way to my clit and even deeper inside. Like a sensual rolling wave, it lifts me, cresting high before it tumbles me over the edge.

"I am not going to fucking last," Brandon gasps.

"Good," Gage says. "Because if you don't finish soon, I'm going to come all over her pretty tits like a green fucking whelp."

Brandon half laughs, hisses, then groans as he stills.

Inside, I feel the swelling of his knot and warmth spread through me as he fills me with his seed.

"Fuck!" Brandon says, grinding me onto his hardness and setting off another sweet clench inside me.

"Don't knot her," Gage growls.

"Too late," Brandon says, lips forming a lazy grin and eyes

dancing with mischief. For so long, he has been my dream, my *obsession*. Now, he is all mine.

I sneak a glance at Gage.

Gage looks like he is in pain.

I giggle, although it is no laughing matter.

"Brat," Gage says, trying to keep his expression stern, although his eyes are alight with humor and hunger.

Then Brandon pulls out, and I gasp.

No sooner does he collapse to the side when Gage takes his place.

"Goddess," I say weakly. I think if I live to a hundred, I will still experience a flare of sharp arousal to be the object of such an intense male's lust.

"Brace yourself, lass," he says. His hand trembles as he grasps my waist in one hand, the other lining his cock with my puffy pussy. "This is going to be rough and fast."

He does not lie. I should not want roughness, as sore as I am. But I do. His thick cock and the pounding rhythm set me tumbling higher and higher. I feel the rough, bumpy ridge of his knot growing with every brutal slap of flesh meeting flesh. I want to wriggle away. But I also want more. I always want more.

"Nuummmmnnn!"

"Good girl," Brandon says, fingers tracing my open lips. "Come for Gage. Come all over his cock."

I squeal as I come. Head back, thighs straining to lift my hips to meet the thrusts, I relish the fierceness of the coupling. With my waist grasped within his strong hands, Gage forces the knot in one more time and stills, growling out his release as he bathes my pussy with his seed.

Still knotted, he rolls to his side so that I am snuggled between the two of them.

"Gods, we will never leave these fucking furs," Gage says

on a gusty breath. "Her breeding scent is enough to keep me insensible with need."

"Breeding?" I say softly, hardly daring to hope.

Brandon kisses my shoulder before nuzzling the side of my throat. "Aye, breeding. Your scent has changed, Jessa. You are with child."

Chapter Thirty-Four

Gage

Somehow, we haul our asses out of the furs, clean up, clean Jessa up, and ride for my clan. Brandon lopes circles around us in wolf form, Jessa naps where she lays over my lap. I keep the horse to a walk, so it takes us a while.

Night is falling by the time we arrive. The alpha on watch sends a lad ahead of us to let the village know. By the time we arrive at my home and hall, Pete is waiting.

"Hail!" he says, grinning. "You have been gone a good while."

Pete's gaze lowers to where Brandon takes a sentry position beside the horse, remaining in wolf form. He does not know the clan well, and he will be on alert until his wolf can be satisfied no danger lurks here.

Pete calls to a couple of nosy servants who have come to gawk. "Prepare the hall, a bath, and some food."

They scurry off.

It might be helpful were Brandon to shift and take the

sleepy lass from my arms. But alas, all he does is growl when Pete dares to take a step forward to hold the reins as I dismount.

"He is not going to hurt the lass, dumb mutt!" I grouch. Rousing Jessa, I put her in the saddle as I dismount before lifting her into my arms.

"I can stand!" she says, voice ripe with querulousness. She is tired and in need of rest in a proper bed. And a bath given her hair is a knotty mess of dried cum. As much as I enjoyed putting her in this state, she will feel better for being thoroughly clean.

"You weigh all but naught," I say. To Pete, I ask, "Has there been any trouble?"

"Aye," he says, nodding. "Jack sent his second, Glen, to find out if we had aught to do with Brandon and Jessa's disappearance. I told them you had passed through with Brandon and Jessa, and that I would send a rider to notify him on your return."

"Good," I say. "Send a rider tonight. He will be here for the morrow. Better to get this over and done with."

"You have bonded," Pete says, eyes shifting to the bundle in my arm. "Her scent has changed. That the wolf is not trying to rip your throat out suggests he has bonded too."

A growl rises from my chest when his eyes linger on Jessa. We have been friends since lads, and I have trusted this man with my life. Brandon, alert to my mood, moves to place himself between Pete and us. Curling his lips, he growls.

Pete lowers his gaze. "You have claimed an omega," he says. "It will take time for your people to adjust. I meant no disrespect."

"We are newly mated," I say. "It will take me some time to temper the feelings the bond invokes."

Pete smiles, and his eyes meet mine without straying. "I

expect that it will. This is a good sign that the Goddess has blessed the clan. The news will give our people hope."

He turns to the side, where a servant casts a nervous glance at Brandon before turning to me. "The hall is prepared, sire," she says.

"We will talk on the morrow, Pete," I say. "Thank you for all you have done, and for having a level head in handling Jack."

Bowing his head in deference, he takes his leave.

"Come on, mutt," I say. I swear the wolf glares at me.

Jessa smiles. "He looks grumpy," she says.

"Are you sure they can't understand humans?" I say, taking the steps to the hall. Brandon's claws clack against the wooden floor as he follows us in. "Mayhap, it is a shifter secret."

A bowing servant swiftly pushes the door shut, just as a scrap of red fur darts inside.

Brandon yips.

The cat jumps up onto the oak table like he owns it and gives Brandon a haughty glare.

"Oh!" Jessa says. A moment ago, she looked like she was ready to fall asleep. Now she is wide-eyed and perky. "What is that?"

"A cat," I say, thinking this is obvious.

"My cat," I correct. "The little bastard has taken to sleeping on my bed of a night when he is not busy mousing."

"Can I pet him?" she asks, trying to wriggle down.

Brandon and the cat are eyeballing one another. I hope the wolf has the sense not to try and eat it.

Do wolves eat cats? I have seen the cat eat rats bigger than he is. I'm confident Brandon's nose will feel the sting of claws if he gets too close.

"No, you can have a bath and eat some supper before we rest."

"Oh," she says, sounding disappointed.

Rolling my eyes, I carry her through to the bedding chamber where a bath is steaming ready for her.

Brandon follows us in, still in wolf form, and sits down to watch. The cat darts in, making a beeline for the bed, and settles in to start his nightly cleaning routine.

I wash Jessa in the bath. She can't take her eyes off the fucking cat! But I like this too, the homely feeling as I work the tangles out of her hair, watched by our audience. How my life has changed. Not so long ago, I was bitter, angry, and heart sore with the ways of my clan.

There is a deep pain in the center of my chest when I think about Danon, still a prisoner of the Halket clan. But that is a worry for another day. First, we must deal with the fallout from the Ralston clan.

After we are done, and she is squeaky clean, I take her to the furs and settle her down for sleep.

It is not long before the cat snuggles in behind me. A little later, as I am falling into a doze, the bed dips, and Brandon, once more in human form, presses in on Jessa's other side.

Chapter Thirty-Five

Brandon

The scents of the clan make me edgy, so I elect to go for a run first thing. It will help my wolf to become familiar with the clan and allow the clan to become familiar with me.

The three of us are bound together now. With hindsight, it has turned out better than I thought it might. When I spoke to Fen on the morning of the festival, he had encouraged me to consider the possibility.

At the time, I was in denial, still hoping that Jessa would say that she did not care for Gage.

That didn't work out so well.

The forest here is mostly fir trees, being higher up the mountain than the Ralston and Halket clans. My paws make a drum against the forest floor soft with fallen pine needles as I take larger and larger loops.

It helps to clear my mind in this form, and the clean forest scents further eases the anxiety balling in my gut. I sense no nefarious goings-on, only wary villagers while I was closer to the center.

They will come today, Jack, maybe Fen as well. I'm nervous, but I'm also hopeful. By now, Fen will have told Jack about our conversation, and learning that the three of us are bonded will not come as a surprise.

With hindsight, I do not believe Jack would have given Jessa to another alpha. But neither Gage nor I were clear of mind when she first revealed. Still, Jack might have tried to separate us, perhaps thinking to protect Jessa. Neither Gage nor I would have tolerated that.

As I near the place where I shed my clothes earlier, I shift. I am ravenous after the many days of Jessa's heat, and my belly rumbles as I shuck on my leather pants and shove feet into boots. It has only been a few hours since I left Jessa sleeping in the bed, but I am eager to see her again.

I take the wooden steps to the hall two at a time...and come to an abrupt stop.

Jessa is sitting on Gage's lap, cheeks flushed and wearing naught but a fur.

He is feeding her.

I frown.

"The lass has two arms," I say. Striding over, I pull out the chair beside them...displacing the fucking cat. My wolf hates the haughty mini beast.

I sit.

Why do I feel so aggrieved by him feeding her?

"Yes! I have two arms," Jessa says.

"I don't give a fuck," Gage says, scowling. "It pleases me to do this, so I will fucking do it."

He is in full alpha bastard mode this morning, it would seem! I raise both hands before dragging the nearest platter toward me. My mouth waters: steak, eggs... I will skip the potatoes. Don't need any vegetables ruining a perfectly good meal.

I eat. I try not to watch him feeding her, but my eyes are drawn there of their own accord.

Her face flushes, but she soon opens obediently for each morsel. Gage kisses her between each bite, and all the while handling her, petting her hair, or fondling her tits. I have seen Jack feed his mate. I should not be surprised.

Yet it is so different to see Jessa treated thus.

I can't tear my gaze away from her engorged nipples nor dismiss the scent of her need.

By the time he is done feeding her, she is restless with need.

I swallow past the tightness in my throat as servants arrive and carry everything away. I'm hoping he will rut her so I can have a turn, but he seems in no hurry.

It is strange to be bonded to an alpha who is also the king of a clan. To the right of Jessa and Gage is a dais where the king and queen sit.

Two chairs.

My gut sours as I wonder at my place here. I am not the alpha. I am merely a beta shifter mated to his queen.

"There is plenty of space for a third chair," Gage says, stirring me from my rumination.

My eyes snap to meet his. I had forgotten about the bond and the way it ties us together. Jessa is also watching me, eyes sensitive.

"I don't need fucking charity," I say.

"You are a dumb mutt and a whelp if you think it is fucking charity," Gage growls. He presses a kiss to Jessa's forehead when she tries to get down from his lap. "When I said I would claim both of you, it was not a fucking lie."

I try to be objective, to let the emotions ripping through me ease their stranglehold. I am being unreasonable, yet it hurts to see Jessa on his lap. Before, she was mine and only mine, and now I must share. He is an alpha and a king. I am only a beta.

"You are mine, mutt," Gage says. "No one would dare think less of you."

His intense feelings pummel me through the bond.

I am upsetting Jessa. And I do not like that.

Swallowing, I nod.

A ruckus comes from beyond the open hall doors. Gage surges from his seat, dumping Jessa on my lap.

My brows draw together. "Jack," I say. Jessa begins to tremble. I draw her closer and purr.

"Aye," Gage says. "Stay here and care for Jessa."

"I will come with you," I say. I'm confident I can diffuse any tension better than Gage can.

"No," Gage says, voice brokering no argument. "I will deal with this. When it is safe, you can both come out."

Jessa frets as he strides from view.

"It will be fine," I say, but I am not feeling fine.

The emotions that assault me are complex. I am a wolf. With Fen, I would have faced any trouble at his side. Only, I don't think Gage orders me to stay here because he sees me as weak.

Does he do this because he thinks it best for Jessa?

No, there is more to it than that. From Gage's side of the bond, the feelings are unmistakably protective...and directed at us both.

I am confused. No one has sought to protect me since I was a pup. I should feel slighted that he treats me thus. And yet, I sense a deep caring that encompasses both Jessa and me.

Jessa is our precious mate. She carries our child. It is her duty to protect the baby in her belly, to nourish it, and Goddess-willing, deliver it into the world. My job is to be close to her and defend her should Gage fail. His job is to protect us both.

My sense of place and purpose is rocked by this determination. For all I am a beta, I am as prideful as the next man. Yet, pride has no place in this. I am Gage's now, and he cares for what he considers his.

He is not a monster.

He is not even a bad man.

I think he might be one of the very best, truth be told.

I am humbled by this understanding.

He is still a grumpy bastard with strange notions of coddling the lass. He is also fucking fierce and brave. But for the first time since two became three, I can start to see my place.

※

Gage

"Come out, and answer for your crimes!"

I am greeted by a wall of alphas keeping an enraged Jack at bay. He has not come alone. No, he has Fen, Glen, and a dozen Ralston warriors with him.

At my nod, my men step aside.

"I let you into my fucking clan, and this is how you repay me," Jack roars. "Where are they?"

He has his fabled ax in hand and looks fit to bust someone open with it.

"They are inside," I say calmly. A lifetime of dealing with my father's rages has paid off, it would seem. "And if you stop waving your ax around like a mad man, I will let you see them both."

"Both?" he says, ax lowering a notch.

"Aye, both."

"They are well?" he asks tentatively.

I nod. "They are well."

With a grunt, he shoves the handle of his ax through his belt. Fen, I notice, has folded his arms and is smirking.

"Jessa's mother said as much," Jack says, swiping a hand over his short beard and looking uncomfortable. "I thought the woman had lost her mind with the stress of losing her daughter twice."

"Well, happen she'll gain a grandchild after this one. Don't know a woman who doesn't lose her mind with excitement when a baby is involved." Turning, I call over my shoulder, "You can come out now."

It is only when they emerge that I remember Jessa is only wearing a fur. Cheeks pink, she doesn't know where to look. Thank fuck Brandon has his pants on.

Jack cuts me a glare.

"We only returned yesterday, and I don't have any fucking clothes for her," I say.

Fen chuckles. "It covers more than the dresses Jack has Hazel wear—uff!" His words are cut off when Jack thumps his shoulder.

At least Jack is no longer glaring.

"I am well," Jessa says. "Please, tell my family not to worry about me. Tell my mama I have gotten my heart's desire."

Jack's face softens in a smile. "Aye, lass, I will."

Jack and his men do not linger for long, keen to return home before night falls so that they can ease the mind of their clan that no wrongdoing has occurred. Not that Jessa's mother was worried, according to Jack.

Jessa and I return to the hall, where I sit at the table with her on my lap. We share a cuddle, both of us relieved that Jack's visit went well.

Outside, Brandon is saying his final words to Fen. He has been the alpha's second from a young pup, but that bond was broken when I claimed him.

It is a strange responsibility and one I do not take lightly. Shifters naturally form much tighter bonds within their pack. beta shifters who do not bond to an alpha, be they shifter or human, can turn feral and become stuck in their wolf form. It is hard to bring them back once that has happened, and more often, they must be killed.

I can sense Brandon's mood inside me, in the same way I can sense Jessa's. Strong and conflicted emotions are swirling through him as he says farewell to Fen. One chapter of his life is closing, and another is opening.

As it is for all three of us.

I understand from my new perspective that when a shifter bonds, it is based upon love and respect that grows ever deeper over time. Unexpectedly, I am jealous of what he once shared with Fen. It will take time, even with the mate-bond in place, for Brandon and me.

There is longing in Jessa as she watches the hall door and a rawness inside her chest that I do not believe is for Brandon.

"You can visit them soon," I say. "Give the news a chance to settle. Then we can all go back together, and I can meet your family."

"Thank you!" she says. Throwing her arms around my neck, she plants a chaste kiss upon my cheek.

"That was not a proper thank you, lass," I say. It feels like too long since I rutted her. Having her pressed against me, my nose full of her breeding scent, has a predictable effect.

The job is done. She is with child. Yet my cock is eager for more. Gods, I can't wait for her belly and tits to grow. If my cock has any say in it, she will spend the rest of her blood moon years plump with whelps in her belly.

Thoughts of rutting are quashed when the cat comes trotting in. "Oh! Can I pet him now?" Jessa asks.

I don't get a chance to answer as she wriggles down from my lap. She has already scooped the tiny killer up and is clutching him to her chest. The cat presents his chin for a deeper petting as she rubs underneath.

Damn cat!

I'm about to demand she put the cat down so I can carry her to the furs before Brandon returns, when the servants arrive with lunch.

Feeding her is more important than rutting, and I can rut her straight after. Barely have I extracted the cat from her hands and put her on my lap when Brandon arrives. He seems different, and his side of the bond thrums with contentment.

"It is my turn," Brandon says, striding over and holding out his arms.

"You did not want a fucking turn this morning," I point out.

"I want a turn now." The mutt has the nerve to scowl at me, and this after all his ridicule this morning.

"Oh, please, do not fight again," Jessa says like we fight all the fucking time.

"We have fought exactly once, lass," I point out. There has been the odd thump in between, but that is hardly worthy of the 'fight' title. "And we will not need to fight again so long as the mutt—"

Cupping my face in her small hands, her earnest eyes hold mine. "Brandon should have a turn. It is only right."

A tic thumps in my jaw. I can sense Brandon's smugness through the bond! I know I should do this, should let him have his turn, but it is hard. He has had her all to himself for many weeks. And he has known her all his life. I feel aggrieved that I barely know the lass.

I want more. I want an equal share. I want her to myself for one fucking moment, but it seems I cannot have even that.

It is our first day in the clan. I have brought them here, separating them from their families and friends.

"He may have a turn," I concede.

Chapter Thirty-Six

Jessa

After a week, I am starting to find my way around the village and get to know the people. I spend the morning with Pete's wife, a kindly beta with three young lads who are the image of their father.

But when I return to the great hall, I find Gage and Brandon eyeballing each other. A few servants are pretending to be doing chores. They are not doing chores. They are being stickybeaks and will doubtless gossip about my fool mates the moment they leave.

I thought they had reached an understanding when we first arrived at the Lyon clan. I was wrong, so very wrong. Gage is an alpha and used to getting his way. Brandon is mule-headed for a wolf and fights him over every point.

Hands on hips, I glare at them. "You are acting like a pair of whelps. This fighting needs to stop."

"We are not fighting. We were discussing matters," Gage

says. "Not that we ever fought. Fighting would imply some level of equality."

"I'm going to rip your fucking throat out," Brandon growls.

"Try it, mutt, and I'll be using your pelt to wipe my boots."

I move to stand between the posturing males, putting a hand on them both. Instantly they stop their bickering and start purring.

Then they both step forward as one, and the air crackles with a different kind of tension.

"No!" I say, planting a hand in the center of Gage's chest. He is the more dominant of the two, and it is Gage I need to reason with. It doesn't help that a flutter kicks off low in my belly.

"She is aroused," Brandon says.

The words of denial catch in my throat as Brandon settles his hands at my waist and leans in to trail kisses up the side of my throat.

I shiver. "This is not the answer to you growling at one another," I say, trying to remember why I was cross with them.

"It is the only answer," Gage says. Hands grasping the hem of my top, he yanks it up and over my head, interrupting Brandon's kisses.

"Goddess! There are people in the hall!"

"I'm going first," Brandon says like the nosy servants and my opinion of them is of no consequence.

"You are not going first," Gage growls.

"Goddess save me," I mutter.

"I am going first. Have we not covered this already?" Brandon says.

Gage's eyes narrow. "There are other places to stick your cock."

"There are, and mine fits into all of them," Brandon says smugly. "But I want her pussy today."

Gage grinds his teeth in a way that suggests he is still thinking about thumping Brandon. I growl.

They ignore me and continue glaring at one another over my head.

"Fine," Gage says, stepping back. "Go ahead."

"Oh!" I am facedown over the table with no idea how this came about.

"I'm going to do her from behind," Brandon says thickly, yanking my hide skirt up.

He stills. *Oops!*

"What the fuck, Jessa!" Brandon says, landing a firm spank on my bare bottom. "Where the fuck are your panties?"

"I don't—" He spanks me again, stoking both my temper and the sweet ache between my thighs. I don't have any panties because Gage never thought to ask the womenfolk to bring me any, and I've not had a chance to make some for myself!

"Yes," Gage says, coming to stand beside Brandon and tugging my skirt even higher like they might be hiding there. "Where the fuck are they?"

"She does this when she wants to be rutted," Brandon says like he is the authority on this. "And spanked. She also likes to be spanked."

My pussy clenches, and I groan. I do also like to be spanked.

Gage chuckles. "Best we see to our mate's needs, then."

Brandon

Gage and I threaten to kill one another on a semi-regular basis. Occasional blows are traded where he reminds me that I couldn't kill him even if that were my desire. Then Jessa appears, and one whiff of her breeding scent and all we care about is rutting.

When we are rutting her, we rarely think about killing one another. And if we do, it lacks genuine heat. Also, she is becoming skilled at distracting us. Gage has even suggested that we pretend to argue when she enters the room just to see what she will do.

I admit he does, on occasion, have surprisingly good suggestions.

Tomorrow, we are due to visit the Ralston clan. Jessa has been beaming with joy at the thought of seeing her parents and the brats.

The separation has been harder on her than on me. I have spent much of the last few years scouting with Fen, which took me away from home as often as not. But Jessa lived for her family and had not spent a single day away from them before Gage claimed us both.

Now Gage has just informed me that we cannot go tomorrow. Furthermore, he doesn't know when we might be able to go. There are reports of raiders snatching stock. The legacy of Gage's recent rise to power has turned some of his father's supporters to villainy. When I spoke to Pete about it yesterday, he said these men were much the same when part of the clan.

"I understand you have matters that must be dealt with. But our mate will be sobbing soon when you tell her that we cannot go. She has talked of nothing but seeing her parents and the brats, and about how Greta will be excited to learn of the babe."

"I do not make this decision lightly," he says, and the bond hums with discord. Instantly, I turn, expecting to see Jessa rush in crying because she has sensed Gage's decision.

There is no one there.

Gage can manipulate the bond in ways I cannot,

preventing Jessa from sensing his emotions and even mine. He says he does it for her own protection. I can see that her knowing every time we argue or come to blows would not be healthy for either her or the growing babe.

"I could help you," I say. "I am a better tracker than the few shifters you have here. I have spent my life in this role. I know how to fight. A beta wolf was meant to fight beside his alpha."

"I don't like to leave her alone!"

"Neither do I, but she will be safer once they are dealt with. How many nights have they snuck into the village? I don't like the thought of the bastards creeping around. I have not slept in human form this past week, my wolf is so uneasy! If you are going to be an ass about letting me help you with this threat, then Jessa and I will visit Ralston on our own."

"I need equal," he growls, chest heaving like this admission hurts.

My brow furrows. A strange, sickly feeling assaults me through the bond.

"Equal? You are the fucking alpha," I say. "You get everything!"

"And you are the lad she grew up with, who she has a lifetime of memories with, who knows her family like they are your own. You are also not the son of a murderous bastard who set the clans to war!"

Equal? I don't even know what that word means anymore. I had not considered that he might be jealous of me. I have been too busy being jealous of him.

"You are not your father," I say, feeling my anger drain. I do not know much about his life, but I believe it has not been an easy one.

"It gladdens me more than you can possibly know to hear you say that. There would be few within your clan who would offer me such charity."

I feel like I have been blind and am only now coming to know the man I have pledged to in the deepest, most intimate bond. He is conflicted. Torn between his duty to keep Jessa safe and his need to be with her.

The bond doesn't lie. He can hide things at times, but it does not lie.

I have come to understand that he is a good man and worthy of Jessa. The Goddess would not have allowed such a sacred bond to form otherwise.

But he does not need to shoulder this responsibility alone. I am a beta shifter. I will defer to him, but I will also speak my mind. I want this to be equal, too. I want to support him, both in the protection of Jessa and the clan, and in the way we love our queen.

This is my home now. I had not considered it so before.

"It is not a simple thing to navigate," he says. "Sharing a lass. But I have no doubt she loves us, and in our own ways. Happen it is us who struggle."

I nod. "I don't think the worries will easily stop just because we have talked."

"They won't," he says. Stepping closer, he places a hand upon the back of my neck. I never let a man touch me there before Gage. But it is comforting. My wolf is not threatened by our alpha touching us thus. "But over time, they will become less and less potent, until one day, it will be naught but a fleeting memory that will make us smile at our foolishness."

I am twice Goddess blessed, I realize. For not only have I gained the sweetest omega lass, but I have gained Gage, a man who is everything I look up to and respect. He is right. We are not yet at the stage where our petty jealousy can be fully put aside, but I can see a future where one day it will be.

"I want to help you," I say. "I want to share the burden with you, both for Jessa's sake and the clan."

He growls.

"I want to help. The quicker I help, the quicker we can all go together to Ralston."

Nostrils flared, he glares at me.

"She is proud to have you as a mate." I smirk as I go in for the kill. "I think she might even want to show you off."

"Now, you are humoring me, mutt." He shakes his head, but he is also smiling and I know that I have won.

❧

Gage

Jessa greets the news that Brandon and I will leave to track the raiders with worry.

Just not the kind I was expecting.

"Be careful," she says, wringing her hands like we are a couple of whelps going on our first hunting trip.

I'm not sure whether to be endeared or insulted that she worries for us thus.

Brandon chuckles and snatches her up for a lusty kiss that is in danger of getting out of control.

I growl. They spring apart.

"Fuck!" Brandon mutters as he adjusts his cock in his pants. "Shifting is painful when it is hard!"

Jessa giggles. I roll my eyes. Life is never boring with the mutt.

Brandon stomps off, muttering about rotting sheep carcasses.

"Remember to stay indoors until we return," I say.

Her brows draw together, and she plants her small hands on her hips. "I am spending the day with Carla. She is not long away from her due date, and I said I would help her with the brats."

Jessa is a queen, yet she is still a sweet lass who is always willing to help where she can in the village. A shiver sweeps down my spine. A forgotten memory of my mother helping the womenfolk in such a way comes to mind. My mother would be proud of the light and grace Jessa has already brought to the clan.

"I will see you when we return," I say. "Once this business is done, we can take our trip to Ralston."

I get a lusty goodbye kiss for that.

It is only the impatience pummeling the bond from Brandon that drags me away.

I find men and horses ready.

We have half a dozen shifters in the community. Fewer than most clans given many left during the worst of my father's years. It is only as I see them standing beside Brandon that I realize the natural dominance of Brandon over them. He is larger, but there is more to it than that. It is neither Pete nor me that the shifters look to. It is Brandon.

"We will scout," Brandon says, nudging his head at the shifters. "We can cover a large distance separately and still keep in communication. Rob will stay with you. When he calls, you will know they have been found, and he will guide you."

Like he hasn't just dropped that mind-blowing announcement, he shucks out of his pants. The other shifters do the same.

"Can you communicate?" I ask. The men around me shuffle uneasily with the same confusion as me.

"Aye," Brandon says, rolling out his shoulders. "I have always been able to communicate with other wolves. At Ralston, my father was the dominant wolf, although that was for hunting."

"And now, you are?" I say, not even bothering to keep the grin off my face.

Brandon frowns. "Aye, I am."

"Their alpha," I point out.

"I—" he turns toward the expectant shifters.

"Fuck!" he mutters gruffly. "I guess I am."

§

We have never had coherent shifter support like this before. Not many clans have a wolf dominant enough to lead the shifters in this way. Most alpha wolves would seek a true pack. I can only think that through bonding with Jessa and me, Brandon has been changed.

He is still my beta, but he is an alpha to the shifters.

I am so fucking proud of him. It hardly seems possible that the lad who stole my fucking trousers and caused no end of mischief could mature thus. I cannot wait to return home and tell Jessa.

I can't believe I am so fucking excited for a whelp that I gave serious consideration to strangling more than once.

But first, we have raiders to catch and to bring to justice.

The wolves pair up and bound into the forest. We ride out, taking a brisk canter that will loop the north-western part of our territory. To the south and east, our lands connect to the Halket and Ralston clans. The remaining borders lead to the sharper slopes of the mountain that are not conducive to settlement.

We have not traveled for long when we hear a distant wolf cry...then another.

Rob lifts his head and howls.

The raiders have been found.

Riding hard and fast, we follow Rob through the forest.

Rob yips and slows to a trot. Ahead of us on the trail stands

Brandon, resplendent in his wolf form among the rest of his pack. As we come to a stop beside him, he throws his head back and howls. His brothers take up the call.

I feel the call burrow under my skin, chilling, rousing... It is the sound of the battle to come.

Turning on the spot, he takes off. We follow.

Thundering into a small clearing, we find them. A hobbled-together community with make-shift tents and small fires. They scramble to gather weapons, but we are upon them, blades flashing as we ride through, cutting them down.

Jumping down from the horse, I wade into the fray. A vicious snarl from behind, and I turn to see Brandon take down a raider. Jaws closing over the side of the man's throat, he shakes the bastard about.

We fight side by side. Carving down those who would harm our people one at a time until there is no one left to kill.

As the last man falls to a blade, the wolves throw their heads back and howl the victory.

The men take up the cry with cheers of their own.

We find a few half-butchered sheep among the broken camp and bodies.

It saddens me to see the wasted lives of men who could not change their ways, living like animals.

They are now dead and must answer to the Goddess.

Setting the camp to fire, we return home, knowing our loved ones in the clan can sleep easier tonight.

Chapter Thirty-Seven

Jessa

I am dizzy with excitement the whole journey to my former home. Gage is dressed smartly in his best hide pants and a beautiful fur-trimmed cloak. Brandon wears his leather pants and jerkin after his determination that only a wuss would wear a cloak.

A few ladies within the clan have taken it upon themselves to make me some fine clothes in secret. I now have a stunning embroidered dress and royal blue fur-trimmed woolen cloak to match. I am a happy wuss in mine.

I cried when Carla presented the clothes to me while a few of the younger lasses who helped her watched on shyly.

Given Carla is fit to burst with her babe, I don't know how she found the time. Happen there will be a babe for me to coo over by the time we return.

But now, my eyes are trained on the familiar scenery.

We are close.

As we emerge through the trees, the village comes into

view. We skirt the shore of a great loch, glistening in the evening sun. Willow, ash, oak, and cottonwood cover the lower slopes of the mountain and butt up to the loch shore. To our left is the valley divided into farming plots. To the center, are the many homes. They sprawl out toward the shoreline and nestle into the lower slopes of the mountain.

"I'll ride ahead to let them know," Brandon says, grinning. Nudging his horse to a gallop, he takes off in a way I wish I could.

Familiar.

"Are you okay, lass?" Gage asks. I sit before him on the horse. It has been a very slow ride, given he refuses to move us faster than a walk.

"Yes," I say, sneaking a glance back at him over my shoulder. "I have a new home now. One I am coming to love just as dearly. But a piece of me will always be here. The Baxter omega still travels every year, and she is white of hair. Now I am an omega, I must learn from her and from my own bond, so I can help bonded betas like she does one day."

"Aye, that would be a fine thing for a queen to do," he agrees.

Queen?

I am really a queen.

My tummy ties in knots as we draw nearer. There is a little crowd assembling at the end of the lane leading into the village.

"Goddess!" I say, feeling the tears spring from my eyes.

Brandon has called them all. Ma, Pa, Greta, William, Amos, Karl, Doug, and Brandon's parents, all waiting and waving as they see us.

Greta squeals with excitement as we draw near.

No sooner does Brandon lift me down than I am surrounded by my family and lost within a giant hug.

"We made honey cake!" Greta announces in an ear-splitting squeal. "I wasn't allowed a slice until you arrived. Can we have honey cake now, Mama? I think Jessa's baby will need to have honey cake straight away."

"Brats," my father says, laughing as he shakes hands with Gage. "You will never get a moment's peace. Welcome to the family."

We spend the evening drinking tea and eating the delicious food Brandon's mother and mine have been preparing for us. Hazel, Jack, and Fen come and join us. We talk until the younger children start to doze. Given we are staying here for a few days, there will be plenty of time for more talking on the morrow.

"Your former home is ready for you," Hazel says with a wink. "Jack said as the old Bennets' home would be kept set aside for whenever clan guests visit. It will be wonderful to have you here for a few days. Our clans are not so far away when you are not with child and can ride a horse fast. But I miss you and hope you take to visiting whenever you can."

She pauses to run her hand over the gentle swell of her belly. "He said we could visit with you in the spring after the baby is born."

"I would love that," I say as we share a warm hug.

Taking our leave, we walk the short distance to the house where Brandon and I first committed to one another. How strange to be staring at the pretty, rambling cottage again. It feels like the world has turned upon its head since I was last here.

"I believe it is customary to carry the bride over the threshold," Brandon says with a wink.

"She is a mate, not a wife," Gage says as though deeply offended by the term.

Brandon rolls his eyes. "Fine, I will carry the lass in.

Although I carried her the first time. I just thought you might want to have your turn."

Brandon chuckles as Gage scoops me up into his arms. "I thought that would work," he says.

"Mutt," Gage mutters under his breath. "You should learn when to quit baiting if you want to rut her tonight."

I giggle as I am swept inside. I'm sure Brandon just groaned as though in great pain.

Carried straight through, I am placed carefully upon the bed.

Gage looks down at me, a familiar hunger in his eyes.

Brandon comes and stands beside him, the same fire lighting his eyes.

I squeeze my thighs together, my body rising at the sight of my two beautiful mates staring down at me.

"So, this is where it all started," Gage says.

"Aye," Brandon replies. "Only she is twice as lusty now. Happen we will need to rut her thoroughly, maybe even awaken the claiming mark before she is satisfied."

The bond hums with pleasure.

"Agreed," Gage says. "Our mate must be thoroughly claimed for her pleasure and ours."

Epilogue

Gage

It has been a long time coming, but Eric has finally relented and allowed me to see my brother, Danon. My claiming of Jessa and Brandon has facilitated the ties growing between our clans. Along with our continuing peaceful ways, allowing tempers to settle. This is only the beginning, but I'm grateful nonetheless for an opportunity to see and speak to my brother.

It has been over year since he was taken prisoner. I have thought of him every single day.

A Halket warrior takes me to a small bare shack adjoining the great hall. A high, barred window lets a little light in, casting weak winter sunlight over my brother.

We take each other's measure. It is good to see Danon, although it pains me that he is locked up like this.

"Did you kill the Halket king?" I ask.

"No," he says.

I believe him. It relieves me that I can accept his words as truth.

I have ruminated over the answer to this question.

Wondered if I would get a chance to even ask him.

Wondered if he would admit that he did kill the late king. Or worse, that he would lie to me about it.

"What happened?"

He sighs. I have a feeling he has told this tale often.

"We split after leaving the clan. Father went north with the first party, I went south with the second, and a third party went east. Scouting was as much as my father said. It was quiet, no attack was coming, and we rode along the border until we met with the third party again. I didn't realize what they were up to, what our father had ordered them to do. Not until I came upon them stringing the body up. I was livid. With them, with our father, with myself. I could barely see straight, let alone think. That was when Eric attacked. He killed everyone but me. And that was only so he could exact his revenge at leisure."

That also rings true. Our late father was ever a man who trusted no one, not even his blood, with his plans. If ever I needed reminding of how little we meant to him, it is manifested here in this shack as I look upon my damned brother.

He looks a little thinner. There are a few more scars on his face, but he is not dead, and although he is a prisoner, he is clean and in reasonable conditions.

"They say you killed our father," he says.

"Aye," I say. "I did."

He nods. I don't know if he is saddened by this news. Maybe like me, he is relieved that the reign of terror is over.

"And that you are king now and mated to an omega."

My lips tug up. It is hard to think of my sweet mate and the not-so-sweet wolf shifter and not smile. Then there are the pup-babies who wake us nightly with their demands and entertain us with their mischief of a day. Were I to glance down at my boots, I would find a few teeth marks there.

"I am. And I have."

"Good," he says. "I am glad. You were always going to make a better king than me."

"Aye, well," I say. "We can also agree on that."

I mean it in a light-hearted teasing way, but my brother does not smile.

"They are never going to let me leave," he says. "I am less than a slave to them. They allow me out of a day that I can labor for them. It is honest work, and I find pleasure and freedom in the simple tasks. But of a night, I return here where I remember what I am. I try not to think about tomorrow and the noose Eric plans to stretch my neck with. But the day will come."

"Don't," I say, feeling a lump settle in my throat and heaviness behind my eyes.

"You need to accept it, Gage."

"I can't."

"I am serious. I looked fucking guilty when they came upon us. They have no reason to believe I am innocent and every reason to find me at fault."

"You didn't fucking do it," I say, anger surging for every word from his lips convinces me more deeply that he does not belong here, rotting in a shack.

"Promise me you won't go to war with them, Gage. Promise me this one fucking thing! I can't have innocent people hurt over me. If you go to war, the people here may be injured. I can't live with that. I've done enough wrong in my life. Maybe this is my dues."

"No," I say. "I can't fucking promise you that. Don't ask me to."

"Don't throw away what you have achieved over this. You

have a mate now. I know you have two shifter babies with your mate and her bonded second. It is all the lasses of the clan talk about. Don't you dare endanger that."

He is right, and I fucking hate that he is right. Knowing this does not make the conflict go away nor lessen the pain within my chest.

We all take different paths through life. Danon's path has been harder than most. He deserves a better end than to hang from a rope.

"I believe in you, Danon. And I believe the Goddess has once more found her way to our clan. Have faith in the Mother of All Things. You have suffered long enough."

The door bangs and rattles as the guard enters. "It is time," he says. "Eric will speak to you now."

I clasp arms with Danon. "Don't lose hope," I say.

"I won't," he says. "Give Eric the bastard my regards. He has not visited me in a while, and I'm starting to think he doesn't care."

I huff out a laugh. For the first time since I entered the shack, I sense my brother is still here. With a look that I pray will not be the last, I leave Danon.

As I step outside, a pretty lass arrives with a cloth-covered tray.

"What's that for, Ellen?" the guard asks.

"You know what," she says, smacking his hand when he tries to peek.

"Fucking prisoner eats better than me," he grouches. "Go on then, lass. He's not tried to strangle you yet, so I don't think he'll try now. I'll be back as soon as I've taken the Lyon King to speak with Eric."

As I turn away, a smirk spreads across my lips.

I look toward the heavens. I have a feeling the Goddess has some plans in play.

۶۵

I am both heartened and sad after visiting with Danon. I sense that he is close to losing hope despite him saying he would not.

He is different.

Some of the changes are for the better, and some are not.

But when I enter the hall of my home, I find a cheery setting that lifts my spirits. Brandon, Jessa, and the pups.

Pups...because they spend more time in wolf form than they do as babies, only changing back when they are hungry or tired. Mostly hungry, since sometimes they remain in wolf form to sleep. A small fur-lined basket is placed to one side of the hearth, and they tend to go there when they are ready to rest or change.

With the onset of winter, it is cold once the sun sets. The fire has been lit, and the pups are playing rough and tumble on the floor. The cat sits to one side, overseeing their antics with a lordly grace only a cat can pull off.

Brandon sits at the table drinking a beer. He lifts his tankard to me in greeting.

Jessa is setting the table for supper. Seeing me, her pretty face breaks into a smile, and she hastens over.

"Pups," I say as I shrug out of my cloak. "How the fuck did you end up breeding her with your small cock that couldn't even—ouch!"

Jessa pinches my arm. I was sure she was going to kiss me before I opened my stupid mouth. She handles our baiting of one another for the most part until we venture into breeding or cocks.

"Do not insult Brandon's cock," she says, planting her small fists upon her hips and trying to act stern. She is an omega, a little waif, and the least stern woman I have met. Even though she has a few more curves after the pups, I can still get my big hands all the way around her waist.

Brandon's grin nearly splits his face. *Damn mutt!* The last time I insulted his cock, Jessa sank on her knees and showed me why she loves it... I need to stop thinking about that.

There was a time when the thought of beating the smug beta shifter to a pulp brought me great joy. Now my dick is rising to attention at the thought of our mate worshiping him! How times have changed.

Brandon leans back in his chair and places his hands behind his head. Fucker!

Risking another pinch, I take Jessa by the waist and claim my kiss...a long, lusty kiss.

When I break away, her cheeks are flushed, and her eyes shining with love.

"Did you see him?" she asks, a little breathless from the kissing.

"Aye," I say, tucking her against my side and sneaking in a pat of her ass. "He was better than I expected. Eric has said that I may visit him again. I hoped the Halket king might be inclined toward letting him go."

Her sensitive eyes hold mine. "It is a start, my love," she says.

Our conversation is put aside as the pups quit their play-fighting and scramble over as fast as their little legs will allow.

"I admit," I say. "They have knocked the cat off the top cute spot."

"Henry," Jessa says. "Our handsome overseer is Henry."

"He has been simply a cat for a good long while," I say. "There is no hope for it."

On reaching me, Fern attacks my boot with her small teeth. Adam is running around us so fast, he is naught but a blur of black fur. I pick Fern up with both hands braced around her body until she is at eye level with me. She yips her excited demand for a cuddle. "Fern, I have told you not to bite my boots."

"She doesn't understand you in wolf form," Brandon says. "And is too young to understand you as a baby, either way. Happen she thinks you are telling her to go at them as often as she likes."

I chuckle. "Given how much she sets her teeth to them, I think you are right."

Tucking her against my chest, I purr how she likes best, and scoop up her little brother. Arms full of wriggling bundles of fur, I follow Jessa to the table. Wet noses poke against my bare chest, small tongues lick, and their bodies thrum with excitement as they clamor for attention.

As I pet their silky fur and rub their ears, it is hard to reconcile that there is a baby in there.

Jessa

"Our little scamps are growing," Gage says with a proud smile.

It warms my heart every time I hear the 'our' word. While Gage is very much the alpha of our house, he loves our sweet pup-babies as though they were his own. Given how thoroughly he rutted me through my first heat when I caught with Adam and Fern, I was as shocked as we all were that the babies could shift. More shocked still that their blue baby eyes changed to the dark brown that makes me think of Gage.

Shifters always have bright blue eyes.

Always.

The sensible part of me accepts that it is a throwback to a distant family lineage. But another part of me remembers how the Goddess healed Gage through me, and I see her work at play.

We enjoy supper together. Listening to Gage talk about his brother, I can feel both his anxiety and his hope. The pups change to babies, and I feed them as Gage tells us about the rest of his trip.

As I finish feeding them, I smile at their sweet human form. I'm about to put them down for the night when there is a knock upon the door.

Pete enters, nodding his head in deference before addressing me.

"Sorry to bother you, my lady," he says. "One of the lads has come home with a nasty cut and it's badly infected. Carla said you would know the best treatment for it."

"I'll come straight over," I say. "Just let me put the little ones down."

"I will take them," Gage says, motioning for them.

"I'll go with her," Brandon says, rising from the table.

Handing my darling babies to their papa, I follow Pete out.

The infection is nasty. But as I mix the balm, I pray to the Goddess that this good lad does not need to lose his hand. As I wrap his hand, I see the color return to his cheeks and know *She* is here with me.

"Leave it on until I can change the bandage on the morrow," I say.

Brandon gives me a look that says he knows what I have done. I have become skilled in keeping wounds bandaged and hidden from all eyes but mine until enough time has passed to avoid suspicion.

When we return to the grand residence that is our home, we find Gage fast asleep on his back among the furs of my nest, a thick pelt covering him to the waist. Fern is tucked into his right side, small wolf head resting over Gage's chest—she loves his purrs best. Adam is on his left side, on his back, legs in the air, snout in the crook of Gage's shoulder. The cat, now known as Henry, has climbed on top and curled up in a ball over Gage's belly.

Brandon chuckles softly, and snagging an arm around my waist, plants a kiss to the side of my throat against the claiming mark. I shiver. He cannot touch it without my body going up in flames.

"His fearsome reputation would be ruined if the clansfolk could see him now," Brandon says, voice low so as not to wake them. "He looks cute—uff!"

I nudge him with my elbow. He grins at me unrepentant. Lifting his head, the cat gives us a haughty glare before jumping down from the bed and padding out of the room.

Night-time is the best mousing time. There is always a slight crack in the shutter of the hall so he can get in and out.

Carefully, so as not to wake them, I lift my beautiful pup-babies and carry them to their cribs. They will likely wake soon in baby form for their feed, but this peacefulness is nice too. Maybe we will get a little time before they wake with their noisy demands.

Having shed his clothes, Brandon stands beside the bed with a big grin on his face and his hard cock in hand.

I bite my lips to contain my giggle. How is a lass supposed to resist? My dress comes over my head and is tossed to the floor before I hurry to join him.

We share a heated kiss, breath mingling and tongues tangling. My pussy clenches, growing *slick* as I anticipate the rutting that will come. Goddess, I am blessed to have two such mates. Kind, brave, caring, and loving me often among the furs. My body, mind, and soul hunger only for them.

Brandon breaks the kiss, staring down at me through the gloom with his beautiful wolf-blue eyes. "Happen we should surprise him," he says, jerking his thumb in Gage's direction.

"What should we do?" I ask.

His hands settle at my waist before rising to cup my full breasts. His thumbs brush over my nipples, drawing a hiss from my lips.

"Are they sore?" he asks.

"Only a little," I say, not wanting him to stop.

Grasping both nipples between finger and thumb, he rolls them roughly, just how I like. I squeeze my thighs together, feeling the flutter inside my pussy as my body responds.

"I want you to go over to him," Brandon whispers. "Pull the pelt from him and worship his cock."

I suck a sharp breath in.

"You know I enjoy watching you struggle to take him down your throat. And you are such a lusty, needy, little omega that you can't help but try."

"Goddess!" I whisper.

He tugs my nipples and twists them cruelly. I nearly come on the spot. Turning me about, he taps my bottom to get me to move.

I throw a look over my shoulder as I near the bottom of the bed. Brandon watches. Turning back, I carefully draw the pelt down. Gage blinks before his gaze settles upon me. His cock jerks, and his teeth flash white in a grin as he waits to see what I will do.

Crawling up the bed, I get on my knees before his bobbing cock. Goddess help me, it will never get any less daunting. But as Brandon says, I enjoy the challenge, and the moment his taste hits my mouth, I am lost.

As I tilt Gage's thick cock so I can suck the tip deeper into my mouth, Brandon comes to stand behind me. My pussy clenches and my tummy does that little tumbling thing. I wonder if Brandon might rut me from behind while I worship Gage.

But Brandon kneels, grasps my ass cheeks in his big hands to open me before swiping his tongue the length of my drenched pussy slit. I all but fall upon Gage's cock, lashing the head with my tongue before sucking it deep into my mouth. I hum around it in pleasure as Brandon eats me out from behind.

"Whatever the fuck you are doing to her, don't stop," Gage says on a groan.

About the Author

Thanks for reading *Claimed for Their Pleasure*. Want to read more? Check out the rest of my *Coveted Prey* series and my other books!
Amazon: https://www.amazon.com/author/lvlane

Where to find me...
Website: https://authorlvlane.com
Blog: https://authorlvlane.wixsite.com/controllers/blog
Facebook: https://www.facebook.com/LVLaneAuthor/
Facebook Page: https://www.facebook.com/LVLaneAuthor/
Facebook reader group: https://www.facebook.com/groups/LVLane/
Twitter: https://twitter.com/AuthorLVLane
Goodreads: https://www.goodreads.com/LVLane

Also by L.V. Lane

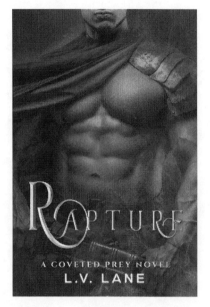

Rapture

Winter

He's supposed to be my protector, the towering male with the delicious scent that drives my body wild.

He's supposed to obey me, although he rides the line of disrespect with infuriating ease.

And when he's injured, I'm supposed to gift him my powerful blood.

Only I don't, and I can't, and now my actions have broken the rules

And the man who once obeyed is going to own me.

Jacob

Beautiful, cold, and untouchable, Winter is all that and more.

The tiny little fairy with the frosty disposition and heart made of ice.

She's supposed to heal me, but my miserly mistress gives me only scraps.

My mind despises her, even as my body craves her blood.

Trapped by circumstance, my broken fairy will break both the rules and me.

But revenge, sweeter than the blood flowing through her veins, will ultimately be mine.

Rapture is a dark and steamy enemies to lovers paranormal, fairy-vampiric mashup. It contains detailed explicit scenes and triggers.

★ Fairy - vampire mash-up

★ Enemies to lovers

★ Action, humor, and heat!

★ Portal fantasy worlds with fairies, humans, orcs, and shifters!

★ Standalone story with HEA

Made in the USA
Las Vegas, NV
03 March 2024

86644694R00217